"Did you see some........" I asked.

"Smelled." The word was curt. "They were here all right."

"They—who's *they*?"

Tucker grimaced. "I smell candle wax, fresh, not two days old, incense and—" He paused a moment and concentrated. "Blood . . . fresh blood. Not today, but . . ." He dropped to a crouch, feet shoulder width apart, arms loose, the long rope of braided hair halfway down his bare back.

I caught a whiff of candle wax, something sweetish, artificial vanilla and cinnamon caught up in cedar, an ashy residue behind it all. Something tugged at my mind. There was something familiar . . . The breeze danced past, and the sweet faded into the normal dusty heat scent and my brother was still standing there as unmoving as one of the cemetery statues. He placed a palm flat on the ground and shut his eyes. He began to hum under his breath. My feet began to sweat in my boots. I could scarcely breathe—the whiff of ozone, of energy surrounded us. I tried to take a deep breath, struggling against the pressure. Something pulled at me, currents tugged at my skin, a whine of electric vibration made my bones sing.

"Here . . . come . . . here." The whispers insinuated themselves in the back of my skull.

Praise for *Blood Bargain*
"Ms. Lima spins a suspenseful tale and packs it with paranormal elements that will hold the reader's attention to the end . . . fast-moving. . . ."
—Darque Reviews

Turn the page for rave reviews of *Matters of the Blood . . .*

Praise for Maria Lima's
Matters of the Blood

"A fast pace that never lags, suspense to keep the reader turning pages, paranormal beings including shapeshifters and vampires, and a personality of its own. . . . It's a complex plot with the requisite twists and turns of a mystery, the passion of a paranormal romance, and the unearthly elements of urban fantasy."

—SF Site

"An absolutely spectacular addition to the paranormal landscape. . . . Novels of this caliber are few and far between. . . . A classy, teasing tale. . . ."

—BookFetish

"Dark, seductive, and bitingly humorous. . . . This is one paranormal super-thriller you should 'bump' to the top of your to-be-read pile."

—Heartstring

"A great page-turner. . . ."

—The Bookshelf Reviews

"An excellent book, readable and gripping with varied characters, an interesting plot, and a great setting in small-town Texas."

—Curled Up With a Good Book (5 stars)

"Keira Kelly kicks butt. . . . A supernatural mystery with guts, brains, and soul. . . . Hot action and spicy romance with a biting sense of humor."

—Dana Cameron, author of *Ashes and Bones*

"A pleasure to read from the first page to the last."

—*CrimeSpree* magazine

"Funny, sexy, mysterious, and lots of fun to read."

—Nancy Pickard, author of *The Virgin of Small Plains*

"Refreshing . . . I loved the story's vividly drawn rural-Texas setting."

—Fantasyliterature (4 stars)

"Maria Lima moves the supernatural to small-town Texas, with nosy neighbors and family eccentrics and a whole lot of magic. Her characters may be psychics, vampires, and werewolves, but first and foremost, they're people you'll want to read more about."

—Toni L.P. Kelner, co-editor of *Many Bloody Returns*

"Grabs you from the start and keeps you turning pages until you solve the mystery."

—Fresh Fiction

"Another kick-ass heroine enters the paranormal arena in Lima's bloodthirsty whodunit. Feisty Keira narrates with a biting sense of humor. . . ."

—*Romantic Times* (4 stars)

"A superb paranormal whodunit with a touch of romance and with plenty of interwoven subplots that will elate fans of various sub-genres, but the center holding this superb tale together is the likable Keira who makes the abnormal seem so normal."

—Alternative Worlds

"An intriguing and diverse supernatural society . . . with a spunky, entertaining lead in Keira Kelly. . . ."

—Bookloons

Also available from from Maria Lima
and Pocket Books

Matters of the Blood

Book Two of the Blood Lines series

BLOOD BARGAIN

MARIA LIMA

POCKET BOOKS
New York London Toronto Sydney

Pocket Books
A Division of Simon & Schuster, Inc.
1230 Avenue of the Americas
New York, NY 10020

This book is a work of fiction. Names, characters, places, and incidents either are products of the author's imagination or are used fictitiously. Any resemblance to actual events or locales or persons, living or dead, is entirely coincidental.

Copyright © 2008 by Maria Lima

This Juno Books/Pocket Books paperback edition October 2009

JUNO BOOKS and colophon are trademarks of Wildside Press LLC used under license by Simon & Schuster, Inc., the publisher of this work.

POCKET and colophon are registered trademarks of Simon & Schuster, Inc.

For information about special discounts for bulk purchases, please contact Simon & Schuster Special Sales at 1-866-506-1949 or business@simonandschuster.com.

The Simon & Schuster Speakers Bureau can bring authors to your live event. For more information or to book an event contact the Simon & Schuster Speakers Bureau at 1-866-248-3049 or visit our website at www.simonspeakers.com.

Cover design by Stephen Segal

Manufactured in the United States of America

10 9 8 7 6 5 4 3 2 1

ISBN 978-1-4391-5675-9
ISBN 978-1-4391-6672-7 (ebook)

*To all of those who have gone
from our lives in the last year:*

Caroline Willner
Ben Bodine
Dan Margulies
Richard Focht

You are all missed.

ACKNOWLEDGMENTS

As ALWAYS, thanks first and foremost to my beta readers, without whose care, thought, insight and eagle eyes, this book wouldn't be the same: Laura Condit, Carla Coupe, Tanya Kennedy-Luminati. *Muchisimas gracias, chicas!*

Thanks to Dina (my number-one fan) and my patient mother, Yolanda Bodine, who answered my questions about real estate and (in the case of my mother) helped me make sure my Spanish didn't suck any worse.

A never ending debt of gratitude to my editor, Paula Guran, who kicks my ass in the best of ways and forces me to write a better book.

And finally, a thousand thanks to my co-workers, fellow authors and friends who listened to me expound, explain and otherwise fill their ears with ramblings, thoughts and ideas. I'm glad you are so patient and supportive!

SMALL TOWNS ARE LIKE GLACIERS. Moving slowly in their majestic beauty, ideas, mores, thoughts frozen in the ice—pretty to look at. Occasionally, you see things happen, slight changes, tiny cracks in the ice, drips melting away piecemeal as Johnny Rodriguez takes a job in Austin and moves himself, his wife, the kids, Mom and Aunt Betty out of the homestead. SueEllen Parker leaves her husband of fifteen years to live in quietly proud defiance with her best friend of even more years, Mary Rose Messing. But overall, life continues as it was, these small ripples hardly changing the face of the ice. Until suddenly, one day, that which you thought was immutable, fixed in stone, carved into eternal ice sheers away, large chunks tearing away with a shriek, crashing and splintering into a million knife-edged shards.

If you're lucky, you're watching this from a safe distance, through binoculars of emotional dampeners. If you're not, you could be closer than you think, the looking glass of your life falsely making items closer than they appear, allowing one or more of those jagged shards to pierce your complacency.

One can even compare small towns to onions . . . you know, layers. As far as I knew, there weren't any ogres in Rio Seco, Texas . . . maybe a few demons. Some of them were even the psychological kind.

Whether or not that's a good thing remains to be seen.

CHAPTER ONE

T HE SOUND was more than a thought, less than a whisper.

"*Here . . . come . . . here . . .*"

I don't know how, but I heard the insistence behind the words and I knew they were meant for me.

"*Sis . . . sis . . . sis . . .*"

The sound faded, even less distinct than before. I strained to hear more.

"*Sisssss . . .*"

The last hissing sibilant was drowned out by the sound of a door shutting upstairs. I heard a shuffle of movement, then muffled steps descending the thickly carpeted staircase.

"Tucker?" My own voice sounded overloud to my ears.

Adam appeared at the bottom of the bedroom staircase holding two open bottles of wine in his left hand, each suspended by the neck. His right hand cradled two wine stems, each two-thirds filled, the red liquid gleaming in the low light.

He was dressed in his usual casual elegance—black silk dress shirt, sleeves rolled back to reveal muscular forearms, collar open to show a small V of pale skin at the neck, shirt tucked into finely woven custom-tailored black slacks. His feet were bare, owing to his habit of removing his shoes at the front door. Adam told me once he liked to feel the textures of the carpets, the fine grain of the hardwood floors, the cool of the tiles as he walked. Occasionally, he'd spend entire nights free of footwear, even outdoors.

He paused on the final stair, giving me a small nod and a smile, lifting both hands. "I'm sorry I'm a bit later than I intended," he said, stepping down. "Did you—" Adam stumbled a little; jutting his elbows out, as he tried to regain balance without spilling the wine. He seemed to waver a moment, then stilled and sank slowly to his knees, sitting back on his heels, arms held carefully in front, keeping the bottles and glasses steady.

"Adam!" I scrambled towards him. I'd been reading in bed the past couple of hours, having decided—since he was working late—I'd skip my usual meal at the Inn's restaurant, have a snack at the house and curl up with a good book. "Are you okay?"

"I'm fine, Keira. Seem to have slipped on the last step." He turned his head to look at the stair, mouth twisting a little, then he shook his head and with the distinctive liquid grace that vampires have, he rose to his feet, still holding bottles and glasses.

The fall surprised me a little—it was so unusual for any supernatural to lose balance and slip like that. But it was probably nothing. He was carrying two bottles and two glasses. He'd done a damned good job of keeping them upright, too.

There was no evidence of spillage, except for a single blood-red drop of wine sliding down the side of one glass. We both watched its slow progression as it followed the curve, went down the stem, then slid across the pale skin of the back of Adam's wrist.

He caught my gaze and without a word, extended his wrist to me, the dark drop of clear red poised, shimmering on the pulse point against the outline of blue veins beneath.

I reached to cup his hand, two fingers extended underneath the offered wrist, holding it steady.

I held Adam's gaze as I bent my head, inhaling the wine's bouquet, deep notes of darkest red-purple woven through with hints of smoky oak and cedar. The scent of Adam's skin lay beneath, soft spice and coolness, with a hint of nutmeg and—

Something else. My nostrils flared. Mingled with the wine, underneath the liquid—blood. Not Adam's, not the living rich scent of life, but concentrated, a heavier weight of *ironmetalcopper* infusing the liquid. The aroma of Adam's own blood lurked under this, beneath his skin, pulsing, heat growing as I drew closer. My own pulse quickened as the scent reached the back of my throat.

This wasn't my wine that spilled, but his. Wine laced with blood extracts. Animal blood, not human, drawn from living donors, the procedure inflicting no more pain than a vet's blood test. Inhaling the rich aroma, I closed my eyes, confused, not certain of his intent.

"Are you sure?" I whispered, opening my eyes to look up at Adam, watching his face.

He held my gaze, expression frozen in a neutrality held by the strongest of wills. A test, then? A challenge? What was he doing?

An eternal heartbeat, two, then the briefest hint of a nod as a word I barely heard escaped his lips. "Yes."

I closed my eyes again, letting myself get lost in the heady scent, then licked the crimson globule from his wrist.

The taste expanded in my mouth, stronger than a single drop should be, dark red *oakironblood* flavor exploding, catching me off guard. I swallowed and straightened, opening my eyes to look at Adam.

"Not what you were expecting?" He'd dropped tight neutrality for a composed amusement, any hint of emotion still hidden behind the mask.

"Not," I answered, stepping back, letting go his wrist and taking the correct glass from his hand. I had to force myself to imitate his dispassionate detachment. We obviously weren't going where I thought we were with his little display of whatever it was.

I took a sip of my own wine, to mask my confusion. The once heady Torre di Pietra Petite Syrah, a favorite, now tasted flat, less real by comparison. I'd never tasted the special blood-laced wine before. Ever since I'd moved in, our nightly wine had become a ritual; Adam would either return from his office up at the Inn with a couple of bottles, one for each of us, or—if Adam had elected to stay in and work from home that night—one of the Inn's wait-staff would deliver the wine. The ritual never varied. The bottles would already be decorked and ready to pour. Adam would pour a glass for me, then one for himself. We'd clink a wordless toast then enjoy, usually sipping in silence.

I'd come to think that Adam drinking his blood wine with me was his way of letting me in, letting me be a part of his life, part of the private side of Adam Walker.

"What was that in aid of?" I asked, finally gaining enough control to speak.

Adam set the wine bottles down on a small table, then took a sip from his own glass before he spoke. "A thought," he said. "Simply that." He sipped again. "You called out for Tucker?" he asked.

Avoiding the subject, Adam Walker? I thought. So that's the way he's playing this. A thought, indeed. More like a whim that turned out to be less whimsical than he'd expected.

"I did," I answered. "Before I heard you upstairs, I was reading and I thought I heard a voice calling me. It said, 'come here,' then I heard it say 'sis.' Tucker wasn't here, was he?"

"He was not."

"I don't think I'd dozed off," I said, "but maybe . . . no, I'm pretty sure I was awake. Maybe I should call Tucker and see if something's wrong."

Adam's hand on my forearm stopped me. "I wouldn't do that if I were you."

"Why?"

"I don't think your brother would appreciate the interruption."

"I'm sorry—what?"

Adam's expression, accompanied by the raising of his right eyebrow, could only be called a smirk.

"Interrupt what? You *know*? How could you possibly know?" My mind zoomed to a place I didn't particularly want to go—to where my brother and his lover were doing things I wish Adam and I were doing. Except Adam and I hadn't been doing anything in that area for more days than I cared to count, which is one of the reasons I'd been so confused about the whole spilled wine thing.

"Niko is tied to me by blood and bond," he answered. "When you called Tucker's name, I instinctively—"

"Holy crap, you can read Niko's mind?"

He laughed. "No, not exactly. I can sense many things, strong emotion being the . . . shall we say, loudest. I don't think either Tucker or Niko would welcome your phone call."

"Huh."

Chalk that up to Vampire Lesson #694. I'd been with Adam for a few months. Some days, I felt as if I knew

everything there was to know about him; evidently, this
wasn't one of those days.

Of course, learning about each other was par for our
particular course. When Adam found out last year that I
was as supernatural as he was—more so, actually, because
I'd been born that way—he'd been as interested in my abilities as I was in his. Problem was, I wasn't sure what those
abilities were quite yet. Like a child entering adolescence,
I was beginning my own Change, moving into what would
eventually be my nature: weather witch, healer, shapeshifter, necromancer. Odds were, since my father and all
six of my elder brothers were shifters, I'd be joining them,
but that wasn't a given. My own experience so far remained
completely out of the realm of the usual. Six months ago,
I started having visions and feeling the power surges that
heralded Changing—some twenty years ahead of sched-
ule. My omniscient double-great-granny—the matriarch
of our clan—figured it out long before I did and sent my
brother to watch over me. So far, my body failed to follow
any sort of normal pattern. By now, I should be Changed.
Six months after onset, I still experienced the odd surge of
power, but nothing more. No wonder I was hearing things.

"Okay, I guess I was dreaming," I said. "I doubt my
brother is calling for me when he's . . . busy."

"I'm quite sure of that." Adam smiled and took another
sip of his wine as he walked toward the bed. He picked
up a copy of this week's edition of the *Hill Country News*
from the nightstand, set the wine down and, as he started
reading the paper, unbuttoned and shrugged off his shirt,
then climbed onto the bed, the picture of domestic bliss,
still reading.

"Hey," I said, walking to the bed, setting my own glass
on the other nightstand and crawling across the mattress,

settling in at his side. "The night's not all that old yet and I've still got a few hours before I need to meet with the realtor guy about the mortuary sale."

"The estate agent, yes. He sold it quickly, didn't he?" Adam said absently.

"Well, now that Marty's dead and my family's moved, no one really wanted to deal with it. I let the realtor do what he thought was best. It's not like the family needs a funeral home. I sign the final paperwork, around eight A.M. or so. Evidently realtors don't work at night."

Adam nodded, still intent on something he was reading. I had no idea what it could be, since most stories in the small town weekly were along the lines of what the week's school menu items would be and discussing area bond voting issues and whatnot.

"So you want to?" I snuggled closer to Adam. Hey, it didn't hurt to try. I wasn't sure why the recent lack, but I thought it was time to end the dry spell and from his action earlier, maybe he'd thought about it, too.

Adam looked at me over the newsprint, folded it carefully, took a pen and circled something before placing both on the bedside table on his side of the bed. "His side" . . . when had we chosen sides?

Six months ago, this thing between us was all "what the heck are you doing in my very obscure little redneck corner of the world?" Now, evidently, we had sides—both of the bed and philosophically. We'd agreed to disagree on whether he should hunt for his blood fix—especially since I mostly sided with his second-in-command Niko. I held the opinion that hunting was fine as long as you ate what you killed and in Adam's case and most of the vampires at the Wild Moon, they didn't even need to kill their prey: local fauna, carefully managed by Niko in his role as wildlife manager. Vampires may not need human blood but they do need blood to survive. Adam refused to hunt, but continued to subsist on the blood extract-laden wine, which I thought was a poor substitute. We managed to sub-limate our difference of opinion most of the time. Tonight had been a bit fraught already, so I figured a little closeness couldn't hurt.

"What did you circle there? In the paper? You seemed so interested."

"Nothing . . . well, perhaps something," he corrected himself.

I made an attempt to emulate the slightly sardonic raised eyebrow that came so naturally to him. I failed miserably and probably looked somewhat demented. My eyebrows had never learned independent movement.

"It's a ranch," Adam said.

"A *what*?"

I sat up from my semi-recline and reached over him to snag the paper with my fingertips. I had a long reach, but it was a very big bed.

"Actually, it's an advertisement for a ranch for sale. I wish to buy it."

Again I tried for the raised brow. Again I failed.

"Ha. Funny. You own a ranch—well, more of a fancy haven for vampires to hang out. You thinking of going na-tive? Working cattle, riding horses?"

Now that was a picture indeed: Adam Walker, undead king of the local vampire tribe, long black hair, green eyes and pale skin, all decked out in faded jeans, Lucchese boots, western shirt and . . . oh my everloving overactive imagina-tion . . . *chaps*. Jesus. I seriously needed either a cold shower or a hot vampire. Ten guesses as to which I preferred and the first nine don't even come close to counting.

I tossed the newspaper to the side and ran my hand up Adam's leg, the fine weave of his trousers smooth to my touch. I dropped my head to his shoulder, tasting his skin as I murmured, "What say we talk about ranch ads later? Let's spend the next couple of hours doing something a hell of a lot more interesting."

My shoulder kiss turned into a neck nuzzle. I moved my hand further up his thigh, across his bare belly and up his chest. Under my touch, his skin was cool at first, his natural temperature heating up as the energy between us built. I wasn't sure if this was magick or something else. It didn't matter.

We'd started having sex a couple of months ago. I'd been willing to go for it right away. My initial reluctance when I knew him in England had been due to the fact I'd thought he was human. When I discovered differently, I was ready to act on the attraction.

But Adam was old-fashioned. He'd wanted to woo me, to court me. So for four months following Adam's arrival in Rio Seco and my cousin Marty's brutal murder, Adam played the suitor.

He'd started with traditional standards, a single rose, elegant dinners at fine restaurants in Austin or San Antonio and then, bit by bit upped the stakes, no pun intended. I'd enjoyed every decadent minute of it.

By week six of the sweet onslaught, I'd been ready to lay down an ultimatum to get laid, but then he pulled out all the stops and handed me an envelope with tickets . . . tickets to a three week holiday in a remote vampire encampment at the Arctic Circle during the height of polar night. We'd spent the greater part of the time in bed . . . not sleeping.

When we got back to Rio Seco, I hadn't even bothered to go back to my own house. I'd taken all my luggage and gone straight to the Wild Moon Ranch and Adam's place. When I asked for closet space, he'd looked at me, seemed about to ask a question, but then shrugged and bowed to the inevitable. I'd been there ever since.

The sex was great, the company even better. Adam would spend a few hours a night doing ranch and other vampire business. I'd amuse myself, something I'd managed to do for two long years babysitting Marty. Compared to that, this was cake . . . with sprinkles on it.

I smiled against Adam's skin, remembering how hard he'd worked, how earnest he'd been to make a good impression. He was definitely different from any of my previous liaisons.

My neck nuzzle turned into a kiss, deep, intense and oh, yes, most definitely a prelude to much, much more. I slid over, moving on top of Adam, letting my hands, my body, show him exactly how much he'd come to mean to me. How much I wanted . . .

Our skin heated with the contact, the energy growing, building, generated by two supernatural people letting down all their walls. Adam reciprocated, his hands skimming my sides, wrapping around my back, his legs twining with mine. Yes.

I needed more—more skin, less clothing. I sat up with a moan, hands scrambling to take off my T-shirt. Adam's hands tangled with mine as he pushed my hands to the side, grabbed the neck of the cotton tee and ripped it down the middle, pushing the pieces off me. We were both sitting up now, my legs wrapped around his hips, only the thin cotton of my panties and his trousers keeping us apart.

I bent my head to his, losing myself in another kiss, taking, demanding, needing to connect. I threw my head back as the heat rose, gasping with the need to breathe.

A low growl issued from Adam's throat as he bent his head, lips to my neck, mouthing, nuzzling, tasting, then nipping a little, teasing me.

"Yes." I arched in pleasure as I hissed the word, palming the back of his head and pressing it to me.

His lips moved against my skin as he licked me again. I felt a sudden scrape, then a sharp pressure/pain.

Finally, I thought. Finally.

Adam's fingers dug into my back, slid into fists as a huge shudder gripped his body. He froze then, every muscle stone. He didn't pull away, didn't continue.

I kept silent, waiting. I knew what he'd nearly done.

After a moment . . . an eternity . . . during which the only sound in the room was our mutual harsh breathing, Adam lifted his hands from my back, placed them on my biceps with a gentle stroke. His head dropped to his chest with a huge exhalation.

"What?" I whispered. There had been a word buried in his sigh.

I pulled away a little, brought my hands up to cradle his face.

"Adam, what?"

With a visible effort, he dropped his hands to his thighs, shuddered again and with a deep intake and release of breath forcibly relaxed.

"No." The word hung out there, bald and blunt.

I blinked, not sure I understood.

"What do you mean, 'no'?"

Adam slid back and off the bed, moving about three feet away. His erection was still visible through the thin fabric.

I scrambled to join him, to confront him. I was sure we looked a sight, both of us half naked, still flushed with arousal, except mine was quickly turning to anger. Damn it all, I was going to get to the bottom of this. He simply could not keep ignoring me.

As I opened my mouth to speak, the not-so-dulcet tones of my cell phone rang.

CHAPTER TWO

A LONG WITH THE ROLE of vampire lover I'd also
assumed the job of occasional Renfield . . . well,
maybe not Renfield, but definitely the daytime repre-
sentative of a nocturnal (duh) vampire. I didn't procure
babies, young virgins or goats, not even blood. Simply
paperwork and legal dealings.

Dealing with humans was part of my resume in the supernatural family business. And, although I preferred night
to day, I could deal with it. It had never been a problem
before, but then it had never interrupted too-long-delayed
whoopie, either.

And now, a supposedly brief early morning appointment had stretched into the afternoon. I was not a happy
Renfield.

It was Adam's not-so-bright idea I should be here, losing sleep and listening to an extremely annoying real estate
broker. Adam was looking to acquire the last bit of ranch
land adjacent to the Wild Moon that wasn't nature preserve.

In fact, it was also Adam's *way* short of brilliant idea to
have given my cell phone number to the brokerage. Kevin,
the annoying real estate guy representing the ranch sale,
had been the one who'd called and interrupted Adam's and
my not-sex. Adam thought he was making things convenient for me—you know, I had an appointment already
to sign paperwork regarding the mortuary sale, why not
spend a little more time and conveniently take care of this

business, as well? Except *my* real estate guy didn't handle ranches. He also did *not* have my private cell number. I was picky about that sort of thing.

Adam had meant to talk to me about the ranch, but I'd distracted him. Or so he said. *Whatever*—it wasn't as if I were alone in that bed. After a confusing phone call with Kevin and then an explanation from Adam about rezoning and a referendum and developers and things I didn't want to talk about right then, I'd given up, agreed to go look at the place and also given up on finding why buying ranches was more important than great sex. It was close to seven by that time, so I'd gone to take a shower and let Adam go to sleep while I'd tried to get ready for the day ahead.

In the interests of keeping it all in the family, I'd risked interrupting *things* and dragged my brother out of his own comfy bed and from the side of his own vampire lover so he could join me in my frustration and sleeplessness. He *totally* owed me. If my great-great-granny could send him here to be my babysitter, then Tucker got to be dragged along on the less fun errands, too.

It wasn't as if I knew anything about ranch land, other than what I'd gleaned over the years living in Rio Seco. Adam had thought (probably rightly) that purchasing this land site unseen (so to speak) was likely to attract attention. So, here we were, Tucker and I, listening to the very unnecessary spiel from a guy who seemed to think my face was somewhere in the middle of my chest. My brother was all too amused.

"It's about five hundred acres all told, got a nice creek running through the middle of it." Kevin Barton gestured, his hands pointing past the smallish house on the left. "The creek's a couple hundred yards back there, past the foreman's house and the bunkhouse. Lots of oaks, most of it's unimproved, but the main house is really nice. And your friend is in luck, property's priced to move quick."

I tried to listen as I shaded my eyes from the afternoon sun. Early morning had morphed into high noon as our original appointment with the broker got delayed. Kevin had called my cell before Tucker and I had been even halfway to the ranch property and asked to postpone the meeting until noon. Didn't this guy eat lunch? After some choice words, I'd agreed and Tucker and I made a detour and spent the next couple of hours getting some power-napping in at my house, a place I hadn't been to in a while.

At least I wasn't completely sleep-deprived, but I was definitely in need of some caffeine. We'd overslept a little and hadn't had time to stop by Bea's café for more than a single to-go mug. As a result, my mood was less than agreeable. All I really wanted to do was to get this farce over with and go back to the ranch to catch some shut-eye.

It was mid-March but the beginning of the Texas heat was already making its presence known. Daytime temps were running in the eighties with a hint of ninety hovering over the horizon. This was the part of the year I hated most. We mostly called it "Summer: Part One." The Texas Hill Country isn't known for mild cool springtimes, except extremely occasionally. I remember a time or two during a late March weekend when a blue norther ripped through and plunged the temperatures below freezing. This was not one of those times. If there were any reason in the known universe to get me to emigrate to British Columbia with the rest of my family, this current hot spell might be one of them. Who says there isn't any global warming?

I'd slathered on some SPF 50 before I'd left the house; tan was something alien to me. All my life, I'd mostly stayed out of the sun since my skin, heritage from my faery mother, was only a shade darker than Adam's and had a terrible tendency to burn. Geared up in jeans and a light long-sleeved cotton shirt over a tank top, I was ready for bear . . . or ranch buying. A black "gimme cap" I'd appropriated from my late cousin's funeral home topped off my attire and helped shade my face. Hard to avoid sun at the peak of the day, though. Even the expensive shades weren't helping much.

"So, okay if I take a look around?" Tucker straightened up from his lean against the porch railing of the main house. The place was really nice: small, but well built, obviously cared for over the years. Not that it mattered. Adam wasn't planning on living here after all; he was buying the place as a precautionary measure. The vampires had been at the Wild Moon since this past October and had managed to keep a low profile. That wasn't too hard, around here, mostly folks kept to themselves.

Kevin shrugged. "Be my guest," he said. "Stay away from the corral, though. Hear Pete's breaking a new horse. He gets a mite cranky with strangers around."

"Pete?" I turned back to Kevin, who was standing in the shade of a giant live oak.

"The foreman," he answered. "Been working for the judge for awhile now."

"Judge?" Tucker asked.

"Judge J.D. Pursell," answered the broker. "County judge. He's retiring at the end of the month and Bitsy's none too fond of the ranching life."

"There's a person named Bitsy?" Jeez, I hope she's twelve and his daughter, I thought, because *really*.

Kevin chuckled. "Elizabeth's her given name," he said. "His wife. Hear she's of the trophy persuasion." His hands started to move, cupped upward. He seemed to think better of it and aborted the motion. Great. I'd already spent close to an hour with this guy ogling my own breasts and now I had to listen to him describe Bitsy, with all the attending male chauvinist hand gestures. Bitsy, evidently, was not so much twelve as twenty-something, tanned, most likely with frosted hair, frosted pink and highly unnatural nails and a penchant for lunch and tennis bracelets. Figured. I didn't know this judge, but there were too many like him around. I'd bet anything that he had a former Mrs. Judge and mother of his children somewhere around.

"I imagine she prefers San Antonio or Austin," I said aloud. "This place a little too remote?"

"Got that 'bout right," Kevin said. "They've got a new place up in one of those new McMansion subdivisions out-side of San Antonio." He leaned in a little, dropping his voice, although there was no one around to hear. "I heard through the grapevine that Ms. Bitsy is buying all new fur-niture for the new house and that's why the quick sell on this one. Kind of surprised me, though. Judge P's old man bought this place dirt cheap during the Depression and it's been in the family ever since. Guess now that it's the two of them, though . . ."

He let his voice trail off as if to intimate there was more to the story. I got the feeling I was supposed to huddle closer and join in the gossip. So not likely. I'd already had enough of Kevin Barton and I was not about to put my breasts in closer proximity to him. I was pretty sure Kevin had his own version of Bitsy at home. Not that I was necessarily in favor of the 'til death do us part type of marriage. Marriage for life wasn't exactly a model in my family. Couldn't be, really, when "life" meant "just short of immortality." But I hated the good ol' boy penchant for dumping the first wife without much warning to marry a younger version. Their first (and sometimes second) marriages never ended well. A lot of times, the original wife and kids suffered from financial hardships, while the second Mrs. Good Ol' Boy raked it in, unlike the more rational arrangements of my own family.

"Their new place is nice," Kevin added in a more normal tone of voice as he realized I wasn't going to play the gossip game. "Three acres per house minimum with private tennis courts, pools and a really amazing golf course."

Sounds like the last place I'd ever want to be, but these types of developments had become too damned pervasive for my tastes. Too much of that going on up Highway 281 and further, places that were once sprawling ranch land cut up for urban sprawl, every year, getting closer to Rio Seco. Come to think of it, that's probably what Adam meant about the rezoning. The state conservation area couldn't be touched, but the Pursell place was an outlet mall and subdivision waiting to happen. Yeah, we were far out from the madding crowd, but the folks in San Marcos, Katy and Allen had thought that, too, and now all those locations had ginormous temples to the retail gods.

"Kevin, you hear anything about any commercial rezoning up around here?" I asked. If anyone would know, he would. He would, of course, have an eye out for new sales possibilities.

He nodded. "There's been talk in town meetings. This could be a decent crossroads once some of the towns get a little bigger. Could be a prime location for a developer. Nothing's come of it yet, though. Judge P said he was fixin' to sell the place, but not to some developer. They've all been arguing the zoning for a couple of months now. Coupl'a real loudmouths thinking to bring in tourist money. Don't think it'll come to a decision on the zoning until Judge P retires next month. He's a big influence on the rest of them."

"He's at the meetings in his capacity as judge?" I asked, confused. Texas politics wasn't my strong suit—hell, most times, politics in this state were incomprehensible even to those whose job it was—but I was pretty sure a county judge had no official place in a town meeting.

"Nah," Kevin answered. "He's there as a private citizen. Thing is, once he retires, some folks are gonna start seeing him as a weekend landowner, since he doesn't live here anymore."

"Yeah, I see that," I said. "Thanks. I guess if he sells the place, then it's all moot."

Kevin shrugged. "Depends. Your friend wanting to move here or buy it as an investment?"

"Neither." I wondered how much Adam had told Kevin during yesterday evening's discussion that I hadn't been privy to. "He owns the adjacent land and wants to avoid exactly what we were talking about."

"'Kay then, guess we should get on with it, so we can get to the point where you want to sign the papers." Kevin motioned with his hand as if it was all settled. Nice realtor's trick, that, but totally unnecessary.

"So, what happens to Pete?" Tucker crouched down near Kevin, idly picking up a stick and making circles in the dirt.

"Happens?"

"When the ranch is sold," I said, understanding where my brother was headed with his question. "What happens to the current staff?"

Kevin snorted a laugh. "Staff? Ain't no one here but Pete and a few, you know . . ." He made a hand gesture that could mean anything from "shoo fly" to "around the world."

"Know what?" He looked around a bit and dropped his voice into the same almost conspiratorial tone he'd used before. "I imagine there are a coupl'a hands, you know, of the exchange variety." He gave us a wink with a bit of a smirk. I wasn't sure what he was getting at, but all it was missing was the "nudge, nudge" to make the look even more disgusting. "Since Pete's foreman, guess he'll be looking for a new job."

"I imagine that would make him a wee bit cranky." Tucker stood from his crouch in one swift movement, startling Kevin, who took a step back.

Kevin grimaced, his jaw setting as he stared at my imposing six-foot-four Viking brother. I knew Tucker was doing this on purpose; for all his amusement at my expense, he obviously liked Kevin Barton about as much as I did, and it wasn't beyond him to use his height and presence as an advantage. I didn't think Kevin was aware of it, but I could see the machismo percolating.

"Imagine so," Kevin said, leaving the shade, moving away from Tucker. He took my arm as he approached, leading me away from the front of the house, toward the other buildings, some fifty yards to the right on a small rise. We'd parked his over-expensive yuppie truck in the muddy drive near the corral. I'd offered to drive, since my Land Rover Defender was meant for this kind of terrain, but Kevin insisted on showing off his new toy. Whatever. I'd left the Rover in the parking lot of the café and he'd be the one scraping mud off a fancy paint job and from the overdone interior . . . or at least paying someone to do it.

Tucker stayed where he was, his face showing no emotion, no feeling. I shot him a glance full of meaning. He grimaced back at me, then threw me an engaging grin. "I'll go look around," he said to no one in particular.

Good. My brother was always able to read me fairly well. "Look around" meant scope out the place as only a 1,200-year-old shapeshifter could. I didn't expect anything

out of the ordinary, but I'd heard of ranch hands doing
some creative growing of less-than-legal herbs on these
weekend type properties. Absentee owners often meant a
very lucrative side business for underpaid hands. Not that
I really minded, but the last thing either side needed was
a delay in the sale due to the discovery of an illegal activity. If Tucker found anything, we could always come back
under cover of darkness and take care of it.

"You do that." I tossed the words over my shoulder, and
turned my attention back to Kevin.

"What about the hands?" I asked as we walked.

"They go back." Kevin stepped in front of me, stopping
to open the door to what was obviously a bunkhouse.

"Back?" I stepped through into the dark interior. It
was slightly cooler than it was outside, but not by much.
I could tell that this building would quickly turn into a
roasting oven during the summer months. No sign of
air-conditioning either. A couple of ratty old ceiling fans
hung up high. Place looked clean, but run down . . . the
opposite of the precisely kept main house. I was betting
the foreman's place was nicer than this, too.

A row of steel-framed bunks lined either side of the
concrete-floored building, small windows broke the mo-
notony of the wooden wall about every ten feet. It looked
very much like an army barracks. Not that I'd ever actually been in one, but I'd seen what Hollywood thought they
looked like.

I suppose it wasn't too bad of a place for a ranch hand to
live. Most of these guys were probably single, drifters; the
last of a dying breed. Places like Texas, Colorado, Wyo-
ming still had cowboys—men who preferred life among
livestock, drifting from place to place in search of whatever. Soft voices in the distance filtered through the hum

of the cicadas. I realized that I could hear the men at the corral. Cowboys, yeah, but here, they mostly spoke a broken mixture of Spanish and English, as if undereducated in both languages. Spanglish, common language of most Hill Country ranches.

"What did you mean by 'back'?" I asked again.

"You know," he said, moving forward to join me. "Back across." He made a swimming motion with his arms.

"They're wetbacks?"

One meaty hand patted me on the shoulder, as the other came up to his lips. "Shush. Exchange students." His eyes twinkled as he emphasized the euphemism that I suddenly understood. Students—more like severely underpaid and underappreciated labor.

"Once the contract is signed and the place is deeded over, Judge'll make sure they get back. Or go work on another place if someone needs 'em."

I shrugged away from his touch. Yeah, I knew this went on in various places, ranches nearby, even. But I'd always thought it was something done by the good ol' boys trying to buck the system. Not by respectable pillars of the community. I should have known, I suppose, should have at least guessed. The ratio of money and power to poverty and hunger never really changed. The powerful would always overshadow the needy—here, or in the bowels of the Welsh mountains where I was a child. Only the venue changed.

"For the love of . . ." I exclaimed. "He's a county judge. How the—"

Sounds of shouting interrupted. Kevin and I exchanged glances and ran outside.

CHAPTER THREE

Two cowboys were holding back a third man outside the horse corral. The man didn't struggle at all; he stood there, a lost look on his face. As we approached, another man split from the group and came toward us.

"Hey," he said, nodding once to Kevin. He looked over at me with that stereotypical I'm-a-guy-and-you-have-tits appraising look that I utterly hated—the one that started at said tits, traveled down to the hip region and then finally, as if dragged there through mud, to my face. Great, another one.

A sardonic smile crossed the weathered features as if giving his seal of approval. He wasn't old, probably close to my own age, maybe thirty-seven, thirty-eight (except he looked it and I didn't); looked as if he'd done this all his life, clothes cowboy rough, dirt-smeared and broken in— the real McCoy. Since he looked about as Mexican as my brother, I figured this was probably the foreman, Pete. The other three men were definitely Latino.

I returned Pete's stare, letting a tiny amount of my don't-mess-with-me-I-could-be-a-predator peek through. Not enough to really frighten, but enough to make most men a little uneasy. Pete didn't disappoint. He shifted his stance, ever so subtly turning toward Kevin.

"What's going on, Pete?" Kevin asked. I could tell he was trying to keep it low-key. After all, I was a prospect. If this ranch sold for the asking price, he'd be making a hefty commission. He'd listed the place, so he wouldn't have to split it with anyone else. Six percent of half a million translated to a whole lot of six-packs and Las Vegas weekends.

Pete shrugged, stepped back a ways and spat into the dirt. He tucked one hand into a back pocket and dug up a battered can of Skoal. He pulled out a hefty pinch and stuffed it into his mouth before answering. I wasn't sure if this was a calculated move, or simply habit.

"Ain't nothin'. Just a couple of the boys gettin' a bit antsy." He didn't look either of us in the eye when he spoke.

"About what?" I asked.

Pete's gaze rose and met mine again. "Nothin' that need concern y'all. I'll handle it."

I extended my senses a wee bit, enough to sense his outer energy, his aura for lack of a better word. Everyone had one, even vampires. A dark muddy brown-red-gray color surrounded him. Ugh. Disgusting. I stopped looking for more. Not a man I wanted to know better . . . in any way at all.

Kevin looked at me, then back at Pete. "Fine. We'll go on then. Keira?"

Kevin's hand was out, motioning forward, as if to direct me. I wasn't about to go that easily. Something didn't sit right with me. The man they were holding back looked tired, run down. Not that the other two guys were spic-and-span; on the contrary, they'd obviously been working hard. Sweat stains on their shirts, dirt and mud streaked jeans spoke of the manual labor these guys did all day. Thing was, the little guy's shirt was nearly threadbare, his jeans cheap imitations of the other men's Levi's and Wranglers. His face, though mostly unlined, was weathered and tired looking and didn't have the telltale hat line that the others had. He couldn't be more than his early thirties, but his eyes looked a great deal older.

"Who is that man?" I stepped forward, intending to walk the few yards to the group. The two men hadn't let up their grip on the smaller one.

Pete spat another disgusting brown glob. This one landed far too close to my shoes for comfort. I was glad I had boots on.

"Sorry," he said. "Didn't mean nothin'. Y'all don't need to worry 'bout this guy. Some spic trespasser. Judge P don't like no strangers on his property."

A defiant glare met my own curious gaze.

"Okay, fine," I said, ignoring the pejorative. "I'm sure he didn't mean anything by it. Why all the hubbub?"

Pete shrugged. "Workin' a new horse. Didn't want her to spook."

I could buy this, except there wasn't a horse around, and though I couldn't be sure from this distance, the hoof marks inside the corral weren't fresh. In fact, I couldn't smell horse at all. If they'd been working a new horse, it hadn't been anytime today.

Kevin tried again. "Look, I've seen enough here. Why don't we go on back into town. We can go over the paper-work—"

"Yo, sis, 'sup?" Tucker sauntered into view from behind the horse barn. His easy gait belied the question I could see in his eyes.

"Apparently, a trespasser," I said, keeping my gaze on Pete's face. His expression didn't change, nor did his posture, but I saw a muscle in his cheek twitch—once. I'd never met this guy before a few minutes ago, but that was standard male-speak for "I'm tense."

"Huh." My brother closed the distance, stooping over on the way and picking up a loose stick. "That happen often around here?" he asked, looking first at Pete and then at Kevin, who was standing as far away as he could from us without actually leaving. The broker was decidedly uncomfortable. He technically represented the Judge in this sale, but he also needed to play the congenial Realtor with me, make sure that I was happy.

Tucker's stance was open, relaxed; his hands played with the stick as if he were bored. I knew better.

"Good question, bro," I said and moved closer to him. "My friend wants a place for privacy," I addressed Kevin. "If trespassers are common, well . . ." I let my voice trail off and watched Kevin's face blanch, then turn red.

"I'm sure—"

"Ain't had any before."

Pete's declaration overrode Kevin's hesitant answer.

"Ah." I moved a little closer to the small group of cowboys. By this time, the other hands had left the barn and joined the party. Two other men joined the first two. None of them spoke a word. "So, how come this guy came here? After all, this isn't exactly the information highway. This piece of land is about as far from anywhere in this county that you're likely to get. Far as I know, there's not really anything that this is between. And he sure as hell doesn't look like an advance scout for a mall developer."

"Between?" I'd obviously confused Kevin.

"You know, between here and there . . . or there and here. Whatever. This isn't a likely property for anyone traveling through to cross." I was right. The reason I was here because it was the one place between the highway crossings and the Wild Moon. Shit.

I shot a glance at Tucker, who'd picked up on my unspoken thought.

He stepped closer to the group of men, towering over the group. He topped me by six inches, and the tallest of the men by at least a foot. They each were compact, tough sinewy cowboys, of the type that roamed Central and South Texas when this was Mexican land.

"So, you looking for the Wild Moon?" my brother asked the captive man.

"Perdoname." The soft voice barely registered at first. *"No comprendo, señor. No hablo Inglés."*

Oh, bloody fucking hell. My Spanish was of the *"una cerveza, por favor"* and *"La plume de ma tante"* kind, semi-remembered lessons in Spanish and French mixed in with the everyday colloquialisms common in Central Texas. I couldn't actually speak the language. I don't think Tucker was any better at it than I was.

"Who can help translate?" I asked, looking around at the men. The ground suddenly became a great deal more fascinating than any of us, because to a man, including Pete, they dropped their gazes and stared intently dirtward.

"Kevin?"

"Sorry," he said with a shrug. "I can barely order a beer." As he spoke, his hand suddenly came up and started groping at the phone on his hip. He murmured an excuse and stepped aside to answer it.

"Perdoname, señorita, señor, busco a mi hermano." The small man tried to step forward, but was blocked by one of the others.

"Callate!" The cowboy hissed at the trespasser, then tipped his hat toward me. "Sorry, ma'am. He don't—"

"I'll handle this." Pete glared at the cowboy, who immediately looked back at the ground.

Okay, I'd had enough of this posturing. I started to speak, intending to tell the foreman exactly what I thought. "I'm thinking that you and your boys need to take this gentleman—"

"Hey, Keira, sorry to interrupt, but I have to get back." Kevin's voice held apology, if not a little relief. I knew this whole exchange was killing him inside. The last thing a broker wants is some sort of dustup at a property he's showing. Especially with a jerk like Pete.

"What is it?" I kept my eye on the cowboys in the corral, their hands still on the small man's shoulder. None of them were moving, they stood still, waiting for some decision to be made.

"Got a double-911-star page from the Sheriff's office. All hands to report. Seems we got some missing kids."

"I'm sorry, what?" I turned to Kevin, who shrugged.

"I'm a volunteer firefighter. Part of the job. Guess they're mounting a search."

Huh, that wasn't good. I nodded at Kevin, then shot a glance at Tucker who was staring at the men, as if trying to memorize their faces.

"Okay, fine, let's go. So, Pete, what are you going to do with this gentleman?"

Pete scowled at me, obviously not wanting to answer. Tucker glared back at him, his silence saying more than I was willing to say out loud. After all, even if I thought that Tucker and I could take all those guys, I wasn't about to advertise our special nature—not to these clowns, and especially not to Kevin.

"We'll take him outside the judge's property." Pete spat out the words.

"Not good enough," my brother growled.

"Where the hell d'you want me to take him, then? Give him a free ride back to Me-hee-co?" Pete spat again, this time spewing out a brown globule of chewing tobacco. He was obviously angry, but not daring enough to stand up to Tucker.

"A humane person would take him into town and drop him at the café . . . or even up to the bus stop up at the main town crossroads," Tucker answered, his voice as neutral as Switzerland.

"We'll take Mr. Trespass into town," I said, striding forward. "That'll get him out of your hair." And answer a few questions for me, too, while we were at it.

Pete grabbed my arm as I stepped past him. "You can't do that."

"Why the hell not?" I yanked my arm out of his grip, impatient with all this crap.

"Yeah," Tucker said. "Why the hell not?" He'd softened his voice even more. A small part of me wanted to see the asshole foreman stand up to Tucker and to see my brother go all hellhound on him.

The sane part of me wanted us to get out of there with that poor scared man. Whatever he wanted, we could figure it out, see if we could get it for him and make sure he had some money and bus fare to take him home. Then I'd make sure Adam not only fired Pete's ass, but I'd talk to the local landowners to make sure he didn't get another job anywhere around here. Whatever the trespasser had done, I was sure that it didn't warrant this kind of treatment. I figured this Pete probably treated most of the hands, exchange or not, pretty badly.

"He . . . we'll . . . I'm foreman here, and I'm supposed to take care of this stuff." Pete straightened his spine at the last, a bantam rooster facing the wolf in the henhouse. I almost laughed as that description skipped through my brain.

"And you did." Tucker sidestepped Pete and put his hand on the trespasser's shoulder. *"Como se llama?"* He smiled at the small man.

"Ignacio Robles." The man smiled tentatively at Tucker,

then lost the smile as he caught sight of Pete's face. The foreman's mouth was set in a grim line, jaw muscles jumping as if to an inner drumbeat.

"*Señor* Robles," I said, "would you like to come with us?" I gestured as I spoke, trying to convey my meaning, pointing to him, to me and Tucker, to the parked truck.

The small man's face was confused at first and I repeated my gestures.

A smile broke over his face. "*Sí, sí, señorita, muchas gracias.*"

"Great, then. Let's get Mr. Robles back to town, shall we?" I stepped to the other side of the man in question, flanking him. "Kevin?"

Kevin looked at us, then at Pete, then at the group of cowboys. I could see the uncertainty in his eyes.

"Shit, man, get your keys and let's go." Tucker dropped his hand from Robles' shoulder and strode forward. Kevin fumbled in his pocket and pulled out the keys, following my brother. I was close behind, keeping one hand on Mr. Robles' back and one swinging loose. I didn't expect any of the other men to do anything, but I wanted to be sure I was ready if they did.

"Back at Bea's okay . . . to get your car?" Kevin asked as he put the truck in gear. "I need to check in with Carlton."

"Perfect," I said. If there was one person in town I could trust to translate, it was my best friend and café owner, Beatriz Ruiz. We'd known each other for most of our lives. Despite everything, she still put up with me.

Ignacio Robles looked like a harmless man, but we'd know soon enough if he had any business with the Wild Moon—valid or in.

CHAPTER FOUR

THAT WHISPER: *"...here...come...here..."*

"Yo, sis." My brother's voice boomed inside the truck. "We're here."

"What? Sorry." I'd started out of my daydream and rubbed my eyes.

Tucker popped open the back door and slid out, motioning for Robles to follow him. I was a little slower on the uptake.

"Did you hear—no, never mind. I'm a little tired," I said to Tucker. I'd heard that whispering again, same as earlier in the morning. I shook my head to clear the fog. I was tired from a great deal of things other than a lack of sleep, but I hadn't yet been able to talk to Tucker about any of it. We'd ridden into town together, but I'd wanted to wait until after the property visit to discuss what was bothering me. Now, it would be later rather than sooner. First I needed to deal with Mr. Robles.

"Thanks, Kevin," I said, automatically opening the door.

"Yeah, sure." He tugged at his shirt collar and turned a little in the seat. "Y'all sure you . . ." He motioned to the parking lot, where Tucker and Ignacio Robles stood waiting for me.

"Yeah, we'll be fine. If he's not a mass murderer or evil terrorist, I'll make sure he gets a square meal and a ride to somewhere less isolated." I cracked a smile. Kevin didn't return it.

"He's probably illegal." Kevin stated a bald fact. "You okay with that?"

"Yeah, well, he still has to eat," I said. "I'm not going to pass judgment on him. Besides, my problem was never with the workers." My problem was with the landowners that paid them a pittance, then hung them up to dry when their usefulness was over.

"Okay, your call," he said. "So, what about the ranch? I'll fax you over a contract, if you like. We've got the number, right? I kind of need to . . ." He waved over toward the Sheriff's office, a few doors down from Bea's and already a buzzing hive of activity. At least five pickups and a couple of SUVs were parked along the walkway that joined the various storefronts. A dozen people were mingling outside, roadie cups of coffee or soda in one hand, cell phones in the other.

"The place is fine, I'm sure my friend will want to make an offer." Unless of course, there was something going on there that wasn't immediately evident. "We'll be in touch. And, Kevin?"

"Yeah?"

I nodded toward the gathering crowd. "You all need help, we'll be inside the café, 'kay?"

He smiled and nodded back. "Yeah, I'll let Carlton know. Could be a false alarm. You know kids."

"Yeah," I replied. I was lying. I didn't actually "know kids."

Kids in my clan were expected to take off and do stupid stuff . . . taught them valuable lessons, my dad would say. Yeah, well. I doubted that lessons like how to stalk deer, gather weather, or hide from humans when you were shifted were on the agenda for whoever these kids were. It was probably nothing. I hoped.

I slid out of the truck, shut the door and waved as Kevin strode over to join the group.

It was still broad daylight. By my reckoning, it was about two-thirty in the afternoon. The sun was still way too high in the sky and the temperature too close to summer for my tastes. I wanted to be indoors, in the cool rock-walled underground bedroom, sleeping next to Adam, despite our argument. Instead, I'd agreed to go visit this ranch in the middle of my night and stirred up who knew what in the process. I was hoping that Ignacio Robles was nothing more than one of hundreds of illegal workers that swam the Rio Grande and hoofed their way hundreds of miles north to find work at the local ranches and that the kids were off doing stupid kid things.

"HEY, *M'HIJA*, what's up? I rarely see you around here during the day anymore."

Bea came out of the back of the restaurant, smiling and wiping her hands on a dishtowel. She knew exactly why I'd stopped hanging out at the café. Good thing we were best friends, or I could take what she'd said the wrong way. That was one of the reasons we *were* still friends, she knew that my not being around didn't mean that I hated her. We'd been friends since she'd taken pity on the new kid in school.

"For that matter, I don't see you around either." She poked a finger at my brother, who laughed.

"You, Ms. Ruiz, are a tease," I said as Tucker laughed.

"You see all that commotion outside?" She gestured with the dishtowel as another pickup came roaring into the parking lot.

"Yeah," I said. "I heard missing kids?"

"Not so much kids as teenagers. Four of them," she

said. "The Wentz twins, Brittany Martinez and Jimmy Stahl. Frances Wentz says Missy and Matthew went out three-wheeling early yesterday morning and they never came home last night.

"This seems awfully quick calling a bunch of sixteen- and seventeen-year-olds missing," I said. "At least, to call in a search party, anyway. It's spring break, isn't it? It's been barely twenty-four hours since they left. Maybe the kids took off somewhere to party."

Bea shrugged. "No idea. I don't know exactly what's up. I heard somebody saying something about a phone call. Maybe one of them got hurt or something."

"Could be," I said.

"So who's this?" Bea motioned to Ignacio, who stood next to Tucker. "Another stray?" Bea's tone echoed the curiosity in her face. She'd gotten used to my bringing visiting cousins in to the café, before my branch of the clan scarpered to British Columbia. We hadn't gotten many familial visitors, of course, over the last couple of years. "This one doesn't look like your typical family member."

"He's not," I said, motioning for Ignacio to take a seat at the nearest table. Not that there was a lack of table space. At this time of day, the place was barren of anyone but Bea.

It was a smallish place, cozy, comfortable and homey. Two round tables that could seat up to six sat to the left of the green Formica cash wrap. To the right, four booths lined the floor-to-ceiling windows. The door to the kitchen was directly behind the cash register. A giant pot of coffee steamed aromatically on a small table behind the counter, complementing the glass case full of homemade goodies, from *pasteles* made from her grandmother's family recipes, to an assortment of pies that Bea bought from Mrs. Tschirhart, a local Alsatian widow who loved to bake.

"So . . ." Bea gave me a sidelong glance as she poured sugar from a large jar into one of the tabletop containers.

"I'm guessing you want to know who he is." I walked over to the coffeepot, still not exactly sure how to explain the whole afternoon.

"You're guessing right." Bea wiped the sugar dispenser and set it down on the table. I heard the thump from where I was standing.

"Have a seat," I said, brushing by her as I seated myself, passing a mug of coffee to Ignacio. The small man watched the two of us, saying nothing. So far, it was fairly likely that he'd not understood word one. A good thing, come to think of it, because not too flattering so far. *Stray* was the word for him, but I'd hate to tell him that.

"Damn, the coffee smells great. What is it?" Tucker grinned at Bea, all but batting his lashes.

"New blend," Bea said, answering Tucker. "Hill Country. A little pecan, a little chocolate, some cinnamon. Here, forget the mug by mug thing. I'll bring us a pot." She eyed Robles cautiously, but busied herself for a few minutes gathering coffeepot and cups. Tucker mimed drinking to Robles, he nodded, then mimed back a hand washing gesture. Tucker smiled and pointed to the dark green sign with the standard white stick figures. The door to both washrooms was located directly beneath the sign, to the left of the cash wrap.

"Con permiso," Robles said in a quiet voice and headed into the men's room.

"Okay, now what the hell is going on?" Bea demanded as she placed the full tray on the table.

I helped myself to a mug before I replied. "Heaven." I took a deep gulp and let the aroma surround me.

There is nothing better than excellent coffee in the com-

pany of friends and family. Not that I couldn't get coffee at
the ranch. I usually wasn't much in the mood for it there. I
preferred coffee at Bea's, hanging out in a booth with her,
yakking. Ranch awakenings were usually about sex and
cuddling and prepping for the night with Adam. I didn't
mind, not in the least, but I did miss this. I used to come into
the café every day around three for coffee, conversation and
breakfast tacos. Now, three o'clock was the prime of my
sleep time. That's what I got for hanging out with vampires.

Bea let me soak in the flavor for a moment. "I repeat.
What are you guys up to?"

I took another drink and put the mug on the table and
looked at my brother who relaxed back into his chair.

"Keira, please, you're a creature of habit. Suddenly, you
and your brother show back up here at four-thirty in the
afternoon with some *mojado*?"

"How do you know he's a wetback?" I asked, genuinely
curious.

She shrugged and stirred more cream into her nearly
white coffee. "It shows. Live here long enough. Live with
enough family from Mexico, you can tell."

"I sort of rescued him." I stirred half-and-half into my
mug of coffee, lightening it up some. Bea's eyebrows rose
as she sipped from her own mug, her gaze cutting over to
Tucker, then back to me.

"Rescued, as in . . ." She left it wide open.

"As in, Tucker and I went over to the Pursell ranch
today to check it out. Said he was trespassing. Looked like
they were spoiling for a fight and this poor guy was in the
middle of it. They wanted to kick him out."

"Pursell?" Bea's voice suddenly got several decibels
quieter. "You mean Judge Pursell's place, over by the
county highway crossroads?" She took a large gulp from

her mug and stared down at the tabletop. Okay, red alert time. This quiet tone wasn't like her.

"Yeah, Adam's looking to buy it. It's on the market." I reached over and grasped her wrist. "Bea, what is it? What's wrong?"

She shook her head, her fingers gripping the sides of the coffee mug. "It's . . . shit." A moment passed, then she looked up at me. "Who else was involved?"

"Involved?"

"In the almost fight."

I shrugged, still wondering what had upset her so much. I knew she'd never laid eyes on Ignacio Robles before a few minutes ago. "Some of the hands were holding him, trying to force him off the property."

Her shoulders relaxed a little. "So, just the hands?"

"Actually," I said, "there was the jerk of a foreman, Pete something. He was a royal pain."

"Pete Garza?"

"No clue," I said. "Why, do you know him?"

"I might." Her answer was quieter than her original question. She dropped her gaze again, staring into her coffee cup as if to read the nonexistent grounds. This was not good.

"I guess he could be a Garza," I continued. "I thought he was a gringo by the accent and the whole 'I'm better than you' 'tude, but around here, who knows."

"Yeah, that sounds like him. *Guero*, fairish hair, chews?"

"You know him?" I was puzzled. Bea and I had been friends for about thirty years. I'd never heard her talk about this guy. Even when I was away in England, we wrote e-mails constantly.

"If it's who I'm thinking about, he's bad news, Keira. As in, really bad."

"Okay, Lucy, you seriously got to 'splain this one," I joked with a fake Ricky Ricardo accent, trying to nudge her out of her evident mood. Hell, I didn't even know what kind of mood it was. If I didn't know her better, I'd have said she was frightened.

"Damn, Keira, I don't know how to tell you this."

I looked over at Ignacio, who'd emerged through the men's room door and stood watching us with a bit of interest. Whatever Bea had to say, I'd bet she didn't want to say it in front of a stranger, no matter if he didn't understand the language. I exchanged glances with Tucker. He took the hint.

"Hey, look, why don't I take Ignacio there to the kitchen? I'm sure he's hungry. Tia Petra can look after him, okay?" Tucker smiled at us both. He knew Bea well enough to know that it was time for the guys to clear out.

I squeezed Bea's shoulder as she looked up at me, a small smile crossing her face as she nodded to Tucker. "Sure. Sounds like a plan."

After a quick exchange with Bea, Ignacio followed Tucker into the kitchen to be overfed by Tia Petra. I could hear the elderly woman's voice through the swinging door. Something about *pobrecito* and enchiladas. No doubt, Tio Richard was cooking up a batch of his special enchiladas and lucky Ignacio was going to share in the bounty. Richard never cooked them for the restaurant, only for family. According to Tio Richard, Tucker was practically a son.

"So," I said as the door stopped its swing. Bea's face was still full of an emotion I couldn't place. "You going to clue me in here, Nancy Drew, or leave me in the dark?"

A sigh escaped her. "It's not that easy, *chica*," she said. "I know should have told you long ago, but . . ." A tear escaped and trickled down her cheek.

"Shit, Bea, what is it?" I handed her a paper napkin.

"About four years ago, when you were still in England, something happened. I never told anyone. Not even my aunt and uncle. Not even Sheriff Larson."

Oh fuck. This was way beyond not good. This was ranging into really, really bad . . . because by Sheriff Larson, she meant Carlton's dad. I could see her not wanting to share personal stuff with a guy we all went to high school with, but Sheriff Larson had been a father figure to all of us, upholding the law with a sense of humor and kindness behind the steel. In fact, since Bea's own dad and mom had died some years back, he'd been a fixture at the café, stopping in right before closing and staying until she locked up. Carlton himself took over that role after his dad died. People tended to look out for Bea, myself included.

"This guy started hanging out here, at the café. This was not long after I'd broken up with Emilio and I was fairly stupid."

"Yeah, I remember," I said, smiling at the memory. Emilio had been nice, but not so much into girls. He'd tried dating Bea to please his mother. When Mama Rojas died, he came out with a bang . . . so to speak. He moved to San Antonio and got a job as headliner at The Bonham, a well-known drag club. He did a fabulous Judy Garland. Bea hadn't been crushed so much as disappointed and a little peeved at herself. They'd been friends for years, but she'd never been so good with the gaydar.

"I'm guessing the guy was this Pete character?"

She nodded. "Yeah, stupid."

"Stupid how?"

"I started going out with him. He was fun, flattered me, paid a lot of attention to me. He really liked me. After Emilio, it was a bit of a relief to go out with a macho kind of guy. Really, that's all it was, fun.

"After a while, though, it was more possession than attention. One night, my nephew Noe and his buddies came over to the café to hang out. Damn, I think they were all of fourteen, fifteen years old. One of the older guys teased me, like they do. Pete came in and saw Chip grabbing me around the waist giving me air kisses. I'd baked some extra cookies for them, you see." The tears flowed freely now. I kept silent, letting her get it out.

"Pete got angry, slapped Chip and told them to stop fucking with his girl. You know me, I got mad right back and yelled at him. The place was full that night, one of our special barbecue nights, I think. Next thing I know, he dragged me outside and started screaming about 'how things looked' and 'my woman' and all sorts of Neanderthal things.

"I screamed at him and told him to go jump in the fucking lake . . ." She smiled a little through the tears. "Or something like that. I really don't remember. In any case, I told him it was over and he could go date some Pleasantville Stepford wife because I wasn't interested."

Bea sighed and blew her nose.

I waited for the rest of the story. I knew there was more. A screaming match with a boyfriend would never reduce her to tears. Never.

She stood up, walked over to the windows and lowered the blinds on the picture window to the right of the café door. Her hands trembled as she stood there, staring at nothing, the white cord wrapped around her index finger. I had to strain to hear her next words.

"I was sound asleep. I don't really know what time it was. After midnight, I guess. Barbecue nights usually end late. I heard something. Thought it was Tia Petra. You know how she gets after eating barbecue and *borracho* beans." Bea made a strange sound. It could have been a laugh, but I doubted it.

"Next thing I know, someone was on top of me, straddling me. I tried to scream, but his hand was over my mouth and nose. I couldn't breathe. All I could do was struggle a little. He had me with his weight.

"I tried everything," she said in a whisper. "Everything. I've been to all those self-defense classes. All I could think of was that I didn't want to wake Tia Petra. I didn't want him to hurt her, too. And Tio Richard's so deaf, I knew he wouldn't hear anything."

"It was Pete?"

"Yeah."

Bea came back to the table and sank into the chair. "He didn't rape me. He didn't really hurt me, not really. He—" She turned away from me. "All I could hear was his breathing . . . then the click. He shoved a gun into my neck and whispered something . . . I don't know what. For four years, I've been trying to figure out what he said, but I can't."

This was worse than I imagined. I got up and walked around behind her, leaned down to give her an awkward hug.

"The reason I'm still alive today is because of my aunt." Bea grasped my hands and pulled them around her, tightening the hug. "The noise I heard was Petra on her way to the bathroom. My bedroom door was open and she heard him in there. She got Richard and they both came in screaming and yelling. Richard had a rifle. I don't know why Pete didn't fire the gun. I think they startled him."

"Holy shit, babe, and all this time, he's been working at the Pursell ranch?"

She nodded. "He was working there when we met and

he never left. He doesn't come in here anymore. Never really saw him again after that night."

"But you didn't tell anyone?"

"I know, I know," she said. "I should have pressed charges. I should have told someone. But Tia and Tio wanted to keep it quiet. They were scared he'd come back. For months afterward, Tio would go to sleep in the recliner in the front room, with his rifle across his lap."

Bea turned in her chair and looked me in the eye. "I'm so sorry. I never told you. I felt so stupid to let myself get involved with that freak. And I knew you'd come tearing back here to do something stupid."

I pulled out of the hug and stood up. "Damn right, I would have," I said. "No one gets away with messing with my best friend."

"Please, Keira, it happened a long time ago. Don't bring it up. I don't want him to know I told you."

"You're still scared of him."

"A little. Like I said, he doesn't come around here at all, and I don't want to give him any reason to."

I didn't like it, but I conceded her point. I simply wouldn't tell her that I'd share this information with Tucker. He'd figure out a way to keep an eye on Pete Gringo Garza.

"So what are you going to do with Ignacio?"

"Figure out why the hell he was trespassing at the Pursell place." I didn't mention to her what Tucker and I were both afraid of . . . that it had something to do with the Wild Moon. She didn't need that.

CHAPTER FIVE

WHEN TUCKER came back out from the kitchen, he shot me a "what the fuck?" look, meaning Bea. I answered back with a silent "later."

He joined us at the small table and Bea poured him a cup of coffee, not looking up to meet his eyes.

"So, did Ignacio spill the beans?" I asked.

Tucker nodded and gulped his coffee. "Yeah, he's coming out to explain to Bea. Tia Petra is one damned fine investigator, but I thought Bea should hear this." He looked at me with another one of his brotherly gazes. I knew what he wanted. He wanted me to watch as Ignacio explained. Tia Petra might be great when it comes to asking questions, but my family was a hell of a lot better at hearing the unsaid.

The kitchen door swung open again and Ignacio came out, a plate of pastries in one hand, his hat in the other. I smiled at him and motioned him to a chair. He smiled back and put the plate of sweets in the middle of the table.

"*Para todos*," he said, quietly. For everyone. No doubt Tia Petra figured we could use the sugar and carbs.

Bea leaned forward and patted him on the back as she began to talk to him in a quiet, steady voice. I took the opportunity to study Ignacio. He was small and wiry; probably no more than five foot four and he'd obviously seen a hard life. His skin was leathered by sun, brown in the way that constant exposure would make it, a life spent outdoors. His threadbare, much-mended cowboy shirt had once been clean and neat. His jeans were worn almost through at the knees and seams. A battered cowboy hat sat on his head, covering hair that wasn't yet gray. He couldn't be more than thirty, yet the weariness in his expression showed many years of hardship. Whatever story he was telling Bea, I was sure it wasn't a pretty one. I understood one or two words in the rapid exchange, one of them being *"hermano"* again. As he spoke, his quiet face became animated, agitated. His dark eyes welled with unshed tears at one point, his hands rubbing them away before they could fall, but he never once shifted his gaze from Bea. Whatever he was saying, it was truth as he knew it.

"Momento, por favor," Bea said with a pat to Ignacio's hand. She turned away from him to face me and Tucker. "I'm going to send him back to Tia Petra. He wants to help out with the dishes, in exchange for the food."

I nodded and smiled at the man, trying to look sympathetic. I hated not knowing the language, not being able to express my concern directly. Mental note: learn to speak better Spanish. It was stupid to be ignorant of the language here in Texas. I could excuse myself with the rationale that I'd spent years learning other things, like martial arts, how to cast spells, how to help people die . . . but not anything remotely useful for this type of situation.

Neither Tucker nor I said anything while Bea escorted Robles to the back. I heard her explaining to her aunt, then more rapid words to Robles. Shortly, she was back at the table, pouring herself more coffee.

"Well?" I asked.

"It sucks," Bea said, "that's the extent of it."

"Sucks?" Tucker chimed in, reaching over for the pot to refill his own mug.

"He's looking for his little brother, Alejandro, Alex . . . at the Pursell ranch. Alex was working there for the past eighteen months. All of a sudden, poof, no Alex."

"Poof? As in he disappeared? And how little—a kid?"

"'Poof' as in he used to send money to the family every month, by the fifth of the month. And *little* as in he's twenty-three."

Not a kid then. For a moment I'd wondered if Alex's disappearance had anything to do with those missing kids. Highly unlikely, though, that a twenty-three year old illegal ranch worker would be hanging around a bunch of high school kids.

Bea continued, "Three months ago, the money stopped. Ignacio works on a ranch about twenty miles outside Piedras Negras. He gets to town a couple of times a month to pick up the money from Alex, but nothing's come in since before the end of the year. He tried calling a couple of times from his wife's cousin's phone, but no one at the Pursell place would tell him anything."

"His brother's been missing since December?" Definitely not to do with the kids then.

Bea grimaced. "That's what he said. He said he got through to someone who kept saying Alex left. That Alex wasn't there anymore. Then they'd hang up on him. Thing is, Ignacio doesn't have any transportation at home, he has to walk into town every time he tries to call. He's even sent two telegrams, but he's getting nowhere."

"Then he came here?"

"Yeah. He crossed over, then hitchhiked here. Took him a week. When he finally got to the Pursell place, they kept throwing him off the property. No one will talk to him."

"He's sure his brother worked there?"

"He's sure," Bea said. "I did ask him that. He said that

Alex told him the name of his boss in case anyone needed to contact him in an emergency."

"Has he gone to the Sheriff?" Tucker asked.

"You don't go to the law when you swim the river," Bea said with a grim laugh. "Carlton would have to turn Ignacio in to La Migra."

"Shit." She had a point.

"Look, Bea," I said. "I don't really want to get in the middle of this if I can avoid it. I don't want Adam and company involved, and these days, I'm part of the 'and company.' I hate the fact that this guy can't find his brother. Tell you what, let me run by Carlton's office, see if he'll talk to me and run this by him as a hypothetical. It won't take long. I can scoot over there while you all wait here. Even if Ignacio gets sent back to Mexico, I'm sure Carlton will help. Maybe his brother went to work at another ranch?"

Or maybe, he took off to find more work and for whatever reason, ended up dead somewhere in the middle of somewhere where no one will ever find him. There's a lot of empty land still left in the Hill Country. More often than not, acres and acres of properties owned by the weekend landowners were never actually seen by human eyes. These types tended to leave the metaphorical "back forty" to nature.

Bea frowned and shrugged. "Maybe," she said. "It's that I don't think Carlton'll want to stir up that hornet's nest. Besides, he's got those missing kids to worry about."

"Nest?"

"You know these good ol' boys hate anyone poking around their land," Bea said. "Carlton's up for reelection this year. You know how it is."

"No, I don't," I said, pushing my chair back. "Carlton Larson isn't the type of guy who puts some damned election above the law. There's a missing person and he'll help find him. I know him. And so much the better, he's already got search crews going out, maybe they can keep an eye out for Alex."

"You *knew* him, sister mine." Tucker's trademark grin flashed across his face for a moment. "Past tense. He wasn't Sheriff then. It changes you."

I stood up. "Like you know. You coming with me, Tucker? We can swing by Carlton's office, then go back to the ranch."

"We need to do something with . . ." Tucker inclined his head in the direction of the kitchen.

Well, fuck me. I was all fired up about justice and finding the man's brother, or at least what happened to him, and forgot about the man himself. "Shit," I said. "We need to find him a place to stay. We can't very well take him with us."

Tucker laughed. "Yeah, that's a good one. Let's take the illegal alien to the vampire ranch."

I slumped back into my chair. What the hell were we going to do? Rio Seco was miles away from any hostelry. The closest place was a small bed-and-breakfast about fifteen miles to the east. I'd happily pay to put him up there, but the place was run by a snotty southern belle with delusions of Scarlett-hood. She simply couldn't abide working folk. She primarily catered to people with more money than sense, overcharging her guests for the privilege of staying in a claustrophobic ten by twelve bedroom decorated like a doll's house version of Tara. She'd never take Ignacio.

"There's always your place," Tucker said. "It's empty . . . more or less. You still out there, Bea?"

She nodded. "On occasion. When it gets too crowded at my place."

"There you have it, bro, no go on that," I said. "Besides, even if Bea weren't hanging out there, that doesn't mean I want someone I don't know staying there by himself. Damn it. Maybe I'll have to move back to the house for a while. I suppose Ignacio could stay in one of the guest rooms and Bea could use the other." I eyed my brother. "Or you could."

"Could what?"

"Move back to my house until Ignacio gets settled and finds his brother."

The look on Tucker's face was priceless. "I don't think so."

Bea laughed. "The two of you are so predictable."

Two pairs of eyes turned to look at her as two pairs of arms crossed. I almost laughed myself when I realized that Tucker and I were clones of each other at that point. These apples did not fall far from our family tree.

"You should hear yourselves. It's really pathetic."

Crap. She was right. I was being selfish and so was Tucker. Here this poor man can't find his brother and we're bickering about leaving our lovers for a few days.

"All right . . ." I started to say.

"Never mind." Bea waved her hands, motioning for me to stop. "Don't get all sacrificial lamb on me. It doesn't make sense for him to go to your place, anyway. He speaks about as much English as you do Spanish. I'll take him to my place. He can bunk in the guestroom above the garage. It's not fancy, but it's clean and none of my cousins are here now, so he'll have some privacy. Besides, Tio Richard already offered."

I threw a sugar packet at her. "Bitch." I threw her a huge grin. "You started that to see what we'd do."

"Yeah." She grinned back. "I love messing with you two."

"So let's go tell Ignacio the news," Tucker said. "We'll leave him in your capable hands and give you a call later."

"Sounds like a plan," I agreed. "Thanks a million, Bea. I owe you . . . and I'll do my best to convince Carlton."

"Anytime." Bea stood up and grabbed the now empty coffeepot. "Here, help me carry these things into the kitchen and I'll tell Ignacio what you're going to do."

The small man listened solemnly as Bea explained the situation to him. When she stopped speaking, he turned to Tucker, then to me, tears forming in his dark brown eyes.

"Gracias," he said, his voice breaking. *"Gracias a Dios. Señor, señorita, eren angeles. Con el ayude de Dios, encuentran a mi hermano."*

I looked at Bea who translated his words.

Oh great. He called us angels . . . and hoped that with God's help, we'd find his brother. Angels we most certainly weren't. Far from it. In fact, in his church, we were precisely the opposite.

CHAPTER SIX

"H EY, CARLTON," I said into the cell phone. "This is Keira. Give me a call when you get a chance. Need to drop by your office when you have time."

I flipped the phone shut and tossed it to my brother who did me the favor of tucking it into my backpack that was at his feet. We were in the car, about to head out to the Wild Moon. The Sheriff's office had been closed when we walked over and all the trucks and SUVs were gone. One of those little clock signs indicated that the Sheriff would be back at nine. A hand-lettered sign was taped up next to it giving the emergency number for the search. We figured the little clock meant tomorrow . . . at which time I'd be sound asleep, or had better be. This sleep deprivation thing was not happening again.

"You think we should volunteer for the search?"

Tucker shrugged. "Officially, probably not. I think we should both probably get some sleep. Later tonight I'll do some unofficial recon. Go sniff around a few places they might have gone. I already heard some scoop from Tio Richard."

"Scoop?"

"You know he knows everything that's going on." Tucker grinned. "He's better than a police scanner."

"So true. What's up?"

"Evidently, the Wentz twins got new three-wheelers and wanted to show them off. Seems there's some sort of crush or something going on with Brittany Martinez, so she hooked up with them. And since Missy and Matt drive sports cars and they needed to transport the three-wheelers, Matt called Jimmy Stahl and the four of them headed out in Jimmy's F-150 early yesterday morning. Richard said the four of them stopped by to get coffee and snacks on their way. He heard the kids say something about going towards the county highway crossroads and the government land. Evidently there's a new lover's lane spot out there, ever since the quarry kind of became off limits."

I flinched a little. The quarry was now off-limits because last October Boris and Greta had dumped the bodies of their two accomplices there. It was also the spot where they nearly killed me, Adam and Niko. The mundane folks around here didn't know what happened, but they'd heard about the blood that someone found there. Now even the teenagers gave it a wide berth.

"Isn't that up by the Pursell place?" I asked. "Also, up towards the far north boundary of the Wild Moon."

"If by 'up by' you mean a mile or so, yeah," he answered. "Not to worry, sis. Niko's got that whole area under patrols and, to be on the safe side, he's working on game fencing it. I don't think that kids hanging out in some clearing is going to be a problem. You don't honestly think there's any connection with Alex Robles, do you?"

"Nah, if he's been gone since December, that's not likely," I agreed. "But . . . I don't like coincidences."

Tucker nodded. "Yeah, I know what you mean. A little too much going on in the same neck of the woods, so to speak. No worries, though. We can talk to Adam and Niko first thing tonight and get some more patrols out there."

"Why do they think the kids are missing? They didn't

come home when they were supposed to, sure, but an all-out search party?"

I was not going to tell my brother that his story sounded a little too much like the beginning of an after-school special, where one of the kids would get hurt on the three-wheeler and they'd consequently all learn a sincere lesson.

Tucker shrugged. "Richard heard Eustace Lovelight say something when he came to get coffee for the searchers. Seems all four of the kids have been acting a bit weird lately. His daughter used to be friends with Brittany, except Brittany started hanging out with the Wentz kids and Jimmy. They're always whispering together in corners and they've stopped hanging out with their other friends. Eustace said they were supposed to come to his girl's birthday party today out at the lake. They didn't show up and when Dina called Brittany's cell phone, she answered, but whispered something she couldn't understand, then hung up. Dina tried a couple more times but Brittany never picked up. She told her dad she thought she heard screaming in the background."

"Oh for . . . they're *kids*. Teenagers. They got drunk or high or both, stayed out all night and are afraid to go home and meet the consequences. How many times did Bea and I do exactly that? You all knew we were safe. Besides, it's plenty hot out right now; they could've gone over to Hippie Hollow Too to cool off and sober up before facing the parents. If they were playing around on the tire swing that would explain the screams . . . and/or the fact that girls tend to shriek when skinny dipping."

Tucker's grin reflected various fond memories we both had of the secluded lakeside area, christened Hippie Hollow Too in remembrance of a popular 1970s Austin-based hangout.

"That's certainly a thought," he said. "Tell you what,

I'll swing by there after we go back to the ranch. You can wait to hear back from your former boyfriend. Think he'll call you?"

Tucker was now staring out the side window, no doubt playing the nonchalant brother card.

"Yeah, he'll call," I said. "Because . . . well, let's say he plays fair."

Tucker looked at me and laughed. "Because his ex-lover is boffing the local vampire king?"

"Shut up." I had to laugh. "You know Carlton's still married. And in spite of everything, brother mine, he still doesn't know about us . . . or the vampires. Okay, so maybe he hates Adam for being Adam . . ."

"Yeah, well, even if he doesn't know Adam's true nature, he's bound to hate him on principle," Tucker said. "You know how much Carlton's always hated the so called 'idle rich.'"

"That he has," I agreed. Carlton had always been leery of people who didn't have to put in what he considered an honest day's labor. Back in the day, it took him a while to warm up to my family, none of whom had done a so-called honest day's labor in centuries. Of course, Carlton wouldn't have had a clue (and still didn't) about the labor we actually did do, nor who we really were. On the face of it, we were all as much idle rich as any ditzy heiress in the tabloids. Except we were a lot smarter and kept a much lower profile.

Tucker placed his large hand on mine, oddly formal for once. "I promise, Keira, whatever it takes, I'll help. So will Niko and Adam. We'll help find Ignacio's brother."

"Thanks. I appreciate it."

"And you, Keira? How are *you* doing?"

I shrugged. "Who knows? Still dreaming on and off. Nothing for the past couple of weeks and nothing as specific as before. Nothing concrete. Except for . . ." I hesitated, not sure I should mention the strange semi-whispers I was hearing on and off.

"Something else?" Tucker squeezed my hand in sympathy.

"Yeah, it's a little off-the-normal path but, so far, everything that's happened to me is not exactly normal for the Change." I took a breath. "I keep hearing whispering."

Tucker's eyes narrowed. "Go on."

"I'm not sure if I'm asleep when this happens or drifting off or what but, I think I hear someone calling me, wanting me to come. At first I thought it was you calling. I heard 'sis' and 'come here.' That was this morning. I was going to call you but Adam told me you were. . . 'busy.' "

"Busy?" He frowned and then beamed as he twigged. "Oh, yeah, I suppose we were. I can definitely tell you I was not calling *you*." He patted my cheek and I caught a whiff of his skin. Salt sweat tang mixed with something foresty and dark underneath, a scent of family, of . . .

Unbidden, my brain formed a mental image of two male bodies glistening in candlelight, moving together in rhythm. Myriad candle flames flickered, light catching on muscled arms, thighs, gleaming on red hair, one nearly strawberry blond, the other a bit darker. The fragrance of some green herbal scent suffused the room, a hint of sweat and musk beneath it. Quick breathing and a quiet murmur of urgent whispers teased my ear, words too low, too intimate. Perhaps if I concentrated, I could—

"Keira?" Tucker shook my shoulder hard. "Keira, snap out of it."

I blinked a few times and stared at my brother, his red hair not spread out on a bed, but neatly plaited. "Sis, what is it?"

I scrubbed at my eyes as if to remove the memory. "Crap, get out of my head," I muttered.

"Excuse me?" Tucker sat back against the car door, facing me. "Oh, please tell me you did not . . ."

"I did," I whispered. "And I'm sorry, I didn't—"

"Do it on purpose. I know," Tucker said. "But wow, that was new."

My eyes widened as I caught his unspoken thought. "Oh crap. You saw that?"

"Saw it? I *did* it. But yeah, if you mean saw it now in your head with you, yeah. We do look pretty, don't we? But if you want to watch, I'm sure—"

I smacked his arm. "Damn it, Tucker, *really*." I sagged into my seat. "Bloody hell, I haven't had a vision in weeks, and *this* is what I get, my brother and Niko shagging? Really not what I wanted."

"So what did you want?" Tucker teased.

"Hell, if I'm going to get visions again, I'd like to figure out what happened to Alex Robles," I retorted. "Then I could at least be useful."

"'S'truth," Tucker said. "In any case, you didn't see something horrible."

I smacked him again. "That's what you think."

Tucker's laugh filled the car.

After a moment, he sobered, his tone more serious. "I know it sucks to be you right now, Keira. It can't be fun not knowing from day to day if you're actually starting to Change or what, but you know I'm here. Whatever happens."

"I'm fine. I'm a little worried that it's taking so long, but I can deal with it. It's probably because of my mixed blood—early onset, longer duration, sporadic symptoms, visions, whatever. Eventually, I'm sure everything will be fine and I'll come out a happy little shapeshifter or something else. I'm not sick. I feel fine." I wasn't sure who I was trying to convince, but on the face of things, it all sounded plausible.

"Maybe we should try to call Isabel? She's a healer. She knows her stuff."

"Maybe. But is it even worth it? C'mon, a few visions, some not-whispers—not the stuff of nightmares. I'm not worried about *that*."

"Then what are you worried about?"

"Nothing." I was lying . . . sort of. I wasn't exactly *worried* about Adam, more angry and frustrated than anything else . . . maybe. His reluctance to take blood in its more pure form did worry me. Although I wasn't familiar with vampire physiology in any scientific sense, I did know that surviving on what was, at best, subsistence nutrition couldn't be good and couldn't be a long-term solution.

Plus, lately, Adam seemed so . . . okay, so he was undead, but . . . lifeless—and the lack of sex wasn't the only sign. He'd stumbled. Fallen. Sure, with a grace no human could have emulated—he hadn't dropped anything—but no matter how uneven a floor, how dangerous a stair, how rough the terrain, I'd *never* seen any of my shapeshifter brothers trip or stumble. I hadn't said anything else to Adam, distracted by the foreplay that ended nowhere, but. . .

It still remained, at this point, a discussion to have privately between Adam and me. I didn't want to involve my brother. He was my brother, but his relationship with Niko put him in an odd position. Niko was Adam's second, and had been at cross-purposes with me since the moment we met. Sharing details of my relationship with Adam and our arguments wasn't something I wanted to do, not quite yet.

"Hmm." Tucker didn't sound convinced.

"Look, really, Tucker, I'm okay. I'm tired and want to get back to the Wild Moon so we can get some sleep. Then, tonight, we can talk to Adam and Niko about Alex. And if the kids aren't found by then, them, too."

"Okay, Keira," Tucker agreed reluctantly. "But you know I meant what I said. I'm here for you, and not simply as Gigi's watchhound. If there's *anything*—" He broke off the fraternal advice, then added: "Look, do one thing for me."

"What's that?"

"For my peace of mind, call Isabel? Tell her about the visions, the whispers and anything else? At least I'll know she knows and if there's anything to be worried about, she'll tell us."

He had a point.

"Okay, I promise, I'll call her soon as we get on the road."

"Deal."

CHAPTER SEVEN

"KEIRA, A DEAD MAN cannot make a baby. You really have to start taking this seriously."

In my not-so-humble opinion, cell phones had to be the work of the devil . . . *a* devil . . . well, whatever evil thing exists if one doesn't happen to believe in the traditional Judeo-Christian dude with a pitchfork and an unfortunate complexion. I think cell phones are damnable not for the usual "they bug other people" reasons, although that alone is enough to consign uncouth users to the lowest depths of the Inferno. It's because I rarely seem to have a normal conversation on mine, even if I was the one initiating the call.

Tucker had dialed for me as I maneuvered the Land Rover out of the strip center parking lot and down toward the farm-to-market road that eventually led to the back entrance of the Wild Moon. Soon as someone answered, he'd turned the phone over to me.

Before I could get a "hello" out, Aunt Jane started talking. Getting her on the line instead of Isabel had been even odds, my luck the wrong aunt answered the phone. I pulled the Rover onto the shoulder. There was no use trying to drive and listen/talk to Jane at the same time.

Jane had been calling me practically daily, for weeks now, checking in on my health, urging me to come to British Columbia, "home to the family, Keira," she'd say. Most of the time, I ignored the calls and let them go to voice mail. As much as I loved B.C., especially the area they'd chosen to move to, I had no intentions of going there anytime soon.

I sighed and hunched over a little, turning away from what was fast becoming an amused look from Tucker. I kept the phone pressed to my ear—not that my dear brother wouldn't probably hear every single word of the conversation on both sides. Preternaturally good hearing came with the very infuriating package.

"Jane, really, I can't talk now. Besides, what makes you think I even want to . . . do what you said?" Crap, I couldn't even say it. Not that the idea was completely out of the question forever. I had no intention of playing the family game yet, not for many, many years to come.

Her gasp was everything I expected—an entire diatribe of words unspoken in a single intake of breath. She and her longtime partner, Isabel, helped raise me. As my semi-stand-in moms when my father pulled me away from my real mother and her own non-human and utterly twisted family back when I was seven, Jane and Isabel made sure I got the female input I sorely needed. Dad wasn't hooked up with any clan woman at the time and hadn't been for years. He didn't know what to do with me once he'd gotten me. Scrawny half-breed daughter, more than half a century younger than his youngest son, of which there were six. I was the first girl in his direct and indirect line. No girl first cousins around, but a hell of a lot of males. In fact, there weren't really many kids around my age at all. My branch of the clan had gone through a growth spurt sometime around the turn of the nineteenth century, and hadn't really seen the need to make more babies for a while. I was a bit of an accident . . . a happy one as Jane liked to explain.

The silence on the other end of the phone made me pause. I knew every dramatic inhale, exhale and tsk-tsk, every accompanying eyebrow raise and eye roll . . . this was a bit different, although I had no doubt that her expressive face was twitching on the other side of that phone line.

Damn it. I couldn't stand hearing this again. Once again, Keira Kelly was different. Not quite clan blood, not quite my mother's family. More of an outsider than Marty ever was, damn his mutant human moldering self. Yeah, Marty's ghost, if you happen to hear this, your favored cousin Keira is a freak. Marty's ghost didn't answer.

Okay, so I was being facetious. I knew his spirit wasn't around. I would have felt him. Nope, Marty was really most sincerely dead, cremated and spread out on the ground at the Point. No lingering spirits anywhere around our small region . . . at least not Marty's. The others, I didn't care about. They weren't family.

"How can you say that, child?"

Child. Yeah, right. Maybe to her I was a child. I *am* really young considering my expected close-to-immortal life span. But I'm waving a serious hello to middle age for a human—not that I am human.

I stared out the windshield at the road I should be on and let my aunt's words flow over me, not bothering to pay much attention. The vocabulary never changed. Aunt Jane had been playing this jolly tune for the last dozen weeks or so.

"Jane, since when have you jumped on the procreation bandwagon?" I interrupted, taking advantage of a pause on her end. "You and Isabel haven't exactly been the model clan citizens. You two could have done the donor sperm thing yourselves."

She and Isabel had been together for decades and, unlike some of the same-sex partnerships in our clan, had never taken advantage of clan donors. Clan relationships being as complex as they were, no one batted an eye to same-sex couplings. For that matter, almost anything went in my family. Long life meant every mix of relationship dynamics you could think of and probably some you couldn't. If you wanted children, there were plenty of temporary partners floating around. There were also plenty of "foster parents" to rear them if you couldn't or decided not to. This really was the whole "it-takes-a-village" concept. Sometimes, like now, I didn't like that part. My father, I could deal with. The rest of the relatives? Not so much.

"I had you to raise, silly child, that was plenty. Besides, you know I'm not from your grandmother's line. I didn't need to pass along genes."

I glanced over at Tucker, who was trying very hard to not look at me. Okay, I give him credit for that much politesse, even though his expression showed how much he was enjoying this.

"Very well, Keira, dearling, I'll try to be brief. You know my life choices aren't the point. Yours are. Why don't you come home? We can work this out."

I sighed again. I could hang up on her, but that would mean we'd pick up where we left off when she called back. And she *would* call back.

"I am home, Jane."

Left unsaid was what I always wanted to say—the part about "when would my family ever get a clue."

"Home means something different to you then," she retorted. "You know I mean family home. But even so, I called your house . . . several times. Left messages on that stupid machine. I know how much you hate for us to track you down on the cell." She paused. "When I called earlier this morning,

I got Bea. She was quite sweet. Told me you weren't there. We had a lovely chat."

"Bea sometimes stays at my place, Jane." I hoped that a statement of fact would be enough.

"And you?" It wasn't.

"I'm where I want to be," I said quietly.

"Bea's aunt and uncle still live with her?"

"Her nephew, too. Once in a while, some cousins come up from town and help out at the café. It's too many people for her tiny house. I offered her a place to stay when she needs it. It suits us. Besides, why aren't you bugging Tucker about coming home? He can do his part."

Jane laughed a little at that, her exasperation showing. "Your brother's already done his part, Keira. You know that. He's added to the gene pool. Now it's your turn."

Bloody unlikely, I thought. There was no way I was going to let myself get caught up in my double-great-granny's let's-make-a-baby games. Yeah, so what if she was head of the clan? There still weren't any guarantees that anyone from my branch of the family would be her heir.

"There's already too damned many of us as it is, Jane," I said, giving voice to my objections. "Because Gigi is who she is doesn't mean her line will win out in the next go 'round. What difference does it make if I contribute? Does it really matter if it's me or my brothers or cousins? They all come from the same genetic line."

"Not exactly." Jane's tone turned sarcastic in a way I hadn't heard in ages. She didn't do sarcasm well, and when she did, she was almost always discussing my not-so-lamented mother.

Well, shit. Yeah, that was certainly true. None of the family, save me, had my mother's blood . . . Sidhe blood.

"Okay, so not exactly," I repeated. "But does Gigi really want me passing that along?"

"Evidently," Jane replied. "Look, Keira, I'm not pretending to understand Gigi's thoughts on this, but her feelings are damned clear. She wants you to be a full part of the clan, so do I. You're one of us, part of the family . . . no matter who your mother was . . . is."

"Yeah, well, whatever, is or was, I don't give a rat's shiny ass about my mother or, frankly, about any of it. You know how I was treated. I'm not saying that indifference and cruelty are genetic, but if the reason Gigi wants me to make babies is because of my Sidhe blood then, no thanks, I'll pass . . . now and in the future." I really didn't want to talk about this anymore. "Look, Jane, whatever her reasons are, they're exactly that, *her* reasons. I'm happy now. Here . . . as things are. Can't I simply be happy for once?"

Jane sighed. I heard anxiety behind the sound. I knew she was trying to look out for me. That's what made it harder and harder to talk to her. She and Isabel were the only mother figures I really had. Gigi didn't coddle her descendants. My dad's style of parenting consisted of asking, "Are you okay, honey?" and dispensing loving pats on the head combined with huge doses of leaving me alone. He loved me, he'd rescued me, but until I came along, he'd had boys.

I had never asked if my dad had expected Mother to get pregnant. I had a sneaking suspicion that they'd all believed it couldn't happen . . . or at least was extremely rare. I knew that Mother's people (I couldn't think of them as mine, no matter what) had an extremely low birthrate. Maybe it was because they usually were fairly insular. There might be something to this expanding the gene pool thing. Not that I planned to tell my aunt that. They could go play musical chromosomes with someone else. Let one of my other brothers go play amongst the Faery folk if Gigi wanted more mixed blood babies.

"How are *you* feeling?" Jane asked.

I closed my eyes and stifled the umpteenth sigh. Jane had switched tactics and was now heading for the end run or some other obscure football metaphor. What did I know from football? Funny how this subject-changing thing worked both ways.

"I'm fine, Jane. Really."

"No sign of . . ."

My aunt's voice held the weight of unsaid words and an entirely different worry. The baby thing was an excuse to get me to what she considered home. This was something else.

"No, not yet."

"You're not worried, Keira?"

I hesitated before I said anything. Granted, I'd called to ask about my visions, the Change process that was taking much longer than any I'd heard of. But as much a healer as Jane was, she was quite different from Isabel. Jane was mostly a homely healer, dealing with cuts, scrapes and other mundane illnesses and conditions.

"A little, Jane, but nothing in particular, nothing specific. I actually had called to see if I could talk to Isabel."

"A good thought, sweetheart. She's so much more knowledgeable about these things than I am, but I'm sorry. She's not around." Jane chuckled. "You know her. She's off on one of her walkabouts. Calls me once in awhile to touch base. She'll come home when it suits. Is there anything I can tell her?"

I hesitated for a moment, but decided that talking to Jane about specifics would worry her. "Thanks, Aunt, but

I think I'll try calling Isabel myself. Did she take her Iridium satellite phone?" The damned thing was ridiculously expensive to use, but it was more or less guaranteed to get a signal from more or less everywhere.

"Yes," Jane answered. "She's been in and out of touch over the past few weeks, but I'm sure if you call and at least leave a message, she'll ring you back. And you know if there's anything I can do . . ."

"I know, Jane," I said. "Thanks."

I flipped the phone shut and turned in my seat to look at my brother.

"Anything I can do?" Tucker's voice was quiet in the stillness.

I shook my head. "Not so much."

"Family." He grinned.

"Yeah, family."

Before I could put the car back into gear and drive on, the phone rang again. I glanced at the display. Carlton.

CHAPTER EIGHT

MY CONVERSATION with our local Sheriff was not going well.

"What do you mean you can't help?"

Carlton stepped around the side of his desk and placed the papers he was holding on top of an already teetering stack of what looked to be faxes.

"Exactly that," he said. "Do I need to make it any clearer?" I couldn't tell if he was being facetious or deliberately being a pain in my ass.

"Why the hell not?"

I folded my arms across my chest and leaned back in the extremely uncomfortable metal and vinyl office chair, shifting around to try and alleviate the ache. The place was a royal mess. The standard government-issue battered steel desk seemed to bow under the weight of all the papers strewn across it. Behind the desk, a narrow folding conference table held an ancient and grubby PC, a coffeemaker and an assortment of disks, plastic stirrers, and Dixie cups. To its side, a Texas flag drooped on a metal stand. The walls were painted that particularly revolting shade of green found primarily in government-funded institutions. The floor was some sort of dingy vinyl tile that once upon a time had been a variation of off white. Now it was nearly as gray as the desk.

Our tax dollars at work. I'd driven Tucker back to the ranch, then turned right back around to catch Carlton at his office. And caught him I had, bedraggled and almost as exhausted looking as Adam was, but for an entirely different reason. Carlton said he'd be there for about an hour before going back out to rejoin the search for awhile before they quit for the night. I debated on touching base with him the next day, because I was so damned tired, but my better nature prevailed. I couldn't let Ignacio down only because I was losing sleep.

"Because, Keira," Carlton said as he returned to sit in the cracked green vinyl rolling chair, "if I look for this guy's missing brother, I'd have to go out to the Pursell place. If I have to go out to the Pursell place, the hands will have to go away and the Judge loses his workers . . ." He leaned back a little, almost copying my own stubborn body language. "Even worse—I go out to the Pursell place, no one warns the hands or the foreman and I'm stuck having to call the boys in green, detaining who knows how many illegal workers and deporting these guys back to Piedras Negras or Nuevo Laredo or whereverthefuck. Again, depriving Judge Pursell of his hands."

I slapped my hands on the desk, and stood up. "Damn it, Carlton, the guy's brother is missing . . . and you're worried about Judge Pursell?" I was getting really tired of arguing. Story of my life these days. Seems like every part of my life these days consisted of one argument followed by another.

There was a small part of me that niggled at the back of my brain. A part of me that whispered that I might need to retreat in the Adam/Keira war, accept Adam's decision, regroup, *think* about what the hell I was doing. I didn't want to listen to it. Not yet. Our relationship was a few months old. There was too much at stake here, pun not intended. I wasn't ready to give this up over some stupid disagreement and I wasn't willing to see him continue to decline.

Nor was I ready to abandon Ignacio's quest for his brother. At least I could do something to help somebody . . . and not sit idly by while—never mind. Keep your mind on the present, Keira Kelly.

"You don't get it, do you?" Carlton pushed over the pile of paper and perched a brown polyester clad hip on the edge of the desk.

"Don't get what?" I asked.

"It's not only the Judge, Keira," Carlton said. "It's everyone around here. You know how it is. I have to turn a blind eye."

"To what? To the exploitation of illegal workers?"

Okay, so I wasn't exactly being very nice about this, but damn it, I really wasn't liking this version of my former lover. Carlton had once been as left-leaning liberal and power-to-the-people as I had. Despite his own father's being Sheriff for most of our growing years and while we were young adults, he'd done his fair share of rebelling—like picketing the local post office when they let Irma Luna go in her second trimester. She'd been the relief postmistress for six years and her pregnancy never interfered with her duties. We'd staged a schoolwide walkout when the board wanted to force a ridiculous dress code. These were ranchers' kids, how on earth did those idiots expect them to wear something other than blue jeans and boots to class? The picketing didn't work, but the school walkout did, mostly because the county officials didn't want to ask the Sheriff to arrest his own son for something so petty,

Even though the years had been very kind physically to Carlton, it seemed his political leanings had shifted much further right. Something I would never have expected.

"It's not that," he began.

"No, it's the fact that you're up for reelection this November, isn't it?"

"Jesus, you really don't think much of me, do you?" He looked hurt.

"I don't know what to think, Carlton," I said. "This doesn't sound like the guy I knew . . . the guy I dated."

"I've changed," he said. "So have you."

He didn't have to say it. Last fall, he'd also returned to Rio Seco and taken the suddenly empty Sheriff's position, leaving a breaking marriage, hoping to rekindle our long-dead affair. Unfortunately for him, I wasn't interested. Never would have been, even if Adam hadn't entered the picture. Carlton was one hundred percent human. I wasn't. Simple as that. He'd always wanted more than I could give him, even when we were in our early twenties. I'd been sowing wild oats. He'd been more interested in planting a cozy garden for two. After Marty's death, Carlton went back to Conroe, picked up the wife and kids and brought them to Rio Seco. Small town or no, I mostly kept out of their way, staying at the ranch as much as possible. No need for me to rub Carol's face in the fact that her husband's former girlfriend was around.

I shrugged at him. Yeah, I'd definitely changed, even if I hadn't yet Changed.

"It's not about the election, Keira. It's about getting along with the ranchers . . . being a part of the community, trying to keep relations cordial." He picked up a couple of the stacked papers, riffled the edges, then put them back down. "I can't investigate this officially, because if I do, it's going to open a can of worms I have to keep pretending I don't know exists. Most of the local ranch owners are barely keeping their heads above water. They have to hire illegal workers. Most guys treat the workers okay. I know this. I make sure of it."

"How?"

He shrugged. "My guys keep me posted. I go around, do the gladhand thing, being neighborly. Nothing official. Nothing in uniform."

I didn't have to look at his face to know how much he hated this part of his job. I could hear it in the weary words. Carlton was a man of action, of doing something, fixing things. He wasn't much for schmoozing the good ol' boys to keep up the old fashioned status quo. That had been his father's strength. Not his. I didn't care. Someone had asked me for help.

"So do the same thing and look for Alex. How hard can it be?"

"It's not the same. I can't go around and ask questions."

"Why not?" I crossed my arms over my chest again. Outstubborning Carlton was an option that I seriously considered. I could very well sit here until he agreed to help or threw me out. He wouldn't do anything drastic. Carlton never really knew what to do with me. Liberal as he was, or used to be, he'd still been raised around here, among the same good ol' boys with Miss Ellie mothers and grandmommas straight out of *Little House on the Prairie* . . . or *Deliverance*. When we were little kids, Rio Seco was precisely that, a dry town perched on an almost dry branch of the Guadalupe River, its town center made up of nothing more than a decrepit Mobil gas station, its red flying horse faded to a puke pink and listing precariously above the twice-mended front door. Next to the gas station had been an equally run down diner that attracted more flies than customers. This suited my family fine. More room for us to remain under the radar.

Not long after my father brought me home, things began to change. Developers bought the Mobil and the diner, tore both down and built a strip center. Bea's parents, not long off the ranch themselves, took out a small business loan and opened the café. Over the years, the strip center became the heart of town, such as it was.

The attraction now wasn't town, but the properties around the area. Resort ranches, weekend retreats for yuppie investors. Some folks sold out and moved away. Others stayed behind, working their ranches, trying to make ends meet. I wasn't sure of the latest census numbers, but after my kin left a couple of years ago, I would guess there were no more than a scant two hundred souls that officially lived in what was counted as Rio Seco. If you included all of those in the county proper, I'd imagine it was maybe a couple thousand. Now, I'd bet those numbers were more than quadrupled.

It was these people who would reelect Carlton in the fall and vote on important things like taxes and levies that paid salaries and benefits. I really did understand. He had to keep them happy. In some ways, it was a bit like my own family microcosm—the fragile juggling of duty versus neighbors—of knowing when to let a local kid go when he really should have gotten a speeding ticket, of when to turn a blind, but still watchful, eye when the senior high class (all sixteen of them) sneaked out behind the Super Suds Car Wash to talk trash and drink a couple of beers a few nights before graduation. Thing was, in the Rio Seco hierarchy, there was a semblance of democracy. Nothing like that existed in my clan, that is, unless Gigi wanted it so. She ruled absolutely which, honestly, was only logical given the nature of my clan. When Gigi had said "move," they did.

I still wasn't sure exactly *why* she hadn't dragged my sorry ass to Canada with them when they'd left. I can only think that she must have been distracted. That and the fact that she needed someone to watch over Marty. Not that I'd done a very good job of it.

In any case, I did understand Carlton's reluctance. I didn't like it. Part of me wanted him to throw off the mantle of law and turn back into the guy who was once my friend. I wanted to hear him say, "Sure thing, Keira, let me help." Unfortunately, I may have killed that part of him last October. We were civil, but not overtly friendly. I didn't know if he'd ever come to accept Adam in my life. I supposed it was a good thing he had no clue about Adam's true nature.

"Look, we're wasting time. You can keep asking me and I can keep saying 'no,'" he said. "We're getting nowhere here." He turned his back to me, muttering a bit as he stuffed a folder into the pile beside the computer. I heard him anyway. "Like always."

I chose to ignore that, like I chose to ignore the fact that this argument was becoming way too close to the other one I kept having—with Adam. What was it about me that I kept asking for things from people I cared about (in various degrees) and kept getting told "no"? Surely, someone at some point had to say "yes." Was I being that unreasonable?

"Look, I get it, Carlton." I leaned forward a little, catching his gaze as he turned around to face me. "I understand, really. It's that—"

"I know, Keira. I know." He watched me for a moment, his expression solid, unchanging, then softening a little. He started to reach a hand out toward me. I could see the emotions flickering, warring, behind his brown eyes. He wanted to help. He wanted—

He pulled his hand back, short of touching me. "Tell you what . . ."

Carlton stood, the words abrupt as his movement. He reached behind him and grabbed his Stetson. "I've got to go back out and rejoin the search. If I can, I'll poke a few snakes and see if anything turns up." He adjusted his Sam Browne and placed the hat on his head. "I can't promise you much and I won't go stirring things up, but if I see anything, I'll let you know."

I rose from the chair and extended my hand. "Thanks, I appreciate it." He gave my hand a brisk shake.

I turned to leave, then paused. "So, the kids, you really think something's wrong?"

He shrugged. "Can't say for sure. We've searched out by Coronado Creek, at the Point and up by any of the places most kids go three-wheeling or even necking. They're not at any of those places. If I weren't getting the feeling something's hinky with the families, I'd have probably figured they're off doing teenage spring break things. I can't put my finger on it." A look came over his face, and he closed his mouth abruptly as if to stop the next words from escaping.

"What?"

"It's . . ." He shook his head. "You ever seen those Wentz kids? Their parents?"

I shrugged. "I know who they are, I think. They're all tall, blue-eyed blond WASP types? Mom and Dad are straight out of some Polo shirt, twin-set and pearls ad; kids junior versions of the same?"

"Yeah," Carlton said. "It was weird. The mom was all ice and polite when I went to talk to her about the kids. Dad's out of town. I couldn't tell if Mrs. Wentz was stoned, drunk or completely emotionless. When I asked for a photo of the kids, she gave me this family portrait thing. The four of them were dressed in matching clothes. Looked like two sets of twins, not parents, older son and younger daughter. Like I said, hinky. Creeped me out."

"By hinky, you meant in a *Flowers in the Attic* way, not a *Children of the Corn* sort of way?"

He barked out a quick laugh. "Oh, Christ, I hope not. I've got enough to worry about."

I chuckled, "Yeah, it's probably some sort of teen rebellion thing. I imagine they're all tucked away somewhere wanting to piss off their parents."

"Probably so, but we've got to check it out anyway." He shot me a measuring look. "Hey, you know, there's one spot we haven't searched yet."

"Where?"

"Out at your new boyfriend's place." He paused a moment, as if considering what to say next. "We've been trying to get in touch with someone out there all day. Left a few messages with the day manager. He tells me he hasn't got the authority to let my searchers in and that his boss isn't reachable. I was planning to go out there this afternoon, but then you called." His eyes narrowed. "Are you here because of that? Did your boyfriend ask you to come?" His tone narrowly missed being sarcastic, but not by much.

"Carlton, seriously, what the fuck? I came out here to talk to you about Alex Robles. Besides, the Wild Moon property isn't entirely fenced, there's a lot of land up to the north of the main ranch complex that's open." And free of vampires during the day, I added to myself. "I promise, if I'd seen any sign of those kids, I would have let you know. Don't be . . ." I stopped myself before I said something I'd regret. I didn't want this conversation to degenerate into the same argument we'd seemed to be having ever since he'd returned to Rio Seco.

"I'm not being . . . whatever, Keira," Carlton said. He started to say something else, then closed his mouth and took a deep breath. "Look, I could use help. I'm short staffed and short volunteered right now with a lot of folks taking advantage of spring break to go on vacation. I've got four missing teenagers and, evidently, a missing illegal worker and I've spent less than five hours at home in the past thirty-six. I know it's a lot to ask but could you mobilize some of the staff out at that ranch and help us look for the kids?"

I didn't respond right away, because yeah, that made sense in more ways than he could know. Mobilizing a cadre of vampires to search thousands of acres of land would be a hell of a lot more effective than even a much larger group of human searchers. If the kids were anywhere in the local area, they'd be found, even if they weren't out in the open . . . or worse. Problem was, none of the ranch residents save the human day manager and his family would be of any use until sunset. Not too far away now, but I'd still have to talk to Adam about it. And there was no way I could explain this to Carlton. He'd have to go on thinking whatever it was he thought. It wasn't as if his perceptions could harm us . . . them.

"Let me see what I can do," I agreed. "And you'll let me know if you hear anything about Alex?"

He nodded and looked at me. Our gazes met and for a brief moment, I saw the Carlton I'd once known behind those now hard-edged brown eyes. Maybe, just maybe, we could salvage what was left of this friendship.

"I'll call you if anything turns up," I said.

"Thanks."

With that, Carlton pushed past me and headed out the door, held it open and motioned for me to leave.

CHAPTER NINE

I WOKE UP to a still dark room, a sleeping vampire beside me. After I'd finished talking with Carlton, I'd driven straight back to the Wild Moon and managed to crawl into bed in an attempt to catch an hour or two of sleep before dusk.

Great, Adam was still sleeping, which meant I'd slept for a whole—I fumbled for my watch, which I'd dropped on the nightstand. We didn't have an alarm clock and the one clock in the room was an antique analog model hung on the opposite wall, which I couldn't see in the pitch dark.

There it was. I found the button and pressed it to light up the display. The numbers blinked and blurred. I rubbed my eyes. Wait, did it say eight thirty-five? What the hell? Sunset was at about seven-thirty this time of year. How could we have overslept? In the time I'd been sleeping with Adam, he was *always* awake promptly at sunset. More often than not, I'd be the one still snoozing and he'd wake me up. The few times I did wake up before he did, it was always before the sun went down, usually a few minutes or so.

I'd easily adopted his rhythms. Promptly at sunset, Adam would go from deep sleep to immediately awake and alert, as if a switch turned on the moment the sun went down. He never slept past that . . . never.

I sat up and turned on the bedside light. Adam lay

unmoving next to me, on his back, all signs of life missing. I pushed back the covers and placed my hand in the center of his chest. His skin was icy to the touch, his body preternaturally still. I waited, holding my own breath, hoping for evidence of the life that usually animated him. It might be magick that made him, but he still needed to breathe, not as often as humans, but his lungs still used oxygen and his heart would beat once or twice in the space of several minutes. Even in sleep, he'd be more than a corpse. He'd never looked like this before.

I made myself wait five extremely long minutes straining to feel movement, to feel breath or the quiet thump of a heartbeat. Nothing. I closed my eyes and concentrated, straining with my other senses, reaching to sense him. Damn it. Nothing.

I didn't want to go further, without permission, it's horribly intimate digging into a person's inner energy, but I *had* to. I couldn't *feel* him. Even when someone is asleep, I can feel an aura. Normally, Adam's was cool, green and calm, a low hum always present underneath the surface. Now, I sensed the same nothingness as in his outer appearance. I reached, letting my consciousness go, past the surface, past the stillness, searching—*there.*

Cold. It is cold, dark, a black hole. All light, heat, sound sucked down into the deep well. I am lost in the darkness, nothingness surrounding me. Something is down there, waiting for me. I do not wish to, but I must go. It calls to me.

With a wrench, I pulled myself away both mentally and physically, moving to the edge of the bed. Wherever he was, was not good.

"Adam," I shouted, reaching over to slap his face

quickly, pulling my hand away before I got caught up in the darkness again. "Adam!" No response.

I scrambled off the bed. I needed to get to the phone, call someone, Tucker, Niko. Get someone here to help me. Phone, where was my bloody cell phone? I couldn't remember where I'd dropped my backpack when I'd come in. Where was—wait, stupid, I could use the regular phone.

A gasp and shudder from Adam stopped me in my tracks.

"Adam?" I moved closer to the bed, watching him.

He blinked slowly a few times and, as if in slow motion, turned his head toward me as he started to lift himself to a sitting position. He braced an arm, paused, blinking again, shaking his head. One deep breath, a pause, then another. With visible effort, he sat up and leaned against the headboard.

"Keira . . . what is it?" he croaked out, his normally smooth, rich voice gravelly and broken.

I approached cautiously, unsure. "It's well past sunset, Adam. I couldn't wake you. What—are you okay?"

"Past sunset, that's—" He closed his eyes, concentrating. A moment later, they flew open and he stared at me, then at the clock on the wall. "How . . . ?"

I got onto the bed and sat next to him. "I don't know. I woke up and you were . . ." I waved a hand. "Out of it." I hesitated, not sure if I should tell him I'd invaded his privacy. No, I had to.

"Adam, I tried shouting, slapping you and finally I looked deeper."

"Deeper?"

"With my senses. Wherever you were was cold and dark. I felt you leaving, going into the darkness."

Adam frowned, a puzzled look on his face. "I don't re-call dreaming," he said. "Was I dreaming?"

Did vampires dream? That was news to me.

"I don't know," I answered truthfully. "It felt real. I was going to call Niko."

"Don't." The bald command surprised me.

"Why?" I asked. "You weren't responding. I'm still not sure you're completely tracking now. I thought you were dying, Adam. I'm not a healer and have no idea about your physiology, but I do know whatever is going on with you is not good. Maybe Niko can help. You haven't been well for a while and this was pretty much the rotten cherry on the top. Something's wrong."

"I'm fine, Keira." Adam crossed his arms and glared at me, eyes glittering in the soft light of the bedside lamp.

"No, damn it, you're not." I got off the bed, going from worried to angry in a flash. "Adam, are we even on the same *page* here?" I stalked to the other side of the room, eating up the distance far too soon. Before I'd walked off my reaction, I reached the opposite wall and had to turn around.

"I'd have thought we were in the same paragraph." Adam's voice remained quiet, a sharp contrast to my own frustration. He sounded stronger now, more like himself. That didn't negate the fact that less than fifteen minutes ago, he was lying like a dead human, the kind of dead you didn't ever wake up from.

"Bloody freakin' hell, Adam. At this point, we're not even in the same *library*." This was it, I was pulling out all the stops. I could not sit by and watch him fail. "You're avoiding sex. You're avoiding hunting, avoid-ing blood and still drinking that half-assed substitute that wouldn't keep a cockroach alive for long. You were asleep well past sunset, which you've never done in the time I've known you. Plus have you looked at yourself in a mirror lately?"

He was pale—not the naturally occurring pallor of what I'd assumed was standard vampire health, but tinged with an underlying tone of grey. Nothing obvious. Nothing that a casual passerby would necessarily notice, but I was far from a passerby and definitely a hell of a lot more than casual. I'd seen variations of this in those I'd helped cross. Relatives who were ready to die.

Adam wasn't there yet. I didn't see any of the calm acceptance, the *need* to pass on, in his eyes. As far as I was concerned he wasn't going to get to that point . . . at least not under my watch. Hypocritical? Yeah, but right now, that didn't matter, because no matter how much I'd sworn to allow people their own choices, I knew this wasn't Adam's choice. It couldn't be. I'd felt his reluctance when I'd sensed the darkness. If that was some metaphor for death, he wasn't ready for it.

"If this keeps up, you're going to die." I paced some more, needing to get my angry energy under control.

"I'm already dead."

"Technically, I believe the term is 'undead,'" I snapped back. "Damn it, Adam, whether you like or not, something is wrong with you. I'm thinking you don't trust me enough."

"I trust you."

"Then what the hell is going on?"

He dropped his gaze and said nothing. I waited, not patiently, because at this point, I was about as far from that state as I could be, but something in me recognized that if I didn't get my own emotion under control, I was likely to walk out of there and not turn back. I wasn't quite ready for that. Not yet. We'd barely gotten started . . . relatively speaking.

"I don't know," Adam said after a long pause.

Well, that wasn't what I was expecting.

"You don't know," I said flatly, all the anger washed out.

"Keira, I know you want answers, so do I. I know I've been avoiding you, avoiding looking at what's wrong. I'm sorry."

I bit my lip before the words *you bet you're sorry* slipped out.

"That said," he continued, "I would prefer to address this at a later time."

"Later—"

Adam's hand came up. "Please, Keira, I promise you that we'll talk about this, but not now. I have some duties in my office I need to attend to, including signing that ranch contract and meeting with Niko and some others. I'm already late."

Yeah, you're late because you overslept which is something you never do, I thought, but kept this to myself. I pondered his expression briefly. He watched me back, his face a study in neutrality. Over the years, I'd learned to read a myriad of neutral expressions. My family was rife with variations on bland faces, but they had nothing on vampires. In my short association with this group, I'd soon realized that for vampires, neutral was less Switzerland and more stone-face. I wasn't going to learn anything Adam wasn't willing to share.

"Okay," I conceded. "After. We'll talk." But this time, buster, you'd better be prepared to face some brutal honesty.

"By the way, I'm coming to the office with you," I said

over my shoulder as I headed to the shower. "Tucker and I need to fill you and Niko in on a couple of things."

"Things?"

I could hear the raised eyebrow.

"I'll tell you when we get there," I shot back and stepped under the hot spray. Two could play the "later" game. I wasn't above being a little petty.

CHAPTER TEN

NIKO LOUNGED against Adam's desk, all long limbs and leather trousers, arms crossed against what I was saying. Adam sat in his chair, dressed in his own version of vampire chic, elbows propped on the chair arms, hands steepled in front of him, face serious. I stood behind one of the guest chairs in front of the desk, my hands on its high back.

"So you want me to muster out my security force to look for these teenagers who may or may not be missing and for some guy's brother?" Niko drawled in amusement. "Some guy we don't even know."

"Look, both Ignacio and Carlton have asked for help and you have people with abilities beyond human. All I'm asking is that you search the Wild Moon lands. The Sheriff's searchers can do everywhere else. Tucker and I will lend a hand." I nodded toward my brother, who sat on a small couch against the right wall.

He'd come in with Niko, with some reluctance, after I'd called and bugged him. He'd made a beeline for the couch, promptly stretched his legs in front of him, crossing them at the ankles, crossed his arms and leaned his head back and shut his eyes. Right now, he was doing a good impression of *Man: Sleeping*. I knew better, though. Tucker was listening. He was letting me do all the talking.

"Keira, do you really think this man is on our property?" asked Adam.

"Honestly? I have no idea," I replied. "He could be, though. The Pursell ranch butts up against the far north-west piece of the Wild Moon and neither ranch is game fenced. Maybe he decided to leave, walked off in the wrong direction and then got hurt or something."

"How long has he been gone?" Adam asked.

"Three months, probably."

Niko's eyes narrowed and he straightened from his slouch. "This means we're looking for remains."

"Yes."

There wasn't any need to couch this in euphemisms with this group. I'd not said anything to Ignacio Robles, but if Alex had gone missing about the time the money stopped arriving, the likelihood was that he was dead. Although someone could live off the land, so to speak, around here, as there was plenty of small game and fresh water creeks, why would you want to? Rio Seco County may be sparsely populated, but there were plenty of roads that were, if not well traveled, at least not deserted. It wasn't that hard to find a ranch or a small farmhouse even if you were lost. No, Alex Robles was either long gone or long dead. In either case, I wanted to find him for his brother or at least establish that he'd left the area.

Adam placed his hands flat on the desk and leaned forward a little, studying me. "Keira, I must ask. Why is it so important for you to find this man . . . or his remains?"

I huffed out a breath and started again. "Because. I promised."

"And you always keep your promises." Adam said it not like a question, but a statement. I could see that, to him, this was enough.

"I try," I said quietly, trying not to think of what had happened to Marty, who'd died on my watch. I walked around and sat in the chair. "It's not that, Adam. I didn't like what was going on over at the Pursell place. That Pete guy. He's bad news and I think he's mistreating the workers. They're illegals and have no recourse."

Niko raised his eyebrows, mirroring Adam's expression. "Recourse?"

"To help. If they report any mistreatment, they'll get sent back to Mexico."

"I thought you disapproved of having undocumented aliens working the ranches around here," Adam said. "You spoke of it once, during a newscast we were watching."

"I am. I'm not against the workers, but this exact situation. They're not treated well. They're paid peanuts and can't do anything about it. I don't know the Judge, but from what I understand, he's never out at the ranch anymore. He may not even be aware of this."

"Keira." Tucker's voice interrupted me. "We don't know that there is a 'this,'" he said. He sat up and leaned forward, his elbows on his thighs, hands clasped in front of him. "Granted, we saw a threat, but in light of the fact that Ignacio was, indeed, trespassing, all we know from that and from what Bea told you, is that Pete Garza is a class-A asshat. We don't have any evidence he's mistreating those workers."

I slumped back in the chair. I couldn't argue with my brother's logic. The man rubbed me the wrong way at the ranch, and then after hearing Bea's story, I'd been sorry I hadn't done something. What, I don't know, but I wanted to get him back for having hurt Bea. "You're right, Tucker. I'm sorry. He's a nasty piece of work, but for all I know, he treats the workers like gold."

Tucker snorted. "I'd not go so far as that, little sister, but I think our primary purpose here is to search the Wild

Moon for signs of Alex and/or the missing kids, not to start a crusade against the mistreatment of undocumented workers."

"You think those children came here, too?" asked Niko.

"They're not quite children," Tucker answered. "At least, to anyone who's not us." His lips curved up as he exchanged a private look with Niko. Niko returned both the smile and the look, his eyes meeting my brother's with a twinkle. Damn. There was definitely an "us" there. I hadn't seen my brother look this besotted in well, ever. Since I've known him, he's been footloose and fancy-free. Looked like his fancy was not quite so free anymore. It was definitely interesting to watch.

"So they're not children and they are missing," Adam stated, an amused look on his face as he watched his second in command and my brother play footsie with their gazes.

"Teenagers with driving licenses and a means to leave town, such as it is, doesn't mean they're missing," Niko said, shooting a look at Adam.

"No," I answered, "but it does mean that they might be doing things they shouldn't . . . and they could *be* somewhere they shouldn't."

"Excuse me." A quiet voice came from the doorway to my left.

A young vampire stood in the doorway, holding a packet of papers.

"Sorry for the intrusion," he said. "I have the contract for you, si . . . sir." I heard what he almost said: sire, not sir. Huh. At first glance, he could have been about sixteen, or perhaps a very young seventeen or eighteen. In reality, he could be anywhere from his twenties to old enough to be my grandfather . . . twice over.

"Thank you, Lance." Adam held out his hand and Lance crossed in front of me to hand over the contract. He gave a quick nod of his head to Niko and to me and turned as if to go, then stopped and faced me.

"I heard what you were saying," he said, fixing me with his brown eyes.

"About?"

Lance shrugged, a lazy graceful gesture. "'Bout the kids. Missing guy, too."

He watched me as he spoke, a lock of dirty blond/brown hair falling over his forehead. He wasn't drop-dead gorgeous like the two other vampires in the room, proof that Hollywood got it wrong again. Becoming vampire doesn't automatically grant you preternaturally good looks and inestimable charm.

Lance stood about five foot five or so, square shoulders and build harking back to Middle European roots, more working class than ruling. His hair hung straight and fine, a short cut, unlike the other three men in the office. He wore nondescript brown denim pants topped by an equally muddy colored T-shirt. Tan chukka boots completed the ensemble. A symphony of earth tones.

"And?" I prodded.

He stared back at me, meeting my own gaze, no challenge in his look, simply the patience of the dead, clear and guileless. I looked for any sign that he was hiding something, but merely saw the calm stare of someone who could wait longer than I could.

He shrugged again. "Don't know if it's anything, but . . ."

"Go on, Lance," Adam encouraged in a soft tone.

Lance glanced back at his . . . boss/sire? Did *sire* mean the same thing in real life as it did in fiction? On *Buffy*,

sire meant the vampire that turned you into a vampire. Did
Adam turn this boy? Because even if he wasn't a boy now,
he was certainly a boy when he'd died. Adam smiled and
nodded. Lance turned back to look at me.

"Last night. Out hunting. Heard screaming."

"The kids?"

"Dunno. Could've been. Didn't go look."

I sprang out of the chair and grabbed his arm. "Why
didn't you check it out?"

At five foot ten, I towered over him. He stood still, as
unperturbed as when he'd come in. I revised my estimate
of his age upward as I stared into the brown wells of his
eyes. Definitely older than my great-great-grandfather
would be if I were human. There were centuries of experience in that gaze. I let my hand fall. No point in trying to intimidate him with my oh-not-so-mighty strength
and abilities. I may be stronger and faster by far than the
average human but to an older vampire, I was so much
papier-mâché.

"I was *hunting*," he repeated, without heat.

"Sorry, I don't get it," I said. "Why couldn't you have
gone over to look?"

Lance got a confused expression on his face, then
looked over at Adam and Niko.

"He doesn't understand your question," said Niko.
"Maybe I can explain."

"Niko." Adam's voice held a warning.

"For Christ's sake, Adam," Niko said. "It's not a secret.
Keira and Tucker live here. Don't you think they should
know?"

Adam dropped his head into his hands with a sigh.

Okay, what the hell? What was going on here? What
else had Adam been keeping from me?

"Go ahead, explain." Adam raised his head, his gaze catching mine. Behind that lucent green was more of the darkness I'd come to know over the past few weeks.

Niko continued his explanation. "When we hunt, we lose a little of our, say, social graces. It's not a good idea to seek out humans in that state. Unless you're very, very good at control, it could lead to—"

"Never mind," I said. "I get it. Bloodlust, right?"

"Of a sort," Niko replied. "It's more the hunger mixed with the exhilaration of hunting. Some of us are better at control than others." He looked at Tucker, who was oddly silent. "I'm sure Tucker understands."

"A little." My brother got a thoughtful look on his face. "I'm not sure that for us it's the same, though. I hunt when shifted. There's not really much letting go involved. I'm not a werewolf, I'm a shapeshifter. I'm wolf, but at the same time, I'm me. I think, I reason."

"A civilized wolf, then." Niko's smile widened.

"You could call it that."

"It's different for us," Adam's voice was harsher than normal. "The part of us that remains human peels away when we hunt. What's left is the hunger."

Was this what was behind Adam's behavior; the reason he wasn't hunting? I couldn't imagine that a vampire of his stature and strength had problems keeping the hunger in check. Even so, who the hell cared? So he went a little apeshit when eating. Not a problem for me, but it obviously was for him. I made a mental note to be brutally honest when we talked later. If losing face in front of me was the key, I could counter it with many stories about watching my brothers and father come home covered in the blood of their prey and reveling in the stories of the hunt over the carcass of whatever they'd killed.

"All right," I said. "You couldn't go check it out. Can you at least tell us where you were so we can go out there?"

Lance nodded. "Yeah, more or less. I can give you a general idea."

Right. Because when you're in the middle of chasing down a deer, it's not like you're making note of landmarks.

"Thank you, Lance," Niko said. "Let's go check out the property map and figure this out so I can send out some teams. Tucker?"

My brother stood and followed them out the door.

I WAITED a few beats after the men had left to let Adam compose himself. We were going to talk about this, oh yeah, we would, but right now, we had other things to concentrate on.

"Who is he?"

"Lance Zarimba. My new secretary. After Andrea left last month to go back to England, I needed someone to help out."

"Andrea was about as much a secretary as I'm Robby the Robot. She was muscle." I'd been sorry when Andrea left. I'd met her shortly after I'd run into Adam. She was the reason I discovered Adam was vampire and not merely a gorgeous man I used to flirt with. Andrea was pure Other. Like Niko, she didn't bother to shield her nature, so I'd twigged to her immediately. Adam, even now, kept up the pretense. Not that I minded, really. I did something similar. My sensitivity to human energies had taught me early on that I needed to keep a mental barrier up 24/7—especially during my fairly hormonal teen years.

He shuffled the papers on his desk and didn't meet my eyes.

"Yes. She was."

"And Lance is . . ."

"My assistant."

"He's new."

"Not to me."

"Not to—oh." Well then. The sire wasn't so much age as relationship. Perhaps he *was* Adam's get.

"He came to us from a cousin of sorts some time ago. From Poland."

"Escaping the war?" I moved closer and perched on the edge of the desk.

"One of them." Adam smiled and reached for my hand. I looked at him curiously, but he kept smiling as if entertained by my questions.

"I pledged to care for him as if he were mine," Adam explained. "When the group of us left England to come here, Lance elected to stay back for a time and assist me by wrapping up some paperwork. He arrived here last week."

"Ah, well then." That explained why I hadn't met Lance before. I hadn't been to the office in several days.

"So you and he . . . ?"

"Occasionally." Adam seemed genuinely amused.

I wasn't jealous, simply interested. I knew Adam had a past; how could he not? He'd met part of my own past when he'd met Carlton. I figured I'd probably keep meeting people from Adam's past as long as I stuck around the Wild Moon. Hell, I even knew Adam and Niko had been partners for at least several centuries and lovers for a portion of that time . . . if not most of it. But as with my own clan, vampires seemed to be less traditional with sexual relationships—at least, what passed for traditional in modern Western culture, anyway. Previous lovers weren't an issue. In fact, monogamy wasn't much of one either. Adam and I had never really discussed this topic in depth, but I could put two and two together and come up with Kinsey.

My main goal right now was to take care of current business—seeing what we all could do to find Alex Robles and the possibly missing kids and then carving out time in a neutral spot (not the bedroom) to have a serious discussion with Adam about what was going on with him.

I gave his hand a squeeze and smiled back at Adam. "Thank you."

"For what?" he asked.

"I don't know really," I said. "For answering my questions and indulging me on this search thing, I suppose—not that I've let you off the hook yet."

Adam caressed my hand, his thumb sweeping over its back. He leaned over and pressed a kiss to my wrist. "I know."

CHAPTER ELEVEN

"**M**ARCO . . ."
 I ignored the caller as I trudged across the rock and cactus laden ground, careful not to brush up against any of the cholla or prickly pear. Despite the oppressive heat, I wore my leather hiking boots, sturdy work jeans and a long-sleeved denim shirt over a cotton tank top. Each piece of clothing felt somewhere between damp and dripping. However tempting, I knew better than to do this in shorts and a T-shirt. The leather and cloth protected me from the cactus spines and the equally prickly mesquite as I literally beat around the bushes.

"Marco . . ."

I took another step forward, avoiding a fire ant mound. Nasty things, those. Good thing that keeping a close eye on the ground in front of me was part of the why we were all here. Yeah, we, as in a scraggy line of searchers, each dressed inappropriately for the weather known as spring in some parts of the world that weren't here. "Marco . . ."

"Tucker, seriously, what the hell? What's up with the 'Marco' business?"

I didn't wait for him to answer, but kept walking and doing what I was there to do: look for signs of the four missing teenagers—the reason for my having woken my brother (again . . . this was getting tiring for the both of us) and the reason we were now poking around land that was best left to the deer, the armadillos and the local flora. This several hundred acre property was adjacent to the Wild Moon and to the Pursell ranch and was owned by some sort of state conservation group.

After the discussion with Lance the night before, Niko had sent out several groups of searchers. Some concentrated in the area Lance had been hunting, others spread out throughout the ranch. I'd tried to talk to Adam several times during the night, but never had the opportunity. The office had turned into a base of sorts, vampires reporting for their search assignments, others coming back to report. By the time dawn rolled around Niko called it all off. There was no trace of anyone that didn't belong. I suppose the results had a silver lining, perhaps Alex's (or the kids') disappearance had nothing to do with the Wild Moon and all the good little vampires could rest easily in their comfy beds. In any case, that meant we were sniffing up the wrong ranch.

Adam and I had gone to bed after he called off the search, each of us reluctant to restart our private discussion at that point. He fell into a deep sleep almost immediately. It took me a little longer. A few hours later, my cell rang.

I was hoping it was Isabel. I'd already left three voice mails for her, hoping that at some point my wandering aunt would end up somewhere where she could check in. But it was Carlton, asking me if Tucker and I could help out. When Carlton told me where they needed help, I agreed and forced myself to get up, rouse my brother and head out into the day. The property they were searching was a little too close to the Wild Moon and a few dozen sleeping vampires for my comfort.

At the very least, Tucker and I could be there and help steer people away from anything that might be unusual.

Not that we'd run into any of the vampires. Even though some of them might be awake during the day, they would all definitely be inside, behind blackout curtains or in cellars blasted out of the native limestone. Like many so-called spring days around here lately, this one started off with a muggy morning and now, nearing noon, promised to be a record-breaking scorcher. Cloudless blue skies and searing heat weren't comfortable for most, but spelled severe discomfort, even death, for the residents of the Wild Moon.

Tucker jogged up beside me, closing the twenty feet of distance between us. He'd been walking to my right for the last hour, being pretty much a pain in my backside.

"You're supposed to say 'Polo.'"

He grinned at me as he wiped his face with a red bandanna, then tucked it into the back pocket of his jeans. He was dressed much the same as I was, though with a long-sleeved tee instead of the denim shirt. His clothing and footwear were nothing more than a concession to appearances. The flora around here couldn't actually do much to his tough shifter hide, even when he was in human shape, but it wouldn't have been prudent to advertise the fact by bopping around in a pair of running shorts and bare feet.

The extra clothes made him miserable, though. My brother was no more used to this climate than I was, despite having lived here a great deal longer than I ever had. His natural body temperature hovered somewhere slightly above a hundred degrees Fahrenheit, something to do with his shifter metabolism. Surviving Texas summers had always been brutal for him. He'd stayed, though, unlike me who, although technically living here for the past thirty years, I'd spent many of my post–high school years traveling, mostly in places with a milder climate, even before I'd left for what was then a more permanent move to London. Tucker, on the other hand, preferred being a homebody, content to be where Gigi planted her flag, whether deep in the Texas Hill Country or now, in British Columbia, where the weather, no doubt, was more suited for his nature. He'd come back to Rio Seco for me. Greater love hath no sibling . . . or something along those lines. I liked to kid him it was because Gigi made him, but I know he'd volunteered.

"Marco Polo? Are you that bored?" I stopped and took a swig out of my giant insulated Bill Miller Bar-B-Q mug. These were the best to-go cups ever. Thank goodness I had a good supply of them, even if I tended to stop at the San Antonio barbecue chain for the giant iced tea mugs instead of the food. I'd packed the container with crushed ice and water earlier, knowing the tricks of staying cooler in the Texas heat. When I was done, I passed the mug to Tucker.

"Bored? How could I be bored when I'm spending time with my favorite sister in the sweltering heat during the middle of the day?" Tucker echoed my own swig, gulping down cold liquid. "Oh yeah," he continued, "all this when I could still be in my cozy bed doing things that don't involve tramping through flora that want to take a bite out of you."

"Once again, I repeat: I really don't want to hear about your sex life, brother mine," I said. "And '*favorite*'? My overheated ass. *Only* sister."

"I was talking about *sleep*, sister dear," he answered with a laugh and a brotherly poke to my side. "But you go right ahead with thinking whatever you want. A little embarrassment isn't half enough punishment for you pulling me out of my extremely cozy bed two days in a row."

I shrugged and continued to walk forward, playing at nonchalant. "You didn't have to come."

"I suppose not," he said. "But someone's got to—"

"Keep an eye on me?" I tossed the words over my shoulder and sped up my pace a little.

Tucker laughed, wiped his brow again and picked up a tree branch he'd been using as a walking stick-*cum*-something to poke into the underbrush with.

"You know I *could* search better by myself." Tucker caught up to me and handed me back my mug. I hooked it back onto the belt clip.

"Yeah, well, good luck with that." I nodded in the direction of the rest of the searchers, each of them with a variation of grim determination on their faces.

"Yeah, well." He looked over at the group and then back out in front of us. "If we don't find anything now, I can come back later . . . after dark. We can both come back . . . with reinforcements."

I looked at my watch. "It's just gone noon. Do you think it's worth coming back? We're bound to cover a lot of territory between now and sunset."

He nodded and started to walk again, toward the unwritten finish line: the county road that bisected the state conservancy. On the other side of the road was land that had been under conservancy purview since 1956: two thousand acres of near pristine Texas Hill Country flora and fauna. We weren't extending the search there since most of the property was game fenced and patrolled regularly by state game wardens.

This was the second day of the search and there was no sign of the missing teens at all. No one had seen hide nor hair of the kids or the three-wheelers, nor Jimmy Stahl's pickup, since they'd headed out day before yesterday. The search teams had already hit up the most logical choices and with the help of the local landowners, the easy-access ranches were also a bust.

Personally, I still figured that we were all barking up the wrong cactus. Four teenagers, at least two of whom were legal to drive? I was betting they'd gone partying in Austin or San Antonio and had overdone it and were crashing at some friend's place. Hell, I'd done much of the same at their age and been too damned embarrassed to call home. Either that or they'd run off, but that was less likely, since three of the four were honor students and were looking forward to graduation in about six weeks.

"I think we still need to try," Tucker finally said. "Niko told me they did a fairly thorough search of the ranch property last night. They didn't quite come out to the property line because some of these search folks had camped out in the area. Too risky."

"Camped out, huh?"

"Yeah, normally, he'd have probably asked them to leave, but under the circumstances . . ."

"Yeah, low profile," I said. "Do you know how far they got? I, um, kind of left before—"

"So I heard," my brother replied drily. "More trouble in ye olde marriage bed?"

"Hardly," I retorted. "Because (a) so not married and (b) we never got to the bed part." Okay, Keira, a little too much information there?

My brother stopped in his tracks and turned to me. "Huh, wow, I was kind of joking, but I'm guessing this is not a joke now?"

"Not," I repeated. I let my voice trail off and took a

deep breath. Now was a good a time as any, I supposed.

Tucker's amused interest immediately gave way to his best brotherly "what's wrong?" stare.

I looked around before I spoke. The other searchers were yards away, walking two-by-two, most of them busy talking to each other. They were all out of earshot. No one seemed to be paying any attention to Tucker and me.

"So," I began, my voice cracking a little. "I have to ask you something. It's a little personal, but . . ."

"So ask."

I inhaled, my nose catching the slightly musky scent that always accompanied my shapeshifter siblings. Behind the closer musk was hot dryness of the dusty ground cut by the sharp green of the mesquite. I wasn't sure how to broach this subject with Tucker, but I knew he was the one that could relate . . . exactly.

"Does Niko sleep every day? I mean, coma sleep, like pass out at dawn and be dead for all practical purposes until dusk?"

"No." Tucker's brow furrowed. "Keira, are you telling me that Adam's doing that? That's not good."

"I know, I know," I said. "That's why . . . he hasn't been completely comatose all the time. Not really and not until fairly recently. When I first started staying there, Adam usually slept about five or six hours—that is, when he slept all the way through a day. He'd do that every few days or so." I looked down to the ground. "Mostly, he slept like that when, um, activities were . . . you know." I shrugged and put my hands in my pockets and looked at the ground.

Tucker chuckled. "So I'm guessing—"

"Don't, Tucker. Don't go there." I was already embarrassed enough. It was one thing to be blasé and worldly when talking about one's sex life in abstract, but discussing specifics with my brother? No. I couldn't do that. Maybe when I was older and wiser or something. Not now.

"Most of the time," I continued, "Adam would be asleep for a few hours, and often up and around during the day. We mostly keep . . . kept, to his house in the daytime. It's easy to avoid direct sunlight when you keep the blinds and curtains drawn." I looked at Tucker again. He looked back, his expression neutral, but concerned.

"The past few weeks, Adam's been sleeping every day, practically from dawn until dusk. At first, I thought it was some sort of seasonal thing. You know, more sun, summer coming, whatever."

Tucker took my hand, squeezed it a little. "I don't think so." I could hear the worry in his voice.

"Then Niko isn't . . . "

"No, he's still keeping to the same routine. Days we kind of laze around, sometimes sleeping, sometimes not. Nights he's outside, doing work-type stuff. Patrolling the ranch. Checking the stock, meeting with Adam, that kind of thing."

"Damn."

I squeezed Tucker's hand and let it go. He knew I wanted to talk, but I wasn't sure how candid I wanted to be. Some things seemed to need privacy even from my brother. Normally, I could talk to Tucker about mostly anything. This, though, seemed more like . . . shit. I don't know what. The kind of thing that you'd talk about with your best girlfriend I suppose . . . or maybe *Dear Abby*. Personal girl things that most brothers would so not want to hear about.

Dear Abby,
My boyfriend won't suck my blood. I've offered, I've

cajoled. I've even begged, even though begging is totally humiliating and degrading because I'm so afraid that if he doesn't, he's going to die. Oh, and did I mention he's a vampire? No, really, the undead kind.

Signed,
Confused in Texas.

Dear Confused:
What The Fuck!?

Okay, so writing *Dear Abby* was out of the question.

What the hell. I took a deep breath. Adam would have to deal. Privacy be damned.

"I think Adam is getting weaker," I said, my hands instinctively curling into fists, as if the words galvanized me to prepare to fight. "You know he's still not hunting, right? The conversation last night in his office? Plus, we haven't had sex in a couple of weeks."

"Why the hell not?"

At first I didn't know whether Tucker meant the hunting or the sex. I was about to say something when he held up a hand, his friendly glare turning into a serious frown.

"Keira, I may joke about it but I really don't want to pry into your sex life, nor in Adam's decisions, but something is wrong. Niko's been working like a fiend setting up hunts, making sure the overpopulated herds are scoped out, marked and tagged so none of the vampires would have to take any of the endangered stock. I don't care what Adam said about losing control or whatever. It's not like the vampires are roaming around willy-nilly and grabbing any which prey."

"I know, I know. That's just it, Tucker. Adam won't

hunt. He's still drinking that godawful wine substitute with the animal blood extracts. I was going to talk to him this morning, when he got back from the office, but he looked so tired, I figured I'd wait. I mean—he slipped on the stairs."

"Huh." Tucker looked thoughtful. "That's a bit unusual."

"Yeah. Vampires tend not to be clumsy—ever," I agreed. "I don't know, chalk it up to whatever, but I ignored it. Then, I tried, well, you know . . . then we had an argument. Tucker, I think he's afraid."

"Of what?"

"Remember last October, after Boris tried to kill him and Niko? He—both of them, actually—took blood from me. Adam said then it's like an addiction. I think he's afraid that he'll slide back into it, not stop with hunting deer, but start hunting humans again."

I tried to keep my voice steady. It wasn't easy. No matter how close I grew to Adam, we couldn't agree on something so substantially fundamental to the both of us.

I'd grown up in a family of hunters: my brothers, my father were all shapeshifters who hunted prey for food. Not human prey—the four-legged kind. No one in my family saw anything wrong with following your nature, your need, least of all me.

It wasn't that Adam would have to kill humans for food. That part of the legend, like many designed to frighten the peasants, was patently untrue. Not that they couldn't kill, but on the whole, vampires didn't need much blood to survive. A little while after I'd moved in, Adam gave me the Vampire Basics class—you know, "No, we don't sleep in coffins. No, holy items don't necessarily bother us," etc. Certainly opened my eyes. I don't suppose I was all that surprised, though. My own family members weren't exactly textbook cases. Tucker was no more like the Wolf Man of Hollywood legend than my mother was a faery princess . . . although, with her, who really knew? The less said about that branch of my bloodline, the better.

When Adam allowed Niko to open up the hunting, I figured that would solve the problem. But it didn't . . . because Adam wasn't hunting. He was still trying to survive on substitutes, worried that his need would grow too strong to ignore and, like the time he was imprisoned in the death camps during World War II, he'd lose control and end up killing.

I knew he was wrong. Hunting was a basic instinctual need for vampires; blood was the source of their nutrition, the necessary ingredient that allowed them to survive. The idea of living animal blood taken from the local deer population made sense to me. Drinking blood extracts that obviously weren't working, didn't. Problem was, no matter how many times we argued, how many times I offered my own blood, he'd continued to ignore it.

"Keira?"

"Sorry," I said. "I'm at my wits' end. I can tell he's growing weaker and he won't admit it. I've offered him my blood—several times. Flat out, he refuses, and he won't even have sex anymore. He fears one act will lead to the next." My voice dropped to a whisper. "I'm afraid he's going to die." I closed my eyes, not wanting to meet my brother's gaze, not wanting to see the quiet sympathy I knew would be there. I didn't want to start crying.

"Big fucking deal."

My eyes flew open at Tucker's blunt words. "What? What happened to tea and sympathy?"

"Is that what you wanted, sis? Because if you did, I'm

definitely the wrong person at this point. I thought you were looking for real advice."

I swallowed my initial retort. He was right. If I'd wanted the "poor baby" routine, I could have easily gone over to Bea's and couched all of this in general terms. Christ, why was I being this stupid? It wasn't like me to be all wimpy lovelorn whatever. I was stronger than this. *Yeah, but you've never really fallen for anybody like this before. You've never had to deal with someone actually possibly dying.* I tried to silence my all-too-honest inner voice.

"No, Tucker, please," I said quickly. "Sorry. I'm . . ."

"Confused, yeah, I know," Tucker said. He put his walking stick down and folded me in his arms. "C'mon, Keira, you know I only want you to be happy."

I hugged him back, grateful for the solid strength of him.

We stood there for a few moments, letting ourselves be silent. "Thanks," I whispered. Tucker kissed the top of my head, gave me a squeeze and then let me go. He kept hold of my arms, his large hands around my biceps, his gaze searching mine.

"Keira, I love you, but I have to be honest with you. Adam's afraid, big fucking deal. So he can get over it and learn to survive."

I pulled away from Tucker and crossed my arms. "Well, then, you bloody well tell him, brother mine, because I'm certainly not having any freaking luck."

"He's a stubborn man, li'l sis. He can't not be and still be in charge of his pack."

"I know. Thing is, there's not really anything you can do. For that matter, anything I can do. Ever try to outstubborn a vampire?"

He laughed, the booming sound ringing across the clearing. I quickly glanced over but most of the searchers were barely in eyesight range, much less in earshot. Thank goodness for that, I'd forgotten we were totally out in the middle of the outdoors with witnesses. I hoped if anyone had seen my mini-meltdown, they'd ignore it.

"C'mon, Keira, can Adam be any more stubborn than a 1,200-year-old hellhound or the hellhound's equally stubborn sister?"

He had a point. I wasn't sure how many years Adam had been on this planet, but my not-so-precocious brother Tucker Kelly had plenty of his own history behind him. My own lifespan, so far, paled in comparison, but I'd learned survival first in the faery mounds, then amongst six half-brothers and the rest of the local clan. My father's great-granny was the proverbial iron-fisted lace and velvet-gloved matriarch. My brothers treated me like any kid sister. I'd learned to be obstinate from an early age.

"Okay, okay, I concede the point," I said. "Adam may have won this round, but I bet we can come up with something. I am not going to let him die."

"Good, now let's get back to the searching," Tucker said. "I'd be willing to let the other searchers continue by themselves while you and I go back to the ranch, but we can't assume these folks won't overlook something, like we can't assume those kids are okay. Especially since Ignacio's brother still hasn't turned up either. This place is close to the Pursell place. If something happened to him, he—or his body—may be out here somewhere."

Tucker was right. We knew after last night that neither the missing kids nor Alex (or their bodies) were on Wild Moon property and even if I didn't know how much land

Adam's security team had covered, if they'd found something, I would know about it.

Tucker and I had checked in with Bea and Ignacio before starting this morning. Ignacio was happily helping by
busing tables and washing dishes, content in the fact that
we were looking for his brother. That kind of faith wasn't
something I knew or understood. I hadn't had the heart, in
the face of his earnest gaze, to tell him how much I'd fallen
down on the job. At least now, though, I could honestly say
we were really looking.

I glanced over at the other searchers, most of them
local ranchers, their wives, some teens and a smatter-
ing of merchants and other Rio Seco county residents.
Weren't many of us around since so much land had been
bought up by outsiders. Still a scant hundred or so ranch
families left in the widespread county, some others who
either worked up near Boerne or commuted to one of the
other larger, yet small towns to work in the Wal-Mart or
the H-E-B stores.

As much as I tried to avoid the obvious, Rio Seco was
a dying town, a dying county. Soon, we'd have to give up
and let the inevitable happen and become a place where
tourists came to live. It wasn't that I was against tourists, or folks who wanted to buy land here. For me, Rio
Seco was Sanctuary. It was the place that had come to
mean safety and love when I was a child and once again
was where I could simply be Keira Kelly, who hangs
out with her best friend Bea Ruiz, alone and happy to
be that way.

Not so alone these days, not with Adam, with Tucker
still there and, by concatenation, Niko, who wasn't exactly
a fan of mine, but tolerated me more than he had when
I'd first met him. We could continue to close ranks, both

Tucker and I removing ourselves to the Wild Moon permanently and leaving the town and county to the incomers, but I wasn't quite ready to do that yet. No matter how many days I stayed at the ranch, this was still my town, my turf . . . or at least close enough.

A far-off shout interrupted my thoughts.

"Something, over here . . ."

Tucker and I exchanged glances, then took off running toward the shouting.

CHAPTER TWELVE

"What is it? What have you found?"

The search group clustered around one of the rocky outcroppings that ran across this part of the area. The land was punctuated here and there with similar walls of rock; some were a part of the next hill, some were small remnants of a long-past geological event, walls of rock thrust out of the ground, hills sheared in two by whatever. I knew that several were artifacts of human intervention; the inevitable blasting that occurs when trying to build in this area. Limestone bedrock mere feet below the surface made construction extremely difficult.

In this case, the rock wall face looked natural, erosion or a long-ago earthquake having exposed it to the outside world, the open face of a hill whose top stood well above our heads, some fourteen feet or so high. Clumps of mesquite and a few live oaks studded the area in front of the rock face.

A dank, dark smell reached my nose, cutting through the dust and rank odor of too many sweaty bodies crowded together. I gasped and stopped still, a shiver running down the back of my spine as the memories crowded in, pushing away the present.

"She's of no use, Branwen, she is not our kind."

The cutting words make me cringe further back into the small corner where I'm sitting, my knees brought up close to my chest, making myself small. It's cold here in my thin shift and they haven't given me back my slippers this time, but I didn't want to ask them for my shoes. We're in a dark room, a single torch lights the damp walls. It's part of the old section and I wasn't supposed to be here. But after they . . . I'd run and found myself here. Found a room. Found a corner.

They came in a few minutes later. My mother first, then the Others. I stayed in the corner on the small ragged tuffet I'd found there, castaway furniture, like me. I'm not hiding exactly, don't really need to be. They never care what they say in front of me, but I still don't want to draw attention to myself. If they notice, it could hurt again. I stare down at the rag doll propped on my thighs. Maybe if I'm very, very still, they'll go away. I am so tired of hurting. Maybe if they forget about me it would be the same as my being like them. Maybe it would be the same as not being different.

"She's my daughter. There must be some *magick in her." My mother's voice is nearly as knife-edged as the other's. I don't know the other's name. They never tell me their names before they hurt me.*

"We've tried a thousand times, Bran." A second voice joins the first, this one softer, but still with the shiny bright hardness that marks all their speech. "It's not going to work. She's not—"

"I know, Geraint," my mother interrupts, impatient as always, except this time, she's impatient with Geraint, whichever one of them that is, and not impatient with me. I hug my knees tighter, smooshing Dollie. "She's not full blood. She's not magick." She looks over at me briefly and then turns back to the two in front of her. "What do you propose we do now?"

"She can be taken Above and returned." The first one speaks again, his misty eyes now staring at me. I tuck my

head down and stare at the floor. I can't stand their eyes.
They seem to see inside, see me scared.

"Above." The one called Geraint seems to agree with
the first one.

"Above?" My mother says it as a question. "She may
not be ours, but she's not human, either, Morcan. We
can't . . . and she is my daughter, my heir."

The first one, Morcan, interrupts her. "She cannot re-
main here, Branwen. She cannot be the—your—heir with-
out magick. Admit it, it failed. Contact her father."

"Keira, Keira." My brother's insistent voice brought me
back to my surroundings. "What is it?" he asked, whispering.

I shivered in the oppressive heat as I shook my head
clear of the clinging cobwebs of memory. Memory I'd
buried long ago, the last icy fingers of that far-away room
replaced by the sticky dampness of the humid Texas air. I
could still smell it, though.

"Nothing . . . the smell," I said as quietly, wiping my
damp face, hoping that Tucker, and anyone else who
might be looking would think the dampness was sweat. I
scrubbed my eyes with the back of my hand, removing the
last of the tears.

"It's a cave," Tucker continued to whisper, keeping his
voice low enough not to be overheard by the others.

"That's what I smelled," I said. "Was there anything
else? Signs of . . . ?"

Tucker shook his head. "Nothing," he replied. "I can't
smell human other than this crowd. Some old animal
bones, I think. Probably squirrel. Been out here too long to
be from . . ." He let his voice trail off. "I can't be positive,
though. All these people."

So no luck at first sniff, then.

I craned my neck and got up on tiptoe, balancing myself by holding on to Tucker's shoulder, trying to peek over the shoulders of the people in front of me. "Have you found something?" I asked, raising my voice.

A ripple of words spread through the small crowd, finally reaching me: "Damn, nothing." "It's nothing." "A cave mouth." "Too small."

I saw someone I sort of knew. "Hey, Chip, what was that? What did you see?"

He shook his head and looked down at the ground. "Nothing. Someone saw what looked to be some clothes, stuck up next to a rock. Thought it could be someone's shirt. Nothing but some torn-up old rags. Look like they've been out here for years. There's a cave mouth, but it ain't much more than a few feet in. Looked different from a distance. Guess we're all tired."

Tired came out as *tarred*. A long-time Rio Seco area rancher, Chip and his wife had spent most of their lives in and around the area. They were the bones and blood of the best of this land, the very people being overrun by the tourists.

"Guess I'd better get on with it," Chip said, and headed back the way he'd come.

People started to turn away, walk back to their designated search patterns, most of them muttering tiredly under their breaths, exhausted from the heat and the fruitless search. I pulled on Tucker's arm and indicated that we should step aside.

"I want to see," I said quietly. "In case . . ."

In case Alex Robles had come this way. In case something was there that the searchers hadn't noticed or that Tucker hadn't scented because of the crowd. And I wanted to not do this alone. Not when I could still feel . . .

I'd always known scents evoked vivid memories; the scent of vanilla and allspice was always the aunts' kitchen during the Winter Solstice as they baked up cookies and pies, anxious to make sure I had treats like the other kids in my school. The dark richness of fresh meat was my father after hunting, my brothers bounding at his side, teeth nipping at each other, matted fur needing brushing and combing, the excitement of a good chase fueling the adrenaline actions of the boys, still boys despite their long years. A spicy dry smell underlaid with a hint of powdery earth meant Adam; a similar mixture tinged with cayenne brought Niko to mind.

But no matter how rich the memory, how evocative the scent, I'd never before lost myself as I'd just done. The closest I'd come was last year, when I'd accidentally touched Boris Nagy and lived his memory; touched Adam and done the same. This, this was all mine. My memory, my fear, my best-forgotten past, triggered by the dank dark odor of the cave mouth. Not that the caves of my mother's family were either dark or dank. The main cave rooms were full of light, of the brilliance of magick and mystery and of the cruel glitter that is the Sidhe. It was only in the bowels of the cave system, rooms long since forgotten and abandoned, that the odor remained. It was in those rooms that I'd played with my *doli*, in hopes of being forgotten and left in peace.

"Y'all coming?" One of the searchers I didn't recognize was speaking to us. The rest of the group had dispersed, back to their search pattern, now yards ahead of us.

"Go on ahead," Tucker called back to the man. "My sister's a little woozy from the heat. We'll rest a while, then catch up."

The man waved a hand in acknowledgment and turned back to the search.

"Why don't you sit down a bit, Keira?" Tucker asked. "You do look a bit paler than normal. I'll take a closer look, peek inside."

I nodded and looked for a suitable rock. Finding one fairly close to the cave mouth, I hiked over there and sat, taking a big swig from my mug. I could smell it, but this time, it wasn't as sharp, didn't trigger any memories. Tucker patted my back and then moved closer yet, feet deliberately scuffing up the ground as he used his shifter senses.

After several minutes of this, I said, "Anything?"

"Old bones, old blood, old fur," he replied. "Looks like a wildcat or something used this as a lair sometime back. Those rags really have been here for years. None of these scents are recent."

"Do you think you'd be able to scent Alex?" I asked. "He's been missing a while. Any of that blood human?"

Tucker wiped his brow with his bandanna and came to squat next to me. "Nope, nothing human's been here in the past few months, I'd wager." He took the mug from my hand, popped the top off and shook some ice into his mouth, crunching it. "I can't tell from the entrance, it's too small for me to go in comfortably. Wanna try?"

I shuddered. "Me? Not so much," I said. "You know how I feel about tight, enclosed spaces."

"Claustrophobic, sister mine?" Tucker chuckled.

"A bit. Besides, what's the point of going in there if you know there's no way Alex, nor any of those kids for that matter, were here?"

"Curiosity?"

I stood up and brushed the dirt off my backside. "Yeah, well, remember what curiosity did," I said.

"Ah, but I'm no cat."

My brother . . . sarcasm became him.

"Well, then, oh hound, shall we?" I motioned in the direction of the search.

"I'm thinking not."

"Not?"

"As in the opposite of—"

"I know what it's the opposite of, Tucker," I broke in, a little annoyed. "I don't know *why* not."

"Because . . ." His voice trailed off. Tucker brought a hand up to shield his eyes, looking around the landscape as if he was searching for something in particular. I mimicked him, hoping I'd see whatever it was, too. Nothing stood out. Same old scrub mesquite, a few live oaks and a whole lot of rocky dirt, studded here and there with cactus. The buzz and hum of the searchers great fainter as the group continued to walk away from us, toward the farm-to-market road that signified the end of their day's goal.

A shrill sound interrupted. Damn. My phone.

I dug it out of my pocket and flipped it open without looking at the display.

"Hello?"

"Keira?"

"Carlton? What is it?"

"You asked me to call you. You know, about that missing man."

"Crap, I'm sorry, Carlton, I've . . . never mind," I stopped myself, because there was no way I could even begin to explain any of this. "Did you find something?"

"Actually, no, not really," he said. "Rick Asher and I have been talking to a few folks on the search teams. Everything seems to be fine . . . more or less."

"More or less?"

"Yeah, well, nothing I could really pinpoint, but when we went out to the Pursell place, they weren't exactly friendly."

"You went out there? I thought you said you weren't going to."

I could almost hear the shrug of Carlton's shoulders. "Had a good excuse, with the missing kids. Figured at the least, I could round up a few more searchers."

Bless you, Carlton, I thought. He had come through.

"I really appreciate that. I know it was tough for you," I said.

"Yeah, well." He did the over-the-phone equivalent of "aw shucks." I decided to cut him a break.

"Did you have any luck? Was Judge Pursell there?"

"Nah, he doesn't go out there much, I hear. Not since he remarried. Too many reminders of Greg."

"Who's Greg? I thought it was his latest wife who didn't like the place."

"Greg was his son. You don't remember that story?"

I wracked my brain for the elusive memory. "Wasn't there something ages ago? He died?"

"Declared dead, anyway," Carlton answered. "Went on a caving trip about ten years ago and was lost. Judge's first wife, Greg's mother, never came to grips with it. She divorced him and moved somewhere east, Maryland or something I think. She died a few years later. Judge did the legal stuff about Greg right after that. He married trophy wife number three a few years ago."

"Bitsy's number three?" Had Kevin told me that? I couldn't remember.

"Yeah, second one didn't last long. She left him less than a year after they were married. This one seems to be sticking around."

"Whatever flips his tortilla, I guess. So who'd you all talk to out at the ranch?"

As I spoke, I moved back over to the rock and sat down, motioning for Tucker to do the same. He shook his head, but came closer and crouched down next to me. I had no illusions. He was following both sides of the conversation as per usual. It didn't bother me—saved me from having to recap it later.

"The foreman," Carlton answered with a snarky tone. "Not the friendliest sort, is he?"

"Pete Garza? Definitely not," I said. "Did you get a chance to talk to any of the hands?"

"Actually, that's the thing. There weren't any."

"Excuse me?" I sat up straighter. Tucker did the same. "None as in 'not home now,' or none as in 'gone for good'?"

"I'm not exactly sure. Got a funny vibe about that foreman, but nothing I can officially do. Kind of got the feeling the hands all left. Not necessarily coming back, either. I don't know. I've got nothing concrete. When we went over to the Coupe place after, to see if we could round up some of those boys to help search back by the old school grounds, Rick talked to a couple of the hands there. They didn't want to say much, but I got a little info. Seems ol' Pete Garza's Bitsy's second cousin. One of the guys used to work for the Pursells, but left when Garza came on board. He told Rick that even though he had to do more work at Coupe's, at least the foreman isn't mean."

Well then, that was certainly interesting. So Pete was family. I filed that tidbit away.

"Did they know anything about Alex?" I asked.

"Nothing specific," Carlton said. "A couple of the guys remember him. They used to party with him from time to time, but that's it. We couldn't get much out of them.

They don't cotton much to the law around the C Note, even though they're all legal."

"I get that," I said. "So now what?"

"Not much more I can do, Keira."

I could hear the apology. Not that it did a whole lot of good, but I suppose he had gone out on a pretty thin limb for me.

"Who'd he talk to?" Tucker asked.

I shot him a "what?" glance.

"At the C Note, which hands? You know, names?"

Ah, I got it.

"What are the names of the guys you talked to, Carlton . . . at the Coupe place?"

"You figuring to go out there?"

"Maybe."

"Hmm. Don't go getting into any trouble," he said. "This isn't your cousin, not family. No excuses."

"No trouble," I agreed. Of course not. None whatsoever. At least no more than was already on my plate.

"Hang on a sec."

I could hear the sound of rustling paper. Typical Carlton. Even with an unofficial "I'm your friendly Sheriff" visit, he'd taken notes.

"One guy was Juan Gutierrez, the other was Paco Ramon. They usually hang out at the Diamondback some afternoons."

"The Diamondback? That old pool hall out Route 1685? That still open?"

"Yeah. Barely, but they get fairly good business from the ranch hands and such."

"Thanks, Carlton," I said. "I appreciate it."

"Sure thing, Keira. You know, if you run across something not right, call me. If it's a matter of a guy taking off on his family and seeking better pasture, do me a favor? Let it lie."

"No worries, I will." I hesitated before I asked, not sure if I really wanted to hear more right now. But no matter, I was part of the search so I figured I'd better. "Carlton, before I go, any sign of the kids yet?"

A deep, heavy sigh on his end was all the answer I got for a moment. "Maybe," he said. "I'm not so sure they're missing anymore. More like ran away."

Now this was a turn of events. "You're sure?"

"Not positive," he answered. "But the more we talked to Mrs. Wentz and her mother, the more I got that hinky feeling I told you about yesterday."

"Still?"

"Yeah. I had one of my female deputies talk to a few more of their classmates. Something's not adding up in the various stories from the parental side. I'm not calling off the official search yet, but if we don't turn anything up by the end of today, I will."

"You're that sure."

"Yeah. My guess at this point—and it's in no way official—is that one set of parents or another, or maybe all of them, were upset that somebody in that group was dating someone else. And the other two kids backed up the unlucky couple. From the sound of things, there was some sort of fight at home. I'm not clear who was involved but it's looking more like Mrs. Wentz and Missy had words. I imagine about Jimmy Stahl. Those Wentzs aren't the type to want their precious daughter dating some no-'count kid from the sticks."

Wow, Carlton, bitter? I thought. Not that this at all reflected on his own marriage to Carol Connors, daughter of Texas royalty: oil money. I refrained from making that observation. Tucker, however, snorted a bit. I poked him and continued my conversation with Carlton.

"Which leads you to believe they took off," I said.

"Makes the most sense. They had Jimmy's truck, so I'm thinking instead of going three-wheeling, they probably ran away."

"Even so, don't you have to keep looking for them? They're not of age, are they? I thought they were sixteen or seventeen."

"So did I at first, but turns out three of them are eighteen," he said. "Jimmy turned seventeen last month, but in Texas, at that age, he's legally allowed to move out from his parent's house. It's kind of like being an emancipated minor. As long as he has a permanent residence and goes to school, we can't force him to go back to his father. The school told me he moved in with his uncle over by the marina last week. So, far as I can tell—no crime here."

"Well, thanks, good to hear. I'll let you know if we find out anything on our end."

I flipped the phone shut and looked at Tucker.

"That's one thing off our list," he joked.

I had to smile. "Guess we're just looking for Alex Robles now."

CHAPTER THIRTEEN

THE DIAMONDBACK was as close as you could get to a Western cliché and not be in a low-budget Hollywood movie. It sat at the curve of a farm and ranch road, about a hundred yards across the official county line into Rio Seco. We'd never been a dry county. Not sure why the sale of alcohol had never been prohibited here, but that meant that tiny ice houses the size of a small cabin and not much bigger honkytonks tended to spring up in the sixties and seventies so folks from neighboring counties could cut across and buy beer and liquor.

By the mid-eighties, most of the surrounding counties had voted wet, so ninety percent of these ramshackle businesses went under, buildings falling apart at the side of the road, so many corpses of entrepreneurship holding mute testimony to the rule of capitalism.

For whatever reason, the Diamondback remained, its weathered cedar and shake shingles flaking, silver gray with age. The entire building listed to the right a bit, not inappropriately in this bastion of conservatism, home of rednecks and Longnecks and a state that spawned one of the worst presidents in history. The Diamondback's wraparound porch was as slanted as the politics you'd find inside, the fading cursive letters of the establishment's sign nearly blended into the background wood. If you didn't know the place was there, you'd probably never find it.

I knew it. I'd been there before, as a reckless teen with

Carlton, Bea and Bea's cousins, ready for drinking and two-stepping and the silliness that goes with being eighteen in a wet county in Texas. It wasn't much of a dance hall, or even a bar, but it was close and we could afford it. Teens from all over congregated at the Diamondback, slugging down longnecks and cans of Coors, struggling through the emotional hell that is dating.

Then the drinking age was raised to twenty-one, and the Diamondback took a dive in both reputation and clientele. Ranch hands could frequent the place legally, but they were often short on money and on women. I'd left Texas soon after the legal drinking age was raised: for England, college, family training—so I didn't really pay much attention to local watering holes and their respective fates. Bea had told me once in a letter she'd heard they were having problems making ends meet. I'd never thought about it again.

Now, as Tucker and I mounted the rickety porch steps, I wondered how they'd managed to keep the place afloat for this long.

As soon as we went inside, it wasn't hard to figure out.

The reek of stale smoke and staler beer hit me as I opened the front door. Tucker held it open for me and motioned for me to go first.

I shot him a look, more out of habit than anything else. I was glad he was there with me.

"Thanks." I smiled a little. He returned it and let the door shut behind him.

It was standard bar-dark inside, the noise of jukebox country warring with billiard balls smacking into each other and voices, lots of them. Hell of a place to be on a Sunday afternoon. Guess this was the ranch hands' version of Sunday services.

Tucker and I stood in the doorway, in the traditional wait-until-our-eyes-adjust pose. For us, it didn't take long. Genetics is a good thing—most of the time.

The Diamondback wasn't really very big, a squarish room with a bar in its center, a sort of dance floor wrapped around the bar, empty of dancers. Tables and booths lined the outside walls. Today, most of the seats were occupied. At the far right corner was a dark and somewhat forbidding doorway, presumably to the restrooms. The jukebox was to the right of that. A couple of pool tables nestled to the left of the bar, in the shadows of the back of the building. A few men, a woman or two, lounged there, holding cues, sipping beers. I couldn't really tell over the disgusting reek of decades-old nicotine and stale cigarettes, but I didn't think the place served any food—that is, besides the ubiquitous chips and salsa, beer nuts and bar snack mix found in most places. No doubt you could buy a bag or two of beef jerky if that took your fancy. I suppose that was for the best. I'm not so sure I'd want to eat food cooked here.

Weathered faces looked at us, eyes glittering in the hazy air as they studied the newcomers. Lean men in cowboy hats, snap front shirts and Levis worn over a variety of boot brands lifted bottles to lips as they checked us out. A few women sat at the tables too, but not very many. The guy-to-girl ratio in here approached that of the Alaskan bush.

The noise level subsided a little as they looked, but then rose again as most of them recognized us. It's not that we were friends with any of these guys . . . but since the Kellys had been residents for so many years, our faces were often seen at the various local establishments: the café, the video store, the deli. We were from around here (more or less) and didn't ping the tourist radar.

"Can I help you?" A heavy twang turned "can" into "kin." No offer of a seat, nor refreshment. No worries, we weren't there to drink.

A smallish woman approached us, bar tray in hand. Her tired face smiled at us, but the expression was a mask. Her eyes remained dull, also a bit wary. We were trespassers here, no matter how well known we were around town. This was not our turf. She wore an outfit that was meant to flatter, but didn't. High cut shorts, topped by a skimpy green T-shirt that barely covered her assets . . . and those she had plenty of. I hoped she'd gotten her money's worth. The shirt was so tiny, the cursive "Diamondback" barely had room to fit alongside the crooked name tag that read "Brandi." Of course. Brandi's streaked blond hair hung limp, the teased "do" a casualty of the job. No telling how long she'd been working today, but I'd bet it was more hours than her feet could stand. She had that pinched look that echoed the ache in her lower back and her arches.

I was beginning to think I'd walked into a movie set with all the ugly stereotypes and clichés. Of course, like they say, every stereotype starts with some truth. Brandi here was the proof of it.

"Hello, darlin'. How are ya?" My brother's voice suddenly turned Texan, the drawling sound nearly a parody of the woman's own heavy East Texas syllables. I didn't have to turn to know that he'd flashed the easy grin that so many women—and men—found irresistible. I saw it in the changed expression on Brandi's face. Her smile widened, the lines on her face smoothing out, her eyes now flashing interest. She shot me a quick glance, unsure of my role here. I could see her trying to work it out. Girlfriend? Wife? Her gaze dropped to my hand and then as quickly back to Tucker. Not wife. No ring. Her smile flashed into calculated smirk, then back to friendly smile.

I stayed quiet. This was definitely Tucker's forte, not mine. He could do the honors.

"I don't know if you know me," he continued. "My name's Tucker Kelly. This here's my sister."

This here? For the love of . . . what was he going to say next: *Fixin' to*? *Yonder*? I hadn't heard my brother lay it on this thick since I was in junior high and he was messing with my cranky adolescent self. If he said *aw shucks* I was going to smack him one . . . right upside the head.

Brandi's friendly smile morphed into a seductive one, a little lip lick and head toss thrown in as garnish. Her attitude instantly changed from wary to wannabe wicked sexy, every bit of her body language straining to shout "Notice me." Obviously, she'd decided I no longer posed a threat to her.

"Hey there, Tucker," she said, her twang now softened deliberately into a drawl. Damn. She was a pro at this. I didn't blame her, though. Tucker was probably as far from her normal clientele as you could get and still be in Texas . . . even if you assumed his humanity.

"Can I get y'all somethin'?" Her smug smile included me this time, the "y'all" a concession.

"How about a couple of Shiner Bocks?" My brother asked, honeyed voice dripping with teasing seduction. I had to fight not to laugh. Brandi was good. Tucker Kelly was better . . . much, much better. Centuries of practice. In fact, if I had to compare, and ignoring my own emotional bias, Tucker was probably better at this than Adam.

"Y'all pick anyplace to sit," Brandi called over her shoulder as she scurried to get our beers. "I'll be right back."

"I'm sure you will," I muttered under my breath.

Tucker chuckled and placed a hand against the small of my back, gesturing graciously toward an unoccupied table to the right of the bar. Not a bad vantage point, all things considered. For the likes of us, an instant and inevitable choice apparent the moment we'd stepped through the door. It was a small, square table, designed to seat four comfortably and was set in a corner made by a small railing and an alcove. With no window behind, and because the table was set at an angle out from the wall, both Tucker and I could sit with our backs safe and still be able to see the rest of the room. Gigi definitely didn't raise us to be no fools. This was Kelly clan primary education. When in unknown territory, take every advantage. Always sit with your back to the wall and don't let them sneak up on you. Not that I necessarily expected violence this afternoon, but safe is better than sorry any day.

Surprisingly, the table was spick-and-span clean. I'd expected worse—half-emptied ashtrays and sticky beer residue. The Diamondback might be a cliché, but the proprietors seemed to take pride in their shabby establishment.

I nodded to a couple of the men seated near us. They nodded back and went back to their low conversation. I wasn't sure, but they might have been some of the hands from the Pursell place. I exchanged a glance with Tucker. He nodded slightly, acknowledging what I didn't ask out loud.

Brandi was back in no time, frosted mugs brimming with dark liquid. I'd expected bottles, but this was much better.

"Thank you," I said, as she placed a mug in front of me.

"Sure thing," she replied, a perky note in her voice. She leaned across the table to serve Tucker his beer. He grinned, she gasped a little in reaction. I could almost smell the pheromones pouring off her. I was sure Tucker could.

"So what brings y'all here?" Brandi asked, bending forward even more. She dropped her left hand to the table and let her weight lean on that arm as she continued her display. I was surprised that she hadn't pulled a Janet Jackson yet. I had to applaud whoever engineered her clothing. I'd have figured that gravity would have won out by now. I didn't really mind this silly preening. I knew Tucker was playing a game and could get information much more easily this way. Problem was, Brandi's pert and barely covered ass was still a too close to my face for comfort. She was practically wriggling at Tucker.

"Why don't you join us?" Tucker leaned forward and pulled out a chair. "It's okay, right?" Thank goodness, he'd noticed my discomfort.

Brandi glanced over toward the bar, then surveyed the room. No one appeared to be in need of anything. "Why sure," she said, beaming an even bigger smile as she slid into the proffered seat. "We don't hold to much formal stuff 'round here. I got some time."

"That's great." Tucker instantly relaxed, draping an arm over the back of the chair, letting his legs splay out even more in the classic posture of strutting male. He was working it . . . working *her*. She ate it up.

I instantly tuned them out, knowing that for the next few minutes, my brother would be exchanging the expected getting-to-know-you small talk, laced liberally with body language meant to tease, to entice. I could watch him and Brandi dance this game, or I could take advantage of the opportunity and survey the room. Give me door number two, Monty. While my brother was reeling in the waitress, I'd check out the patrons.

There were maybe twenty-five people in the place, the dance floor barren for now. Sunday afternoons were for chillin' and drinking. It wasn't football season, so the small television at the back of the bar was dark. A second waitress moved around the pool tables, passing out beers and emptying overflowing ashtrays. She could easily be Brandi's twin, hair a different shade of blond, legs a tad bit longer—the deep country Texas version of Hooters—a little less leg showing, a lot more hair, about the same ratio of natural to purchased.

A few wives or girlfriends accompanied their men, each with the same rode hard and put away wet look, Mary Kay troweled-on faces worn by too many kids, beers and cigarettes. These were tough women who ran homes on thinner than shoestring budgets, hoping that *La Migra* or the bad economy didn't take their man and their livelihood. Most of the women worked outside the home. They had to. Working a dead end desk job didn't bring in enough money to really help, but at least it was steady and sometimes the jobs even came with health insurance. Some of them were watching me, watching my brother.

I didn't blame them for looking at me with both envy and hatred. Despair colored their expressions like Miss Clairol colored their hair.

My family had been part of this area for as long as theirs had. The main difference was exactly that—difference. My family had been different from the get-go. Not wealthy ranch owners like Judge Pursell—those types, they knew how to handle. They were the bosses, and the bosses had trophy wives and trophy kids who had to be tolerated. We weren't like them, either, not because we weren't originally from here, nobody really was, except for the *Mexicanos*, and it was no longer their land. A lot of these guys' families emigrated here from Germany, Alsace-Lorraine, and other places in the heart of Europe. Names like Schneider and Tschirhardt were as common as Lozano and Garcia.

Again, another point of difference from us, the Kelly clan: most of us were Celtic fair and dark or red of hair and freckled. When I was little, I wanted to have olive skin like Bea. It was such a contrast to my own paleness. Bea darkened in the sun, her smooth tan the envy of many girls in school. I couldn't stay out for long or I'd lobster up quicker than a microwave dinner. Even the lighter-skinned European stock had all come from peasant roots, hardy, sturdy bodies that thrived in the country, long family histories of working the land.

Some of the locals accepted our family, at least the ones who traded with us—Bea's parents, Jonna and Drew Crofter who owned the laundry, Carlton's dad, who accepted us as law abiding, thus easy to leave be. Most of the time the folks in the county, if not friends, came to tolerate and include us as part of the community.

The ranch hands and their families—not so much. They hadn't *hated* us, not really, not like they hated Arabs (pronounced *Ay*-rabs) or homosexuals or even city folk. With us, mostly it was the discomfort kind of hate. The kind that meant "I don't understand you, but you've been around for a while and haven't messed with me, so maybe you're okay" . . . on the other hand, maybe we weren't, and that's why we never fit in. We, meaning the so-called younger generation. Tucker, me, Marty—who'd been more like them than they'd ever known, and the rest of the clan that looked to be in my generation, even though they weren't.

Most of our so-called contemporaries finished at the high school and then went to work locally, at some ranch somewhere, or maybe in Boerne or Kerrville, or maybe even in San Antonio. These shrubs didn't grow far from the family roots.

They never understood our free and easy traveling ways. I'd gone off to college in England, returned briefly and then went back overseas after my affair with Carlton. Tucker had come and gone between Rio Seco and Europe with as much ease as if he'd been driving up to Austin for a weekend. My father and other brothers had been much the same. Our life, our internal family culture (at least the public side of it) was as far from theirs as New York was from Outer Mongolia. I'd wondered recently if this constant outsiderness was one of the reasons that Gigi had decreed the family relocation. Yes, the area was filling up with incomers, but that surely couldn't have been the main reason to pull up stakes and move. Surely a clan as ancient as ours could figure out how to exist here, in a place that had grown used to us. Surely we'd have been able to purchase more than enough land to keep our hunting grounds. I didn't know. Maybe it was easier being an outsider when there were fewer people to be an outsider from. This wasn't something I'd ever discuss with Gigi, as the matriarch and clan chief, she'd admit to no weakness. Kind of like Adam in that respect.

"So you know Alex, then." The words penetrated my thoughts and I turned my attention back to my brother's conversation.

"Why sure, sugar," she said. "He and those boys from Judge P's place, why, they're regulars. If it's Sunday, at least a handful of 'em are here. 'Cept I haven't seen him since the last big party. 'Bout two, three months now." Brandi shimmied a little in her seat. "Don't know where he went, but a big bunch of 'em were out here last Sunday, another party. Jolene and I worked a double on account of they paid extra. Brought in fried chicken and taco fixin's and such. Even had barbecue from Rudy's. Those boys stayed until closing. They had a grand old time."

"Yeah, and look where it got us."

Fuck. I'd been so caught up in listening to Brandi's story, I hadn't noticed the man approaching the table. Pete. Judge Pursell's foreman. He didn't appear to be any friendlier than he had been at the ranch.

Tucker and I both stood, keeping our backs to the wall. Brandi slid out of her chair and scurried over to the bar. I had to appreciate that. She obviously was a survivor.

"What do you mean?" I asked, keeping my voice steady and quiet.

"I got fired." Pete challenged us with his expression. "You people bought the ranch, and I don't got a job."

CHAPTER FOURTEEN

I EXCHANGED a quick glance with Tucker, unsure of what to do. It was obvious that Pete was more than a little worse for wear. He listed to the left, a half-empty bottle of Lone Star dangling from his lax fingers. Bloodshot eyes completed the picture.

"You damned yuppie wannabes," he growled, fingers tightening on the neck of the bottle. "Buying up all the land 'round here, taking over real people's land. Puttin' us all out of work."

"That's ridiculous," I said. "Don't play poor pitiful me on this one, Pete."

Tucker's left hand moved in a slight gesture, a warning. Nope, didn't see it . . . or at least, not caring about it.

I stepped forward, moving closer to the foreman. "You can't tell me that Judge Pursell did any serious ranching. You know as well as I do that the reason he keeps stock and horses on the property is for the agricultural exemption. He's about as much of a rancher as I am."

I looked around at the other hands, some of who had stood themselves. Now I was sure I recognized them. The two at the back of the table next to us were the ones who had restrained Ignacio Robles.

Pete raised his bottle and took a long deep pull, then dropped the bottle back to his side. He leaned forward a little, still unsteady on his feet, opened his mouth and belched. "Whatever, at least he's not some wimpy, limp-wristed fag freak. Yeah, Judge don't take to those Eurotrash fags. Pro'ly a good thing I don't have to work for no freak."

Sounds of agreement filled the room, cowboys nodding and muttering "yeah." Intermixed with the variations on "he's right." The words "Judge P's fag son . . . ran off his own kid" reached my ears.

"Who said that?" Both Pete and I spoke at the same time, each of us looking around. Silent faces stared back at us, no one admitting to anything. The room was suddenly quiet, the sound of the jukebox blaring out some nouveau Nashville crap, the only thing audible.

"What's all that about?" I looked at Pete for an explanation. "What did they mean about the Judge's son?"

He glowered back at me. "Don't know, don't care. You and your hippie brother gonna make something of it?" He threw his chest out, jerking his chin in challenge.

I stared back, giving no ground. At the other tables, some of the other cowboys were standing, a few of the women patting arms and silently pleading for their men to sit down. The Pursell . . . or former . . . Pursell ranch hands stood still, staying in their space, waiting.

I sensed the nervousness around me, from the hands, from the other cowboys, the women. Bar fights have started for less, deaths happened for sillier reasons. I knew none of the others wanted us to go there. Still, there was a frisson of excitement underpinning the tension. No matter how civilized humans seem, their animal nature still recognized challenge and reveled in the adrenaline rush.

My brother's calm voice broke the charged atmosphere. His hand touched my back, at once soothing and cajoling. "No, we're leaving, actually."

I relaxed into Tucker's touch, letting him know that I wasn't going to pursue the challenge.

"Right, we're leaving," I said, echoing my brother's calm tone. I dropped my gaze from Pete's and conceded the staring match. He instantly relaxed a little, but didn't move.

Tucker pulled out a couple of bills and placed them on the table for Brandi. Without another word, we each walked around the table, skirted the still unmoving Pete and headed for the exit. Every eye in the place followed as we opened the front door and stepped out into the late afternoon sun.

I waited until we were nearly to my Land Rover before I exploded in quiet fury.

"What the hell was that all about, Tucker Kelly? We left before we found anything. We had a good—"

Tucker grabbed my arm and dragged me over to the left of the building, around the side of the sagging porch. "Sshh. We're about to have company."

Before I could say anything else, a door on the side of the building opened and the other waitress stepped out. She was a little older than Brandi, maybe late thirties, her strawberry blond hair as lusterless as her expression. Her nametag read: JOLENE.

"Hey," Tucker said, a gentle smile on his face. This wasn't his wooing smile, this was the big brother version.

"Hey," Jolene echoed. She looked around and leaned up against the wall, pulling a crumpled cigarette from behind one ear and a lighter out of her back shorts pocket. Head bowed, she cupped her hands together as she lighted her smoke. After a deep drag, she let out the smoke along with a sigh.

"Damn, that's good." She smiled a little, turning her

face from plain to pretty. "Sorry about that in there. Old Pete's a pain in the ass. He's been in here since about noon drinking up what's left of his last paycheck." He must have come straight here after talking to Carlton, I figured.

"No worries," I said. "He was bluffing."

Okay, so I was lying. Pete would have started something if I'd pushed him. I looked at her, then shot a glance at Tucker, trying to figure out what was going on. He sent me a clear message: Wait.

Jolene ignored us, smoking in silence for a few minutes. I sympathized. These smoke breaks were probably her sole moments of quiet during her entire shift.

"Look," she said, as she straightened and dropped the remaining cigarette stub to the dirt and ground it out with her shoe. "I'm not so sure I should be talking to you." She shot a glance to the closed door. "He'd . . ." She looked down at the ground and toed the remains of her cigarette.

"It's okay, Jolene," Tucker said. "Go on."

She hesitated a moment, biting her lip. "I hear y'all were asking about Alex Robles," she said, then looked at Tucker, her gaze flickering from him, to me, to the door.

I started a little at this, but kept silent, watching her expression.

"We were," Tucker agreed softly. "Brandi told us he was last here about three months ago with a party."

"Yeah." Jolene looked away again, and pulled the elastic band from around her ponytail and shook out her shoulder-length hair, then re-fashioned the ponytail and rewrapped the band. "They were all here," she continued, still looking in the other direction. "All the hands from the Pursell place. Payday and Junior's birthday."

"Junior?" I asked.

"One of the hands." She shrugged and tucked her hands

into the pockets of her shorts, as if it didn't make much difference which particular guy it was. "They started partying at about noon and didn't leave out of here until we closed. Weren't a one of them fit to drive, but wasn't mine to mind or worry about, so I didn't." She dropped her gaze back to the ground, her foot worrying at the stubbed out cigarette butt again. "Guess it was okay, then, 'cause they all came back the next day."

"Alex?" I prompted gently.

A quick smile flashed across her face, then vanished equally as swiftly. Her gaze wandered away from the fascination of the ground to the far horizon. "Alex didn't leave with them. He stayed." She looked at me then, her expression changing a little, sharing the secret look that girls give one another. The look we all know the meaning of.

"So he went home with you." I wasn't asking.

Jolene pressed her hands against the rough wooden boards, behind her back, leaning against them. "Yeah, I took him home. It was nice. He . . . was nice. We partied a little more. I had some crank. Then, well, you know . . ." She turned a little toward me, her gaze seeking out mine. "I heard he was missing. I'm sorry. I wish I knew . . ."

"So you don't know where he went?" I looked at Tucker briefly. He, too, was leaning against the side of the building, arms crossed loosely.

Jolene's expression crumpled a little, then she stood up straight. "I'm sorry. I had to go to work that morning. I used to work a morning shift three times a week at the Denny's over off 1694. I had to be in by five A.M., so after . . . I . . . Well, I asked him where to take him and he wasn't sure how to get to the ranch. Me neither. I've heard of the place, but I don't know how to get there."

She fumbled in her pocket, looking for something, probably another cigarette. "We drove around a little while and then it was getting late. I dropped him at the old cross-roads back about a mile or so from the main county road turnoff. You know, right where those little white crosses are. I don't recall if there were road signs." Her expression turned defiant. "He said he recognized it and could walk. I couldn't be late. I couldn't afford to get fired. I gotta go back inside. You got what you want?"

Tucker moved forward then and touched the woman on the arm. "Thanks, Jolene. We appreciate it. Really. If you could do me one tiny little favor before you go inside?"

Her mouth thinned.

"Could you possibly give us directions to where you dropped Alex off?'

She glanced at the door again and nodded quickly. "Yeah, okay." Jolene pulled a crumpled bar napkin out of her pocket along with a stubby pencil. She thought a moment, then scribbled some lines and words. "Here," she said, handing it to Tucker.

"I truly appreciate this," he said. "For your trouble." I caught a flash of a folded bill as he slipped it into the pocket of the little bar apron she wore.

She nodded and patted the pocket, then without another word, turned to go back inside.

"Wait. Please," I said. "What those guys were saying in there, about the Judge's son. What was that all about?"

She froze in her tracks, one hand reaching for the door handle. After a couple of seconds, she turned back toward me and stepped away from the door. "Heard tell that the story was Judge P ran off the kid because he liked boys. I dunno. Could be made up." She seemed reluctant to say more, but at the same time, I thought I could detect something in her eyes. What was she wanting me to ask?

"I thought his son disappeared while caving," I said, encouraging her with a smile and a nod.

"Yeah, that's what I heard, too." She pulled out another cigarette, lit it and took a deep drag, then another, staring out across the porch, watching a squirrel chase another one up a tree.

"Which one is it, Jolene?" I prompted softly. "Did the Judge kick his son out for being gay or was it a caving accident?"

Jolene spit a crumb of tobacco out onto her thumb and wiped it on her apron, leaving a yellow-brown smear among the assorted other food stains. "I guess it was a little of both," she said finally. "My mom's friend Arletta did Mrs. Pursell's hair every week. Arletta'd come over to our house talking 'bout how sweet that Pursell boy was and wasn't it a cryin' shame his father was such a bastard." She choked out a cloud of smoke along with a raspy laugh. "My momma would rock and smile real wide and agree. Then they'd get all whispery and tell me to go play in my room."

I wanted to knock my head against the wall. This was not getting us anywhere.

I didn't know that any of this made any difference, but a man who'd kick his son out for being gay wasn't someone I could trust. I knew that having issues with homosexuality was common amongst the Judge's generation, especially in this part of Texas, and that didn't automatically mean he let his workers get mistreated or, worse yet, cover up the fact one of them was missing, but it sure as hell didn't speak well for his character.

"So, was he gay?" Tucker asked, smiling at Jolene.

Jolene tapped the ash off the end of her cigarette. "I suppose, but I don't really know for sure. I know that Momma and Arletta had some good times gossiping about that boy. They were both pretty tore up when he disappeared like that."

"Any chance of a quick chat with your momma?" Tucker broadened his smile and touched Jolene's elbow. He'd gone back to seduction mode.

She blushed like a twelve-year-old girl and fluttered her lashes a little. "Wish I could help you out, but my momma passed some ten years back. Arletta, too, last year."

My brother nodded solemnly. "Sorry to hear that. Appreciate your help, though."

With that, Jolene dropped her cigarette, and with a hint of a flirtatious flourish, stepped back into the bar, leaving Tucker and me outside.

My brother and I looked at each other.

"How?" I asked.

"What?"

"How did you know she wanted to talk and how did you know she knew something about Alex?"

"When you were playing face-off with Pete. I was looking around the room and she caught my eye." He smiled. "I'm good at reading body language, sis."

"She motioned to the door, didn't she?" Body language, my ass.

"Yeah, well." He shrugged and smiled.

"Speaking of body language, you think something was off with her? She was nervous the entire time she was out here, that is until you turned on the charm."

"Charm is it?" Tucker laughed and gave a light punch to my arm. I punched him back.

"Yes, 'charm.' Don't pull that crap with me, Tucker Kelly. What do you think was up with Jolene?"

"She was definitely nervous about someone finding out she was talking to us."

"That's exactly what I was thinking," I agreed. "You think it's her worried about getting caught gossiping or something else?"

Tucker shrugged. "I'm not sure. But I bet if we go check out this crossroads and then, maybe pay a visit to the Judge, we might be able to find out."

"That, dear brother, sounds like a plan."

CHAPTER FIFTEEN

"KEIRA, THANKS for coming by." Kevin Barton surprised me by actually looking at my face this time as he stuck out his hand. I shook it and stepped into the relative cool of the real estate office. "Your brother not with you?"

"I dropped him off at the café on the way over," I said. "We were on our way to run an errand when you called. I'm going to pick him up after we're done. Where's the paperwork you need me to look at?"

"Hey, I like that," Kevin said. "Direct and to the point."

Actually, yes, I thought. Let's get to the point so I can get out of here and back to what I was doing. Tucker and I had barely set out from the Diamondback when Kevin's call came in. He'd apologized for having to bother me on such short notice, but he needed me to come get some paperwork for Adam. Something that needed Adam's review and countersignature before they could proceed. I'd agreed to come right there, mostly because it wasn't much of a detour on our way to the crossroads, at least not if Jolene's map was accurate.

"Sure, sure," he said. "Come on in."

I followed him further into the small building. The office was a stand-alone faux-log cabin style building, located a mile or so down the main drag of town, next to the post office. Inside, it was divided into two sections: his office and a larger reception-type area with a few visitor chairs, a long table with a variety of brochures and ad circulars and a coffee machine. The walls reflected the pseudo-rustic design, photos of ranches fighting for prominence next to the numerous heads of dead deer, boar, javelina. I swallowed the sarcastic comment I was going to make as I took this in. Crap. This was something straight out of I-shop-at-Cabelas-weekly. Even the chairs fit with the theme: brown and tan plain canvas upholstery on some of them, the others a ridiculous camouflage pattern.

"Come on through to my office," Kevin said, motioning me inward.

I stopped gaping at the trophies and went on in, stopping short as I realized that the decor in the reception area was a tasteful introduction to what I'd find in Kevin's private office. Directly in front of the door was a large, wooden desk stacked high with papers. Above it, looming over the leather executive chair, was the front quarter of the largest example of a bighorn sheep I'd ever seen. Horns curling defiantly, it stood as proud in death as it did in life.

"You like it? That's one of the coolest things I've got. 'Cept for that, of course." He pointed to our right.

I clenched my fist, breathing hard. In the far corner, in a place of honor under a small spotlight stood a full-grown arctic white wolf. Mounted on a pedestal, its dead fur gleamed in the light, glass eyes glittering in something too close to living. Beside it, a fox carried the broken body of a quail in its mouth. I looked away, swallowing the bile in my throat. My brother Rhys often looked like that when he shifted. His twin, Ianto, would emulate him. I grew up watching two white wolves playing tag with each other, often nipping at each other in playful glee as Tucker chased them.

Kevin, oblivious to my reaction, nattered on. "Got a

guy up in Alaska. He finds me all sorts of trophies. This shipped in a few days ago. Never thought it'd get here."

"Shall we get on with it," I said through clenched teeth. "I'm busy."

"Sure, sure," he said, bustling around to the other side of the desk and grabbing a stack of papers. "Here you go. They're marked. Mrs. Pursell finished her part. If you could have Mr. Walker initial where the stickies are."

I nodded and turned to leave, needing to get out of there. This was nothing but a wannabe's ode to the worst of Texas macho. He didn't even hunt the trophies, ordered them like a mail order bride, props to an image he couldn't achieve on the best of days.

"I'll get the papers back to you—" The front door opened, a burst of wind scattering some of the brochures out front to the floor.

"Oh, I'm sorry, Kevin. Dratted wind." The blond woman shut the door quickly. "Seems to be blowing up a little out there," she said. "Sorry to interrupt. I realized when I got halfway down the street. I forgot my phone on your desk." The woman's breathless drawl was punctuated with an accent thick as her mascara.

"No problem, Mrs. P, come on in. Keira, this is Mrs. Pursell. Mrs. P, Keira Kelly, she's representing the buyer."

So this was the infamous Bitsy, trophy wife number three.

A flash of would-be debutante smile lit up her face as she entered the inner office. She stood about five-foot-six or so and was dressed in the epitome of nouveau-riche chic. Hot pink denim jeans hugged every artificial curve and flared out over tidy white sandals. A pink-and-white polka-dotted cap-sleeved knit top fit like a second skin, molding to every inch of tan and showing off her extremely unlikely breasts. A diamond and platinum tennis bracelet graced her right wrist, while her left sported a diamond-encrusted Rolex in white gold. A rock the size of a small monument flashed on her ring finger, more diamonds sparking on her ears, under the fashionably streaked blond mane. A wealthier version of Brandi the waitress, but no less a soul sister, down to the accent and the frosted pink artificial nails tipping each finger. Bitsy's just cost a lot more.

She stepped forward, her smile bright and extended her hand. "Pleased to meetcha."

I looked into her blue eyes and smiled back. "Likewise." Her handshake was short of the proper ladylike limp, but not dead-fish worthy. Tanned skin felt like leather underneath my own. She'd spent too many days in the sun. Easier to remove that evidence from your face via surgery. The hands will always tell. I revised my age estimate from thirties to early forties.

"Hope your client likes the place," Bitsy said, as we concluded our ritual of greeting.

"Oh, I'm not a realtor," I replied. "My . . . friend asked me to take care of the business end of the deal since he has other commitments during the day."

"Oh, okay then." Confusion flashed across her pretty face as she worked this through. "Anyhow, that's real nice. You seen my phone?" This last was directed at Kevin, who'd dropped into what he did best, evidently: staring at Bitsy's bits. Not that I really blamed him. She did have most of them on display and it was rather difficult to ignore the expanse of smooth tan above the low-cut top.

"Uhm, yeah, here." Kevin fumbled on the desk and handed her the bright pink (naturally) cell phone.

She took it from his hand and deposited it in her purse, a gold leather monstrosity studded with silver buckles and trim. "Thanks, sugar," she said with a smile. "Wouldn't do to lose that."

"No, no it wouldn't," Kevin agreed. "Thank you again for stopping by, Mrs. Pursell. Now that Keira has the final paperwork, once Mr. Walker signs it, we're nearly there. About a week or so for the title search and we can close."

"That sounds great, Kevin. Then I can concentrate on getting that pool house built." Bitsy giggled. "It's been such fun picking out the tile and stuff. Shoot, I might have to build me something else when it's finished."

I nearly rolled my eyes at that. She sounded like some giddy ten-year-old girl with her first Barbie dollhouse and unlimited funds to buy accessories at the toy store. I would never understand the attraction of empty-brained arm candy wives. Never.

"Well, gotta run," she said. "I'm meeting the girls for lunch at the club." Of course she was.

"If you don't mind," I said. "I'll walk out with you. Kevin, we're done here, right?"

"Yes, of course. Thank you. When you've got the signatures I need, drop off the paperwork or give me a call and I'll come get it."

"Will do."

Bitsy and I walked out together.

"Nice to meetcha," she said, heading toward her car, an overbearing white Escalade.

"Mrs. Pursell, if you don't mind . . . . could I ask you a couple of questions before you go?"

"Why sure, I suppose."

"I'm sorry this is kind of blunt, but I have my reasons for asking. Can you tell me why the Judge fired Pete Garza so quickly? I kind of figured that he'd keep him on for a bit, at least until we close on the sale, seeing as how he's related and all." I tried to mitigate the question a little. "You know, we might have worked something out for the hands, even though Adam, Mr. Walker, isn't going to live on the ranch." Not really, but it didn't hurt to pretend.

Bitsy fiddled with her key fob, a leather and metal piece matching the handbag. She dug her other hand into her purse and pulled out her sunglasses, putting them on and effectively hiding her eyes from me. Was she doing this consciously or was this a sign of nerves?

"How do you know that?" she finally asked. "He called me this morning. I didn't even know."

"Sorry, I don't mean to pry," I said. (Yes, I do.) "But I was up at the Diamondback a bit ago and Pete was there. He was drunk and angry. Saying things about getting fired and about the Judge and his fag son. He says the Judge kicked Greg out for being gay. Is that true?"

"No!" Bitsy's exclamation was immediate. "Carl didn't kick him out. Greg ran away."

"I'm sorry, I thought he went missing in a caving accident."

Bitsy sighed. "Yes, that's what Carl wanted people to think. He didn't like folks thinking that his son ran off. But he didn't go caving. Carl told me the truth right after we were married. He's real honest that way." I kept my mouth shut. Honest, yeah. Like lying to everyone as to what happened to his son.

She continued. "Greg and he kept fighting. Carl says it was a father-son thing. I remember a bit about this. I was working up at the club then. I'd see them fighting down by the locker rooms, out by the pool. Carl would want Greg to come play golf and Greg wanted to stay by the pool. I thought he was sick. We all talked about how sick he looked. Dottie English told me once that she'd heard Greg was under the treatment of some sort with a doctor in Austin. I know he kept getting skinnier and skinnier losing lots of weight and looking pale." Bitsy played with the fringe on her bag. "Carl never talks about it, even now. I'm pretty sure he had it."

"It." The disease that no one talked about back then. AIDS. In many places, including Rio Seco, obituaries often stated the cause of death as "long illness." No one faced the truth until it was too real not to.

Bitsy scrabbled in her bag and pulled out a small leather book. She flipped it open to the back. "Look, here's a picture of Carl and him at the lake."

"Why do you keep a picture of Greg?" I asked. After all, she'd not been married to the Judge until recently, long after Greg's disappearance.

She smiled widely and pointed with a pink tipped finger. "Carl. He's so handsome in this, I couldn't bear to let him toss it."

"He was going to throw it out?"

Bitsy nodded. "Oh yes, he cleared all the reminders of Greg out of the ranch house when we decided to sell it. I rescued this picture from the trash."

"May I?" Bitsy handed me the book and I studied the photo, trying to see if I could tell from a years-old grainy picture if Greg Pursell had been gay and/or stricken with AIDS. Two men beaming at the camera, each of them holding one end of a line on which a huge striped fish of some sort hung. Greg squinted out under a billed cap that nearly hid close-cropped fair hair. His build was slender, not muscular, small bones in his wrist prominent, and both hands held up his end of the line. A loose tee, cargo shorts and a fishing vest matched those of his dad's—an older and sturdier copy of the young man. Did Greg ping my gaydar? I had no idea. I wasn't all that good at this with real live people standing right in front of me. For all I knew, Greg could as easily have been a dyed-in-the-wool neo-Nazi as a card-carrying member of the Nancy squad. Being gay doesn't automatically mean you have a pink triangle sewn on your clothing . . . at least not here and now.

"They're both quite handsome." I returned the book to her. She shoved it in her bag and smiled.

"Yes, they are."

"By any chance, do you know anything about a worker that went missing from the ranch about three months or so ago?" I kept my tone casual, as if this was simply a random question.

Bitsy twisted her lips a little, seeming perplexed. "Why, I don't rightly know," she said. "I do know that over the years, though, there've always been one or two guys up and leave without notice. Carl was really way stressed about that. He'd come home to San Antonio after coming here to check on the place. Pete would tell him someone else left and Carl would be all grumpy and moody for days. I mean, poor Carl. He's so good to those workers. They really are ungrateful. After all, he provides free room and board and pays them on top of all that. That's a lot more that they'd get back home."

Oh, yeah, Judge Carl Pursell was a real Daddy War-bucks and Norma Rae all mashed together. Why I bet that he even paid those boys in cash so they didn't have to deal with a bank. Mighty kind of him. I fought the urge to whap Bitsy with a clue bat. She wouldn't get it. In her mind, her husband was the epitome of a kind landowner, saving those poor ignorant Mexican workers. Yeah, definitely clue-challenged.

I forced a smile. "Well, thanks, anyway," I said. "I appreciate your time."

Bitsy scrunched up her face again, frowning, then quickly smoothing it out again. "You're welcome," she responded automatically, and with that, got into her SUV.

I watched her drive away.

CHAPTER SIXTEEN

"So Bitsy lived up to her name," Tucker chuckled as he drove.

We were headed out to find the crossroads, going by the directions Jolene gave us earlier. After I picked Tucker up at the café, I'd filled him in on the conversation with Pursell wife number three.

"Yeah, pretty much," I agreed. "She wasn't much help, really."

"At least we know what happened to the Judge's son," Tucker said. "Not that it has anything to do with anything."

I shrugged. "Oh well, it was an opportunity and I took it."

I peered at the napkin trying to reconcile the sort of map with where we were. I hoped we were on the right track. Jolene's recollection of a place she'd driven to after a night of sex, speed and liquor three months past might not pan out. There were dozens of similar crossroads in the local area, and by local, I meant anywhere within thirty minutes driving distance of the Diamondback.

Tucker maneuvered the car over a short rise, squinting into the sun. "Hey, am I totally off base here, or are we heading toward the Wild Moon from a different direction?"

"What?" I looked up from the directions. "Are we?"

"I think so." Tucker pulled the car over, the nonexistent shoulder making it difficult for him to get completely off the road. We'd been on a winding two-lane back road for a few miles, having had to drive to Jolene's place first so we could follow her directions precisely from point of origin. "Are we in the right place?"

I squinted at her writing. "Fuck if I know," I said. "This woman has no sense of direction. She has us going east on Hawaii, but that road runs north-south."

"Let me see that." Tucker leaned over and peered at the napkin. "I think that's not Hawaii but *Valley*."

"Oh for . . ." I looked around. We were on a small rise in the road, about to reach the intersection of Mauna Loa and Waikiki. I'd always thought these were stupid names for streets in the middle of the Hill Country, but some long-ago developer had purchased the land, planned a subdivision around some sort of island theme, and the roads had been named appropriately. After one too many oil busts, the money for the housing development vanished, leaving acres and acres of unimproved land intersected by roads with tropical names.

"If you take this road for another half a mile or so, we should find Valley," I said. "It's that windy bit that parallels the conservation area for a while and becomes a county highway when it curves around—"

I stopped as I realized where Jolene's map was leading us. "Shit, Tucker. Look at this." I pointed to a smudged bit of the map. "She's got the proportions all wrong. That short piece here that I thought was Hawaii. If that's Valley, then that crossroads she told us about sounds like one particular place." I looked at my brother.

"Well, shit is right," he said. "That's the main crossroads at the back end of the Wild Moon."

"Yeah, up by the old cemetery."

We looked at each other.

"You thinking what I'm thinking?" I asked.

"I'm thinking that I am," Tucker replied.

LESS THAN half an hour later, we were there, having by-passed the crossroads for the old cemetery. It wasn't Rest-lawn Burial Park, which folks around here tended to use, but a semi-historical (read *abandoned*) and nameless place where the newest grave was about fifty-some-odd-years old. Once at the intersection of three large ranches and the place where these ranch families laid their beloved dead, time and modern sensibilities had turned it into a long-forgotten garden of cracked stones and long-dusty remains. The locals knew about it, but no one ever really came out here, not even kids on a dare, it was too damn hard to get to for a casual make-out session or Hallowe'en hijinks.

The land the cemetery occupied no longer belonged to the ranch families, but was part of a no-man's land tucked into a curve of foothill, on the extreme opposite of where we'd been earlier and only accessible by a good off-road vehicle and some hiking, or, someone walking from a de-serted crossroads trying to get back to the Pursell ranch. Not a horribly tough haul and conceivably doable even under the influence. If the moon had been out that night, Alex could have probably seen fairly well and may have sought shelter. The cemetery was directly in the crow's flight path from the crossroads to the Pursell land.

Adam could probably claim the cemetery as part of the Wild Moon holdings, as it was completely surrounded by the ranch but, legally, it belonged to no one. The original three families had owned the land jointly. Two of them had sold portions of their adjoining properties to the state, and those properties eventually became the conservation site.

The remaining pieces and the third family ranch had sold to the original owners of what was now the Wild Moon. The cemetery itself remained in legal limbo, none of the distant descendants willing to pay for the red tape laden paperwork to establish ownership.

"I can't believe I forgot about this place," I said as we approached the entrance. "It's been years." I stopped and took a deep breath before I went in, reinforcing my mental shields. Although no one had been laid to rest here in decades, I still could feel the whisper-tug of death at the edges of my awareness. Not really strong enough to matter, but enough to distract me a little.

Tucker nodded and walked up next to me, his face somber. "I think this was my first babysitting chore with you," he said. "You were what, twelve?"

"Thirteen . . . barely." I wiped my hands on my jeans. "I'm a little surprised Gigi didn't leave someone behind or hire someone to keep up the place."

"I suppose she had her reasons," Tucker said. "Although, I do wonder a bit. They may not be family, but many of them were friends."

"Which is why I had to come once a week and clean up the place," I remarked.

"With my help."

"With your help." I closed my eyes a moment, remembering myself as a somewhat stubborn newly minted teen, arguing with my aunts about having to clean up some moldy old graveyard when all my friends were going out to the lake. It took about three seconds of Gigi's intervention and I had trudged out here with Tucker at my side, still fuming and still resentful. After I spent about five months of prime spring and summer Sunday afternoons in the company of the long-dead, Gigi released me from that duty.

"You know, I think I was eighteen or nineteen before I realized why she made me do this." I looked over at my brother, who was still regarding the graves in silent contemplation.

He smiled at me. "Obedience?"

I shook my head. "No, more like exposure."

Tucker gave me a quizzical look.

I motioned to the gravestones. "To the dead. To the fact that no matter how much we look like them, we're not them. They die."

"Ah."

"Yeah."

Tucker squeezed my shoulder in understanding. I smiled back at him, ever the practical, yet sympathetic big brother. He'd always been there for me. When I'd first arrived in the company of our father, when I'd first realized that I wasn't like the other kids in school, when the reality of human death hit. He'd even been there for me during all my silly teenage crushes and subsequent heartbreaks.

I covered his hand with mine and squeezed back. "Thanks," I said quietly.

"For what?"

"Being here, then and now."

"No problem." He grinned. "So. Shall we?"

"Let's to it," I said.

There really wasn't much to the place, nothing at all like modern acres-large burial grounds. This unnamed place of rest measured slightly over an acre and was studded with old-fashioned standing markers interspersed between a few live oaks. The whole place was overgrown, prickly pear and cholla vying with mesquite for dominance, and sat in a natural hollow semi-surrounded by limestone outcroppings. A decorative wrought-iron fence enclosed the entire graveyard, its opening ungated, marked by a pair of matching trumpeting angel statues, their heads a bit higher than the fence line. The fence was short, a couple of feet high, and for the most part, still intact. The gravestones within ranged from the typical round-edged flat-surface kind, carved with names, dates and sometimes a Bible verse or two to more modern markers (and by modern I meant in the last century). A few elaborate statues stood out in proud testament to those whose deaths they commemorated.

"You know," I remarked, after pushing through a particularly vicious mesquite bush and skirting the tall leaning stone marking the grave of Sidney Jeremiah Halfstock, Beloved Husband and Father, d. 1835, "I don't even think we need your special tracking talents for this one, Tucker. I'm thinking that there's one real place to look." I brushed some loose dirt off the top of Sidney's stone as I passed, the old cleaning and tidying habit returning. I felt nothing when I touched the warm stone. Sidney had been dead much too long and whatever was left of his essence long since dissipated into the Texas air.

"If you were lost, confused, highly intoxicated and definitely not in your right state of mind, *plus* you were brought up in what I presume was a traditional Catholic household, where would you go?"

"I've never been Catholic, but I've definitely been all the rest." Tucker chuckled and motioned forward. "But I get your point. On to the grammatically incorrect *La Angel,* I presume?"

"Got it in one."

I avoided a nasty clump of cactus and headed northeast to the far corner of the cemetery. There, shaded by three old-growth live oaks and tucked into a natural alcove formed by a limestone outcropping was The Angel. Known as *"La Angel"* by the locals, dubbed so somewhere in history by someone who didn't know the word "angel" was always masculine in Spanish, she was a typical angel statue one would find in many graveyards—this one, like the famous Urrutia angel in San Antonio, was intentionally headless. I had no idea if this particular statue was a tribute to the more well-known one, which was modeled after Nike (the Greek goddess, not the shoe) or if, at some point in history, headless angels were all the rage. In some cemeteries, weeping angels dominated the landscape; obelisks were fashionable monuments at one time.

Whatever the case, this statue was probably the largest one in the small cemetery. The Angel sat on a large rectangular limestone base upon which local women of past years would come and lay down offerings. During the days of what I'd considered my penance, I'd often spend more than an hour or so scrubbing candle wax and cleaning dead flower petals off the statue's base. Sometimes, the offerings had been somewhat grotesque, at least to me at the time. Tiny baby teeth, locks of hair tied lovingly with faded ribbons, fingernail clippings and other less savory and unexamined substances smearing the dark marble. I'd seriously hated that part.

"I didn't think people still knew about her or came to her anymore," said Tucker as we approached the statue.

"I can't be sure," I replied, "but it's a better guess than pulling something out of our collective asses. I mean if Alex didn't make it back to the Pursell ranch, and he didn't turn up anywhere else, what's to say—if Jolene told the truth—that he didn't come out here, crawl over to *La Angel* and expire of an overdose or something?" I stepped over a piece of a broken headstone.

"Shit." Tucker stopped walking and threw out his arm to bar my way.

"What is it?" I asked as I stumbled and grabbed onto his arm. "Did you see something?"

"Smelled." The word was curt. "They were here all right."

"*They*—who's *they*?"

Tucker grimaced. "I doubt it was Alex Robles, unless he decided to spend the last three months camping out here. Too recent. I smell candle wax, fresh, not two days old, incense and—" He paused a moment and concentrated. "Yeah, I'm not wrong. Blood . . . fresh blood. Not today, but . . ."

"Fuck."

This was not good. As far as we knew, the four teens were still missing, whether or not they had run away. Blood and missing kids is not a combination I either expected or wanted to hear. Of course, there was the off chance that this hadn't anything to do with them, but could be some random person who'd stumbled across the place. We got our share of drifters throughout the Hill Country, like anywhere else. Except, of course, around here, it was a lot harder to hide or keep a low profile, since most everyone knew everyone else, or at least knew the faces that belonged.

"Stay here a sec, Keira, and let me do a little recon."

Tucker swiftly pulled off his T-shirt and tossed it behind him. He dropped to a crouch, unlaced his hiking boots, then stood and kicked them both off, along with his socks. He stood there a moment, facing away from me, feet shoulder width apart, arms loose at his side, the long rope of braided hair halfway down his bare back.

I waited a beat, then two, then another. The insistent buzzy hum of the cicadas permeated the air, occasionally interrupted by scattershot bird chatter or the rustling of leaves in the slight breeze. I caught a whiff of candle wax, something sweetish, artificial vanilla and cinnamon caught up in cedar, an ashy residue behind it all. Something tugged at my mind: sounds, voices, a memory? I chased after it mentally, concentrating. There was something familiar . . . The breeze danced past, and the sweet faded into the normal dusty heat scent and my brother was still standing there as unmoving as one of the cemetery statues.

"You going to shift?" I asked what seemed to be the obvious question, although he hadn't stripped down to skin yet.

"No."

"No?"

"Be patient." He motioned to his right. "Stand there."

I shrugged and walked around beside him, about three feet away. "Here good?"

He glanced over, still distracted, still staring forward, concentrating on whatever. "Yeah, fine."

I shrugged, and leaned back against the nearest gravestone. *Alice Olivia Lovelace*, it read. *Beloved.* I crossed my arms and watched my brother. Whatever he was doing, he'd eventually let me know.

Although, I had to admit I *was* curious. Of all my family, Tucker was the least likely to go all woo-woo mystery and magick. Two of my other brothers, Rhys and Ianto, plus several close cousins, tended to get off on that whole "I am magickal, look at me sweep my velvet cape" posturing, a la Draco Malfoy. It amused them to play the game, even amongst clan. My mother's family? From everything I remembered, they were even worse—more Lucius than Draco with a touch of Bellatrix Lestrange thrown in for good measure.

Tucker never got into that. While he didn't exactly eschew magick, it was as much a part of his nature as the wolf. He definitely preferred utilitarian shapeshifting to any hocus-pocus. With him, you always got what you saw. That is, mostly. We all had our private bits, I supposed. I'd never seen Tucker go the magick route. Right now, I watched, waiting to see what he was up to.

My brother shook out his arms, crouched down, placed a palm flat on the ground and shut his eyes. He began to hum under his breath, a low tuneless melody punctuated by whispers of sound. The humid air seemed to grow thicker, stiller, denser. The background sounds of cicadas thinned, faded, elided into a faint hum, teasing the edges of my awareness. My feet began to sweat in my boots. My socks, too warm. All my clothes suddenly felt too tight, too heavy, too much. I slipped out of my denim overshirt, but that wasn't enough. I was suffocating, drowning in the thick humidity, the air too close, too dense. I could scarcely breathe. Like the worst of the worst summer days—hundred-plus temperatures with nearly hundred percent humidity—the whiff of ozone, of energy surrounded us. Could it merely be Tucker's magick? The feeling reminded me of the atmosphere before one of the famous gullywasher thunderstorms so prevalent in the area. I tried to take a deep breath, struggling against the pressure. Something pulled at me, currents tugged at my skin, a whine of electric vibration made my bones sing.

"Here . . . come . . . here."

The whispers insinuated themselves in the back of my skull, sliding past and fading into the thick air. Was I really hearing this or was this another manifestation of whatever my brother was doing?

"Tucker—" I began to complain as I tried to shake it off, but stopped as I saw his face.

"Something is very, very wrong," he said, his voice low and angry. "I can't . . ." He stood in a swift motion, his attitude all predator. The muscles on his back rippled, tensing and releasing, tensing again.

"What is it?" I concentrated on my brother, trying to ignore the feeling of suffocating energy swirling around me, causing my skin to tingle. My muscles tightened as the energy increased.

"I'm not sure." Tucker clenched his hands into fists and closed his eyes, sniffing the air. His brow furrowed. "It feels off. Like . . ."

"Damn it, Tucker, what?"

With a low growl, he tore open the buttons on his jeans and skinned them off as if the fabric was burning him. A couple of deep breaths and a shimmer of light later and the wolf that was my brother stood next to me. With an almost audible pop, the energy vanished.

CHAPTER SEVENTEEN

"T UCKER, what's going on?"
I did not like this one bit. Tucker rarely changed in broad daylight in front of people, even if "people" meant me. Not that he was shy, but changing required a certain level of concentration and focus that was difficult to achieve when in the presence of non-shifters. Tucker had always preferred to do it in private.

He shook his head, his shaggy reddish fur glinting in the sun. I smiled a little, despite the situation. In whatever incarnation, my brother was a handsome beast. He stood tall when human. As a wolf, his shoulder nearly reached my waist and he probably weighed in at well over 170 pounds. Large for a wolf, and definitely not someone you'd like to run into in a dark alley—in either form. Good thing he was my brother.

Tucker crouched a moment, head down, eyes shut. I held still, waiting. With a shudder and shake, his form quickly shifted back to human and he fell to the ground, still panting, bare sides heaving as if trying to catch a breath.

I crouched next to him, my hand on his shoulder. "Tucker, you all right?"

He groaned, eyes screwed shut, curling into a fetal position. "Hurts a little," he mumbled. "'M a'right."

"Hurts? It's not supposed to hurt. What sort of all right is that?" I couldn't keep the fear out of my voice. I'd never seen him like this. Shifting back and forth took energy, yes, but never like this.

"'M all right," he insisted, voice stronger now. "Give me a minute."

I patted his shoulder, feeling helpless. What the hell *could* I do? I had no idea what happened.

Tucker lay there breathing heavily, hands clenching as if trying to work out a muscle spasm for a few more minutes. Then, with a lurch, he got to his hands and knees, arms shaking a little with the strain. I stumbled back and sat down hard on my backside as the effort of his trying to get up upset my balance.

"Damn it," he said. "I feel like a newborn shifter, a first-timer." He panted through the words then, with a groan, sat back on his heels, fighting to keep upright. "What the fuck *was* that?"

"You're asking me?" I snapped back, my worry evident. "One minute, you're all silent stoic spellcaster dude, and the next, you're tearing off your clothes and shifting . . . in the daylight . . . in front of me. Then you shift back a few minutes later and tell me you feel like a newborn."

"I don't know, Keira," Tucker answered. "I thought if I did a casting, tried to feel out the ground, the site, tried to get an idea of what had been here . . ." His voice trailed off and he got a thoughtful look on his face. "There was something, some energy I couldn't pinpoint. I reached for it, grounding myself, but then it—I don't really know. Like a backlash or something and I had to shift."

I got to my own knees and put a hand on his arm. "It *made* you shift? Holy shit!"

"No," he said. "Not exactly that. More like, it built and built, and the only thing I could do was shift or . . ."

"Or?"

"I don't know, really. I knew that shifting seemed to be my best bet. But even that, when I was in wolf shape, I felt weak, exhausted." Tucker scrubbed at his face, then stared at the Angel, his eyes narrowing. "I do not like this," he said. "Whatever's around here is not a good thing."

"What do you think it is?" I asked. "A spell? A ward?"

"Possibly both. In any case, I don't want to try to get at it again without some help."

"At it?"

Tucker inclined his head toward the statue. "Back there, behind the Angel. That's where it came from."

La Angel stood about nine feet atop a fifteen-inch tall base. The base itself created a sort of shelf all around the statue and the whole thing was tucked into a depression in the limestone overhang, which created a natural shelter. The whole setup reminded me of those *Virgen de Guadalupe* statues often found on the lawns of devout Mexican Catholics. I'd always thought it was supposed to be a seashell behind the woman's figure, but evidently, the icon's background signified a full body halo. Our angel had its own backdrop. If you looked at her from the front, you got a similar feel to the *Virgens*. Except of course, our statue looked completely different.

In any case, I'd always figured that whoever placed the Angel here either had a whacked sense of humor or hadn't noticed the resemblance. Or better yet, maybe they were actually creating a shrine. Years ago, when I'd first come here, I'd wondered whose grave this was because there was no name carved into the plinth. I'd meant to ask Gigi or someone if they knew. But the question got lost in all the rest of life's teenage angst and I'd never learned the answer.

The statue itself sat close to the stone wall. Once upon

a time, when I'd been assigned to clean this place, there had been no overgrowth, no snarled mesquite to block the way, a live oak behind and on either side of the statute to provide shade, as if *La Angel* needed protection from the Texas sun. They effectively blocked the area behind the statue, but a person could fairly easily squeeze through if they wanted to. I'd never bothered to clean back there, figuring no one would notice if I skipped that.

Years of neglect meant that the mesquite, blackbrush and other types of underbrush had taken over and for all intents and purposes, completely closed off the space between the Angel and the wall. Countless rains washed debris and junk into this hollow, creating a six-foot-high deadfall, denser than some hedgerows.

"You want to go back behind there and check it out?" I asked.

"No, not right now," Tucker said. "I'm certainly not up to it yet and like I said, I think we need reinforcements."

"Who the hell do you think we can get? Unless you want to call in the family, and that will take at least a day or two for someone to come out here from B.C." I stood up and brushed the dirt from my jeans. "I vote we go tell Carlton we saw some evidence of recent activity here and let him and the searchers take over."

Tucker braced his hands on his thighs and with a visible strain, hauled himself to his feet. "Hand me my jeans, would you?"

I picked up the jeans and his shirt and brought them over to him. "So, your idea?"

"I'm not so sure bringing the humans is a good idea," he said as he fastened the jeans and held out a hand for his shirt. "Even non-magickal folks might be affected by it."

"I wasn't," I said bluntly.

Tucker grimaced at me, his lips tight as if holding back words. He stayed silent until he'd finished dressing, pulled on his boots and laced them. "You think not?"

"Not," I answered. "I felt it, the air was thick with it. But that's all. Then when you shifted, it vanished, like a bubble popping."

"Huh," he said. "Wonder what that means?"

I laughed, getting a little of my humor back. "I'm immune?"

"Smartass." My brother grinned back at me. He was beginning to look more like his normal self, except for the free-flowing hair hanging down his back. He rarely left it loose, but shifting so quickly had wreaked havoc with his usual braid.

"Who were you thinking could help, if not the local law?" I asked.

"Our friendly neighborhood vampires."

"But they're not so much about the magick," I said.

"Even so, I'd rather have Niko and Adam at my back, in case this happens again," said Tucker. "Wouldn't you?"

"Oh, by help, you mean: we come back with them," I said. "Not, turn this over to someone else."

"You'd give up now?" Tucker looked at me with a quizzical look on his face.

"Maybe." I dug into my pocket for a coated rubber band for his hair. "Here."

He took it gratefully and started to twist a braid. "I kind of thought you were invested in finding Alex Robles and those kids."

I crossed my arms and leaned against the nearest headstone. "I was," I said. "But that was before you got all Scooby-Doo on me. I don't like the fact that there's some sort of wild energy there that forced you to shift. Neither you, nor I nor any of the vampires have any experience with this kind of energy . . . at least, we don't. I guess I can't really speak for the vampires, but I seriously doubt it. I mean, what's Niko going to do—bite it?"

Tucker's head went back as he laughed. "You, dear sister, crack me up."

"Well? I mean, really."

"Honestly, I was hoping that maybe we can call someone in the family and see if they know about this. Then we can come back with a vampire or two and try to get back behind the statue, scope it out—without me trying to do magick this time. Should be safe enough."

"Here's the thing, Tucker. Are *you* doing this because of Alex Robles or the kids—or because of the energy? Because I don't exactly see how either those kids or Robles could have gotten back there without disturbing that deadfall. That thing's been like that for a while."

"I do think those kids were here," he said. "There's candle wax on the base of the statue, and that's less than three days old. And next to the wax, see? A smudge of incense." He made show of sniffing the air. "Patchouli? No, something darker. Myrrh, maybe?"

I took a few steps closer to *La Angel* wanting to get a better look. He was right. Smears of wax, some smudges of ash and the remains of at least one incense cone next to the various smears.

"Some sort of teenage ritual or hanging out smoking weed?" I asked as I poked at the melted wax with a stick.

"Why they were here, if it was them, isn't really important, I imagine," Tucker said. "Maybe this is their version of a make-out place. Or a place to tell ghost stories and such. I bet they were here and maybe saw something."

"Something or someone?"

"Yeah, exactly."

The wax was soft in the late afternoon sun, thick but pliable. I poked the stick through it, stirring it as I thought. I knew what Tucker meant. It could be either. Perhaps some leftover stray energy from a long time ago built up for some unknown reason. Wasn't unheard of. Maybe someone who created whatever caused that energy surge. A ward, a do-not-disturb spell? I wasn't sure what it could be as this was absolutely not my cup of witchbane. I'd never been that good at warding or identifying such. Problem was, neither was Tucker.

"So, what next?" I asked, dropping the waxy stick as I straightened up. It touched my thigh as it fell onto the statue's base. Damn, I'd have to get the wax out before I tossed these into the machine, I thought.

"I don't know about you, but I'm wiped," Tucker said. He peered up at the lowering sun. "I vote we go back to our respective abodes, crash for a while and then talk to Adam and Niko. It's more than an hour till sunset, but I think both of us need to sleep first. We can come back in a few hours."

"I like the idea of sleep," I agreed. "But much as I hate to say this, before we do any more exploring, like you said, we may want to call family. For all we know, one of our dear departed-to-B.C. clan members left behind a booby trap they forgot about and you triggered it. Could save us some flailing about." Or a trip back here, I didn't say. As much as I loved my brother and as much as I wanted to find out what the hell we'd encountered, I'd be happy to discover this was some old warding left by some Kelly years ago—because if it wasn't, that meant something else was responsible.

Tucker chuckled. "Point to you, sis. How 'bout this:

Sleep, then let's regroup in Adam's office at nine or so and call Jane?"

"Nine? That's what? A whole couple of hours or so of sleep? Hate to break it to you, but I really want at least four or five hours. I'm not as young as I used to be. And really, could we try Isabel again instead of Jane?" I asked. "I really don't want another lecture along with any information she can give us."

My brother's chuckle turned into a full-out guffaw. "I can see that—full-blown family-style lecture in front of Adam." He ruffled my hair. "Yes, dear sister, we can call later. Let's plan to meet around eleven or so."

I glowered at him. The idea of having to listen to my aunt Jane's "you ought to have babies" diatribe in Adam's presence was absolutely not my idea of a good time.

"Eleven. Adam's office," I said. "We'll call Isabel. If she's still incommunicado, then I vote for calling Dad. He'll at least know who to ask, even if his idea of magick is having dinner ready at a decent hour."

"Sounds like a plan," Tucker said and motioned to me. "To the car, then?"

I nodded and fell into step beside him.

As I got into the car, my hand brushed against the side of my leg and touched part of my jeans soiled with the candle wax. Instinctively, I rubbed my hand on my thigh, trying to get it off, then raised it to see if I'd gotten it all. The aroma of sage and sandalwood hit me and I collapsed into the car seat.

"Shh." The girl's anxious shushing sounds loud in the dark. "Be careful." The small circle of the flashlight illuminates four pairs of feet, two clad in matching hiking boots standing side by side, the boots nearly pristine and fresh out of their boxes with $200-plus price tags. Another

set of feet, small and in battered Doc Marten ripoffs stands to their left, facing the same direction. The last pair, clad in well worn cowboy boots, stands to the right, inches from the larger pair of the hiking boots. A pair of hands clasp together, between Larger Hiking Boots and Scuffed Brown Tony Lamas.

"Where's the candles?" demands the high clear voice of the second girl. "We've got to do the candles right or this won't work."

"Here." A male voice answers her. "I've got the lighter, hang on." The clasped hands squeeze, release and the boy digs into a pocket of his nearly pristine jeans.

A metallic sound and the smell of butane fills the air as the Zippo wavers, then catches. Four pairs of eyes watch the boy's hands as he lights a candle, drips some wax onto the stone and sets it down, holding it steady until the puddle of wax hardens enough.

"Flashlight, B," the boy says quietly as candle by candle, he lights, drips, sets and holds, face grim in the flickering light, blond hair white, ethereal. His somber expression is mirrored by the other three faces, another blond, so alike to him as mirror image but female, dressed as he is in Polo shirt, khaki shorts and matching hikers. The difference is that her shirt is pink. His is a pale green. Both have a little man on a horse embroidered on them.

A dark-haired girl, the one with the flashlight, the one he'd called "B," her clothes a discount imitation of vintage Goth chic via Wal-Mart, right down to the footwear. The second boy wears Texas ranch standard: plain one-pocket tee, faded jeans and shitkickers. His light brown hair is cut in a shaggy mop. He stands tense, hands now jammed in his pockets. The Goth girl's small hand moves and the flashlight goes out.

"Is this going to work?" The second girl's whisper barely breaks through the quiet sounds of the night.

"It has to," replies the fourth person in a well-modulated tenor. *"It has to."*

As the first boy starts to light the final candle, a scream rips through the air. Startled, he whips around, the edge of his elbow catching the standing candles, knocking all of them from the gravestone onto the ground, plunging them into utter darkness.

Ten seconds later, when the small flashlight stutters back on, they all begin screaming.

CHAPTER EIGHTEEN

"KEIRA. KEIRA." Tucker's voice seemed loud to my ears. Why was he bothering me when I was asleep? Didn't he know I was tired? "Damn it, Keira, are you all right?"

I batted at his hand on my face. "'M fine, leave me alone," I said. I rubbed my eyes and sat up in the car. The car. What the hell was I doing in my car? With a rush and a chill, the vision came back to me.

"Tucker, you were right," I said. "They were here."

"You okay?" He peered at me with concern. Crap, how long was I out?

"I'm okay," I reassured him. "The smell of the wax. It was on my hands. Triggered a vision. I saw them . . . at least, I figure it was them. Four teens, at *La Angel*, doing some sort of ritual with candles." I quickly described the rest of the vision. "They were screaming, Tucker."

"Damn, that's intense," Tucker said. "Sounds like it was them, though. Look, let me drive. I think we should go to Carlton and tell him what we saw after all. Maybe they did see something."

"Before we go home?" I couldn't help sounding a little whiny. I'd gone from tired to exhausted.

Tucker smiled at me and tucked a strand of loose hair behind my ear. "I know, you're tired. Visions will do that to you. What say we go over to Bea's for some serious caffeine and something to eat. We can check to see if Carlton's still at his office or call him from there and tell him. Then we'll go home."

"Yeah, okay. You drive." I switched seats with him.

Twenty minutes later I regretted agreeing with my brother. Twenty or more teens crowded the small café, a couple of sets of parents cowering in the furthest corner booth on the right, merrily ignoring the utter chaos.

"Keira, Tucker!" Bea's happy voice cut through the din. "Good to see y'all. There's a free booth over there." She whirled through the teens, a loaded pizza tray in either hand. "Sorry for the craziness. It's pizza and pasta spring break special." Bea dropped the pizza trays on a table seating three gangly boys. A fourth joined them as he scented his prey. "There you go, guys, two extra large with the works. Feel free to fill up the Cokes at the fountain." With that, she vanished through the kitchen doors, no doubt in search of more food to satisfy the ravenous horde.

A gaggle of girls sat behind the boys, heads bent toward each other, whispering and gesturing. I grabbed Tucker's hand in self-defense as we maneuvered our way past the mob to the one lone empty booth in the far corner of the café. It was next to the door to the restrooms, so rarely got occupied.

"Stay here, Keira," Tucker said. "I'll get us something." I nodded in mute awe at the hubbub. Was I ever this young? This insanely loud? I buried my head in my hands and tried to mute the sounds as best I could. The overwhelming din was a bit too much after my recent vision. All my senses were on overload. I concentrated. Breathe in, breathe out. Calm, even rhythm. Imagine the shield walls thickening, holding, muting the cacophony.

"You okay, *m'hija*?" Bea's welcome voice cut into my focus.

"Yeah, I'm fine," I said, smiling. "It's a little much in here."

She gave me a rueful smile as she plopped down across from me, two mugs of coffee in her hand. Passing one to me, she took a sip. "So, what brings you here on the busiest night of the year?"

"You do this every year?" I asked.

She laughed. "Every year, first Monday evening of spring break, five to eight. Except usually . . ." She shrugged and took another sip. "It's not normally this hot and we set up picnic tables in the parking lot and serve everyone outside."

"Now that makes more sense," I said, laughing. "Did you see where my brother went?"

"He's in the kitchen. Trying to wheedle some tortillas out of Tia Petra."

"Figures. He was supposed to be getting us both food."

As if on cue, Tucker emerged through the kitchen door, bearing a tray laden with two steaming plates of pasta, a tortilla warmer and a plate of shredded cheese. Behind him, Ignacio Robles carried a full pitcher of ice water and two large glasses, both filled with crushed ice. I could have kissed them both.

Less than twenty minutes later, I was hydrated, satiated and ready to sit for at least an hour. Bea and Ignacio had gone back to work, both of them hustling to make sure the voracious teens' appetites were satisfied.

"He's working the floor now," I observed.

Tucker nodded and wiped the last of the spaghetti sauce from his bowl with the remaining tortilla. "So Tia told me. His lack of English is a factor, but he knows enough to help serve, refill water and Cokes and such. He's also helping with nightly clean up."

"So did you say anything to him about what we heard about Alex?" I asked.

"I did. I told Tia and she explained it to him. He didn't say anything, just stood there, quiet. Then he nodded his head and went back to work. I guess he needs time to think about it."

"Either that, or he's better at accepting the inevitable," I said.

"True. We're not that good at death, are we?"

"Not the involuntary kind." I stretched in my seat, feeling a thousand times better. "We should go over and see if Carlton's there. Fill him in." Then, we could go home and sleep. Even if it was night. My body clock was so fucked up now, I'd probably sleep the clock around and wake up tomorrow night. Of course, we still also had to call the clan about the wards.

"He's not," Tucker said. "I mentioned it to Tia when I was in there and Tio Richard told me Carlton's gone over to talk to Mrs. Wentz again."

"Damn, I guess I'll call him." If I could hear over the racket. Although, now that I'd eaten, the noise wasn't quite so nerve-wracking.

I got Carlton's voice mail, so I gave him the quick and dirty overview of what we'd found, leaving out anything remotely supernatural, including the screams.

"Time for more coffee," I said as I put the phone away.

As I neared the urn, one of the girls in the gaggle group broke off from the gang and approached me.

"Hey, Ms. Kelly, right?"

I nodded and topped off my mug. "You are?"

"Crystal," she said. "Crystal Rodriguez." She looked like any of the other kids, about sixteen, seventeen, medium height. A little rounder than some, less round than others. Her dark brown hair was cut in an imitation seventies shag, complementing her imitation seventies wide-leg jeans and granny top. Doc Martens completed the bizarre ensemble. I supposed if you live long enough, all the fashions make a comeback, even the ones that were ugly to begin with.

"What can I help you with, Crystal?"

"I heard what you said on the phone, about Brittany and the others?" Like many teens, the statement got turned into a question as her voice lifted at the end.

Suddenly, I was interested. I'd been polite up to now, not sure of what the girl wanted. "You know something?" I asked.

She looked over her shoulder at the others, who by now were ignoring her in favor of something on someone's iPod screen.

"Can I come sit over with you? I don't want . . ."

"Sure," I said. "Come on."

I slid in across from Tucker. Crystal, after a shy glance at my brother, followed suit, settling in beside me. I turned so I could see her better. "Crystal, this is my brother, Tucker. Tucker, this is Crystal Rodriguez. She wants to tell us something about Brittany."

"Hello, Crystal," Tucker said, giving the girl the big-brother smile.

Crystal smiled back, still a little shy. "She's a friend of mine, you know. Sort of, anyway," she began, breathlessly, words rushing out. "Anyhow, I heard what you said to the Sheriff about the Angel and she went there."

"She did? You know this for sure." I studied Crystal's face, trying to determine if she was serious.

Crystal nodded emphatically. "Yes, I know. Look, we weren't *über* close or anything, not really BFFs, but in fourth grade, we were. So the other day, I ran into her in the locker room after fifth period gym. Friday, I think, yeah, because we had volleyball." Crystal's fingers rubbed a random pattern on the tabletop. "We were alone in there. She came over to me and told me that she had a secret but she had to tell someone and that I wasn't totally stupid." The girl looked up at me and Tucker. "It wasn't an insult, really, I knew what she meant. Everyone thinks she's weird on account'a how she dresses and all, but she's really super smart. Like scholarship smart. She got a full ride to Tech and to someplace East. She's just gotta pick." Crystal stopped a moment. "Can I get a Coke?" she asked.

Tucker nodded. "Sure, what can I get you?"

"Dr Pepper," she said. "Thanks." Tucker slid out of the booth.

"Was that the secret?" I asked Crystal after Tucker left. "Her scholarships?"

"No, no, not that," she replied, a hint of scorn in her voice. "Everyone knew that. This was different. She told me they were going to ask the Angel to show them a way to make it all work."

"It?"

"Yeah, that's what she said. I don't know what she meant. She wasn't religious or anything." Crystal looked around and then moved a little closer to me, dropping her voice. "I think, it's that a bunch of kids at school are always teasing her and calling her a dyke, 'cause she hangs out with that rich bitch Missy Wentz. People think that she's got a crush on Missy. Maybe she wanted them to stop?"

"Why would they think that?" I asked. "Because she's friends with Missy?"

Crystal shakes her head. "Not that. Missy's not friends with anyone really. So the kids think they're dykes."

"Are they?"

"No, I know for sure."

At this point, Tucker returned with a frosty ice-filled glass of Dr Pepper for Crystal. She took it with a grateful look and took a couple of deep swallows before continuing. "I don't know about Missy, but Brittany likes guys. She's been half in love with a guy she knows from Austin. She met him at the basketball tournament a couple of years ago. They're always texting."

"What do you think Brittany was going to ask the Angel?" I asked.

"My guess, it's for a way for her to go away to college." Crystal chomped on a piece of ice.

"I thought you said she got a full ride to a couple of places."

"She did," Crystal said in that oh-my-God-how-stupid-can-adults-be tone of voice. "It's her mother. Brittany's mom is always sick, always telling her that she needs her to stay and take care of her. There's no other relatives, so Brittany feels like she can't leave her mom alone."

Oh, for the love of all that's eternal, that one took the cake and the icing, too. Nothing like a little maternal—or any type of familial—guilt to really fuck up a kid's chances.

"Crystal, we heard something about the four of them going three-wheeling. You know anything about that?" Tucker asked.

Crystal snorted. "Yeah, right. Like Missy Ice Princess Wentz would ever do something outdoors."

"I take it that's a 'no,' then?" Tucker remarked.

"That one's more at home on a shopping spree at Neiman's than on some crappy three-wheeler," Crystal replied. "I have no idea what idiot came up with that story."

"I did," broke in a male voice. A tall teenager walked out of the restroom doorway.

"Hey, Andy," Crystal barely managed, as her face flushed red.

Andy approached the table, but waved away my gesture to sit down. "Thanks, but I need to get back," he said. "It's 'cause I heard y'all. I know that it sounds weird as shit, but I swear I saw them all at the gas station. I work there after school and weekends," he explained. "The four of them were there in Jimmy Stahl's truck, you know that old brown thing that used to be his grandpa's? The three-wheelers were in the bed. I saw Jimmy first, at the pump, then when I came around the counter to pick up a piece of paper I dropped, I saw Matt, Missy and Brittany all crammed in the front. Pretty fucking wild." He ran a hand through his shaggy brown hair, the other one was crammed in his jeans pocket. "Matt came inside then, picked up a coupl'a six packs of Coke and some water. I said something to Matt about having to straddle the gear shift and to be careful of his boys."

Tucker snorted a laugh and I rolled my eyes at him. Didn't matter the age of the boy, nor his origins, certain stupidities were endemic to the gender.

Andy kept talking, either ignoring us or oblivious to our exchange. "Jimmy walked in right then and paid for the gas. He didn't say anything. He looked at Matt and then they both got in the truck. I don't know where they were headed, but I heard Missy say something to Brittany about angels. They were driving away, so I wasn't positive that's what she said, though. Anyway, that's where all of that came from." Andy shrugged. "Hope they find them. Gotta go." He ambled back over to a table and sat down.

"Crystal, have you ever heard of *La Angel*?" I asked her.

"La Angel?" She scrunched her brow in concentration. "I think so. Isn't that the statue up at that old cemetery somewhere out on one of the ranch roads?"

"Yes. Is that somewhere you all go to hang out?"

"Nah, it's too far. It's better out at the lake. I know about it because Brittany was talking about angel statues last—" Her eyes got really big as she clued in. "Oh, wow. That's right. All last week, she kept asking Mr. Marks about angel statues and cemeteries in the area. She said she'd found something online and it reminded her of something from Texas history class in seventh grade."

Bingo! There's the connection we'd been looking for.

"Crystal, thanks so much," I said. "You've been a great help."

"You think they'll find them?" she asked, her voice suddenly childlike. "Are they going to be okay?"

"I'm sure they are," Tucker said. "Sheriff Larson has the best people looking."

"Thanks," she said. "I'll go now if that's okay?"

"Sure."

She scooted out and rejoined her friends, none of whom had paid one iota of attention to what was going on outside their immediate circle. Teenagers. I thanked my lucky stars I wasn't one anymore.

CHAPTER NINETEEN

B EA CAME OUT of the kitchen, and joined us, sliding in next to me. Her face was rigid, unsmiling. Her hands trembled.

"Bea, what is it?"

"I'm okay, really," she said. I wasn't convinced. She sounded tired and shaken. The first wasn't exactly out of the ordinary. I never knew how she managed to run the café practically by herself. Even with help from her elderly aunt and uncle and sporadic help from a nephew, she did the bulk of the work. Hiring staff never panned out because soon they'd be off for greener restaurant pastures as new eateries opened in nearby towns. I admired her for it. I'd never had that kind of stubborn tenacity to succeed. I'd never needed it.

"Anything in particular?" I asked after a few beats of silence. Tucker sat still, watching the both of us.

"Sort of," she said. "Something a bit strange, actually."

"Strange?"

"Well, not so much strange as . . ." Her voice trailed off and she clasped her hands on the table in front of her. She was doing a damned poor job of okay. From what I could tell, she was one second away from wringing her hands and bursting into tears.

"Seriously, Bea, what's up?" I placed a tentative hand on her back, reinforcing my shielding before I did so. With the latest developments in Vision Central, I wasn't about to take a chance in the middle of a crowded restaurant. "Tucker, go get her some coffee."

"No, wait, don't," she said. "I'm good. Only . . . I was out back a few minutes ago, taking some trash to the Dumpster. Remember what I told you about Pete Garza?" she asked, glancing over at Tucker briefly.

"You mean the grade A asshole part?" I replied.

"Yeah, that." She took a breath and paused again, probably glad that I hadn't brought up the story she'd told me in confidence. "Since that time, he hasn't come around here at all. Not even close by. When I was out back, I could swear I saw his truck drive by."

"You saw the truck behind the café? Why the hell didn't you come get us?" Tucker demanded.

"Calm down, Tucker," I said. "Let her explain. Bea, was he right out behind here? Isn't that a service road for the strip–doesn't go anywhere?"

"Mostly, yeah, but you remember that one place where it connects out to Lohmann's Crossing? It's part of the easement back by the old deli."

Strange that in a few short months, the abandoned store once run by the elderly brother and sister that became my cousin's murderers was now the "old" deli.

Bea continued. "I had some trouble with the Dumpster lid, so I went around back of it and when I did, I saw a white Ford F-150 pull out onto Lohmann's Crossing from the service road."

"You're sure it was him? There are a lot of white Ford pickups around here. F-150's got to be the most popular."

"Mostly sure," she replied. "I know it was a few years ago since I last saw him, but yeah. It's pretty beat up, and he has a couple of bumper stickers on the back. Something about Jesus being his master and some disgusting thing about women. I couldn't tell in the dark, but it sure looked like the same truck, bumper stickers and all."

I snorted and blurted out the first words that came into my mind. "So if Jesus is his master, does that mean Pete likes to sub?"

"You did not just say that!"

Bea sounded more amused than shocked, which I silently applauded. Whether or not she'd seen Pete Garza, I wanted her to laugh. I missed our camaraderie. As much as I was . . . or had been . . . enjoying my time at the Wild Moon, some nights, when I was hanging around waiting for Adam to stop playing Lord of the Manor for the evening, I wanted nothing more than to curl up on the sofa with Bea, both of us sharing a big bowl of microwave popcorn, some decent wine and some sappy romantic movie. Not that anyone or anything stopped me from doing that, but the timing was always off. These days, Bea worked too many late nights and by the time she was done, she was usually too pooped to enjoy any friend time. I made a mental vow to rectify this soon, by conspiring with her aunt and uncle to liberate her for a girls' night out. Even if we simply hung out at my house, it would give her a chance to relax a little.

"Sorry. I couldn't help it," I said. "Look, why don't Tucker and I go out back and take a look?"

There wasn't much behind the strip center but an undeveloped plot of land about an acre deep. Another one of those red-tape real estate deals caught up in the hell of what happens when financing goes bust. About a year ago, it was slated for some additional retail spaces, intended to complement the strip center. I'd never been sure how anyone thought they'd support said retail, being as how Rio Seco's population was falling instead of growing. We had a ton of weekenders and summer vacationers, but not enough to warrant new shops.

"That's fine, but I think it's okay," Bea said.

"Okay or not, I'm going out there." Tucker slid out of the booth and vanished into the kitchen.

I patted Bea's back, positive she was more rattled than she'd let on. Seeing Pete's truck like that was like my turning a corner at the Wild Moon and running into Gideon—although as bad as he'd been, he never pulled a similar stunt on me as Pete Garza had with Bea. I'd have emasculated him without a second thought. My papa . . . well, my great-great-granny actually, hadn't raised us to hesitate. Bea, however, was a human woman who rightfully feared a crazy man with a loaded gun.

"You think he was looking for you?" I asked.

"Or maybe Ignacio," Bea replied. "I've told him that I saw Pete and to not go out back tonight."

"Good point. You know, here's a thought. It's already eight, the spring break special's over. Get a couple of those high school boys to take out the trash for you and do some of the heavy clean up. Offer them some free pizza or something. I'll hang out here until you close. Then you and Ignacio can go stay over at my place. Pete may know where you live, but I'm sure he has no idea where I live."

"Babysitting me?" I could hear the small smile in her voice. I was glad that she'd told me. I'd been so caught up in events the past couple of days that face time with Bea would be great, even though it was a direct result of her seeing Pete Garza around. Of course, she could be wrong about who she'd seen. Old beat-up white Ford F-150s were a dime a dozen around here, including bumper stickers extolling the virtues of everything from Skoal to Jesus. The distance from the back of the café to the easement road was close to two hundred yards. In the dark, with the poor lighting back there, it wouldn't be hard to mistake one truck for another. Still, I wasn't going to take any chances. Pete Garza stalking either Bea or Ignacio: definitely a bad thing.

"You know I'll feel better if I do," I said. "Seriously, Bea, come stay at my place tonight. We'll hang out, watch a movie or something. Ignacio can watch Univision on the cable in the guest room."

"Thanks, *chica*, I think I will. I miss you."

"Yeah, me, too. Life keeps getting weirder. We were out searching earlier, then we had a run-in with Pete at the Diamondback."

"You did? What happened?"

I filled her in on the details of our trip to the bar, then subsequent events, up to and including the cemetery.

"Wow, I'd forgotten about that place. You guys find anything?"

"Yeah, actually, Tucker thinks the kids were out there, and based on what young Crystal over there says and the wild but whacky vision-o-rama, so do I. Then freakish energy, the ward or whatever."

Bea looked a little confused. "Ward as in Cleaver?"

"No, more like ward as in something family might have left behind."

"*Your* family, I'm guessing."

"Got it one, sweetie," I said. "We ran across some sort of energy or something, more on the freakish side than not. Tucker and I decided to table it for now, get some rest and figure out what it is later."

I didn't really want to go into any more details with Bea. She knew about us, knew about Tucker's ability, but I wasn't at all comfortable with explaining what happened, especially since she was already a bit unnerved. The fact that some sort of energy forced my brother to shift wouldn't help her stay calm.

Tucker came back a few minutes later.

"Anything?"

He shook his head. "No, there's definitely signs of at least one vehicle out there, but too many scents, too many tracks to distinguish one particular one. All I could tell is that someone drove through there at least once in the last hour." He settled back into the booth. "Bea, I think to be on the safe side—"

"She's going to come home with me, tonight," I interrupted. "So's Ignacio."

"Good." He gulped down the dregs of his coffee. "We'll hang out here until you close, Bea. When we leave, you two ride with Keira and I'll take your car and go back to the Wild Moon. That way, if Garza is trying to follow you, he'll pick the wrong victim this time."

"I need to come in to work in the morning," Bea protested. "I've got to open."

"All settled," Tucker said. "I spoke to your aunt and uncle. They're going to take the breakfast shift and you're going to sleep in. Keira can bring you in and we'll work out the car situation later."

Bea capitulated. "Thank you."

After all, she knew better than to argue with common sense. Especially when it was presented by a more-than-a-millennium-old hellhound.

CHAPTER TWENTY

I HUNG UP the phone and stretched. We managed to herd the rest of the teenagers and attending parents out by eight-thirty, but cleanup and prep for the morning took a while. Both Tucker and I pitched in, neither of us complete strangers to kitchen duty at the café. In my own teen years, I often hung out here in the afternoons, "helping" Bea and snagging free munchies. With everyone helping, we wrapped things up in about an hour.

"Good thing you don't own anything smaller, Bea." Tucker packed his body into Bea's subcompact, grumbling good-naturedly. "Everything cool at the ranch, sis?"

"Suppose so," I said. "I left a voice mail. Adam's not answering. I imagine he's in a meeting."

"Makes sense. Damn, this seat doesn't go back far enough," Tucker complained.

"I sure hope that Pete Garza does follow you, bro," I laughed. "I'd love to see his face when you get out of the car."

"You take care of Bea, you hear?" he said, quietly. I glanced over at Bea, who was explaining to Ignacio what we were doing.

"I will. You call me if anything happens, okay?"

"Ditto."

I nodded and he drove off. Bea, Ignacio and I piled into my car and we headed to my place.

As I pulled up into the circular drive, it occurred to

me that this was more Bea's home these days than mine.
Other than the short nap when Tucker and I had sacked
out here before going to view the Pursell ranch, I didn't
think I'd been back to this house in at least a month.
Once, not that long ago, it had been a refuge. My own
small comfort zone and a place where I was free to be
me. After Adam came back into my life, my comfort
zone changed and home became his house at the ranch.
Fickle? Maybe. More a realization that "home" signified
a concept more than a physical place. For Tucker, home
was wherever he could relax. Sometimes that was with
me. Sometimes with Niko. I didn't know what home was
for Bea.

"I can't believe I'm hungry again," I said, as we entered
the house. "Didn't we eat a little bit ago?"

"Three hours," Bea replied. "Let me get Ignacio settled
in the small guest room and I'll help you fix something."

"Fix something? There's no food here, is there?" I
racked my brain. "I can't remember the last time I've
bought any groceries for the house. Months ago? There
might be some boxes of microwave popcorn or something,
but real food, not likely."

Bea laughed. "Yes. There is. Remember, I stay out here
sometimes? I like to eat and I don't always want to fix
something at the café or eat old microwave popcorn."

"Oh." I flushed, embarrassed at my gaffe. "Egads, I'm
a terrible host."

"You're not a host, *chica*. You're family. I'm perfectly
capable of stocking the kitchen and cooking for myself. I'll
be back in a minute."

Bea spoke briefly to Ignacio and motioned for him to
walk down the hall with her. I'd suggested he take the
smaller guest room, primarily because the other cable feed

was in there and he could watch the Spanish language stations and not be bothered by us gabbing.

There were some clean men's clothes in the guest room closet, some of Marty's stuff that had never been worn. I'd pulled them aside when I donated the rest of his stuff to Goodwill after his death. My cousin, on the most part, had had execrable taste, but a few items, including some jeans and some nice button-down shirts and Polos were still in their original packages. Flotsam and jetsam from his final life's spending spree, I supposed. Purchased with blood money. In any case, I'd meant to donate these to a place I knew of in San Antonio that helped folks get jobs. They were always looking for presentable clothing. Some of the items might fit Ignacio. Even though he was thinner than Marty, they were about the same height and build.

Bea came back out into the living room, Ignacio trailing her. "He's offered to cook for us," she said.

"He has? He doesn't have to."

"He knows, he would like to do something for us, for you."

"Por favor, señorita," Ignacio broke in. *"Les agradezco lo que hicistes por mí. Dejame cocinar para ustedes. Les cocinos algo muy bueno."*

Bea translated quickly. "He wants to cook. Says he's grateful for what we've done for him and that he'll cook something very good."

"Oh for— Bea, he *really* doesn't have to do that." How could this guy be so grateful, so patient? "I mean, all we've done is establish that his brother took off with some waitress for a night of drugged up sex and then probably got himself lost and died of exposure or something out in the middle of nowhere. We haven't even found his body, for pity's sake. And here Ignacio wants to cook for us."

"Let him, Keira, really," Bea said. "I know how you feel, all I did was put him to work. But, we need to let him do this."

"Okay, okay," I said. "But he needs to sit with us and eat, too."

"Done." Bea turned to Ignacio and spoke to him, then they disappeared into the kitchen. Thirty minutes later, the three of us sat down to fluffy cheese and mushroom omelets, accompanied by pan fried potatoes and slices of garlic bread.

"This tastes wonderful," I said, stuffing my face. Eating dinner at the Inn's restaurant every night was fabulous, but they tended to cook elaborate meals, since their primary customers were the resident vampires. The vampires usually wanted meat dishes, heavy on the rare, which I loved, but occasionally a simple sandwich or omelet would do me fine. I hated to ask for special treatment there, so tended to have something off the night's menu.

It didn't take us long to demolish the excellent food.

"Thank you very much, Ignacio," I said. "*Muchas gracias*. This was excellent."

Ignacio ducked his head. "*De nada, señorita.*" He stood and started to gather the empty plates.

"Wait a moment, please." I put a hand on his arm. "Please sit down and relax." I motioned to the chair. "Bea, can you tell him that I'd like to ask a few questions? About Alex? I don't want to upset him or anything, but there are a few things I need to ask."

Bea quickly explained to him. Ignacio hesitated, then sat, his hands folded on the table, like a particularly obedient school kid at his desk, waiting for the teacher. Opposite him, Bea sat patiently, ready to play interpreter.

Something Bitsy had said to me earlier had been nagging me so I opened with that. "Ignacio, when I spoke to Mrs. Pursell today, she told me that other workers had left the ranch before. Do you know anything about that? Was that something your brother talked to you about?"

Bea translated and his face immediately grew animated. *"Sí, sí,"* he said, and spoke rapidly. I caught a word or two, "Alejandro" and *"dinero,"* but couldn't follow most of it.

"He says Alex told him about that in a phone call a week or two before he last heard from him," Bea explained. "They talked for a long time, Alex saying how much he missed home, but the money was too good on this side. He made a hundred a week cash and got nearly every Sunday off so he could call Ignacio twice a month and send two hundred a month home to the family via Giros Postales."

"Seriously? He made that little and still sent half of it back home?"

"I know," Bea said. "That's way less than minimum wage, and you can bet those men aren't working forty hour weeks. A couple hundred dollars goes a long way in Mexico, but not here."

She said something to Ignacio, and he responded. "Oh my. Ignacio says that the men get room and board plus their wages, so it's really good." Bea shook her head in disbelief. "Damn, and I have trouble keeping kitchen workers at minimum wage. That's wrong."

"Totally," I agreed. "But that's what happens when they bring in these guys. They have no recourse since they're here illegally. I suppose that's a problem for another day, though. You and I can't really do anything about this now."

"True. It still sucks."

"Very much so," I said. "Bea, ask him if he thinks the men who left, left of their own accord."

Ignacio shook his head at the question and shrugged. He spoke for a long time and then waited for Bea to translate to me.

"He says he doesn't know, but that Alex thought at least one of them was odd," Bea said.

"Them?"

"The situation. He says Alex worked for the Pursells for nearly two years. Most of the time there at the Pursell ranch, but sometimes he'd get loaned out when some of the Judge's pals needed extra workers. One of the *patrones* had a great ranch house and paid Alex nearly double his weekly wage to help build a stone barbecue at the pool house. Ignacio says Alex worked with two other guys there and that one of those guys knew the worker who had gone from the Pursell ranch. He told Ignacio he would ask about it next time he worked at the new place, but that was the last phone call he got from Alex."

"Damn," I said. "I can't help but wonder if there really was something going on and Alex stumbled across it by asking questions."

Bea chewed her lip. "If he did, I'd go directly to blaming Pete Garza."

"Yeah, that's kind of where I was headed," I said. "From what you've told me, and the little I've seen of him, he's the type to either run off workers or do something nasty. Except in this case, I'm pretty sure Alex never made it back to the ranch after his little party with Jolene."

"You're probably right." Bea yawned and stretched. "Man, I'm so beat. Why don't we clean up and then we can sack out? I'll tell Ignacio to go on back and get some rest. He did all the work, so we'll take care of the dishes."

"Sounds like a good idea." I picked up my plate and Bea did the same with hers. She spoke to Ignacio, and although he seemed to protest, he bowed to the inevitable and after saying goodnight to both of us, went back to the guest room.

Bea and I made short work of the cleanup, mostly because Ignacio had already done most of the heavy lifting. The kitchen was spotless and he'd already washed and dried the pans he'd used to cook with.

"Go on to bed, Bea," I said after she yawned a third time. "It's late and you've had a stressful day between the teenaged hordes and then everything else."

"Mm, yeah, you're right." She folded the dishtowel she'd been using and placed it on the counter. "Sorry I'm so wiped. I was hoping to have some time to sit and chat with you."

"I know, sweetie. Me, too, but we're all tired." I ushered her out of the kitchen and shut off the light. "Let's plan on a girls' night, soon, okay?"

"Cool." Bea trundled down the hall and into the second guest bedroom, shutting the door.

THE DARK enveloped me as I sat curled in the armchair. After taking a quick shower, I'd changed into a tank top and some loose sweatpants and come back out to the living room. I'd thought about sacking out, getting the sleep I sorely needed, but at this point, I'd moved from tired and sleepy to tired and wired. A low energy buzzed through me, the kind you get when lack of sleep and too much stress keep your mind whirling and unable to let go. My muscles ached with exhaustion, but the last thing I wanted to do was to lie down in bed and stare at the ceiling.

The porch light peeking through a gap in the curtains gave me enough ambient light to see by. I saw more than most; my night vision enabled me to make out the nap of the couch, the leaf pattern on one of the throw pillows. I wrapped my arms around my legs and closed my eyes. So here I was. Back in my house, Bea in the guest room, like it once was. Before Adam. *Plus ça change*, I suppose. Tonight *was* nice, spending time with Bea, even though the reason wasn't so good. I was lucky to have her as a friend. We'd known each other since I was seven, since my father brought me here, straight from the Sidhe stronghold underneath the Welsh faery mounds and with no idea what was going to happen to me. Over the years, our friendship deepened and grew and despite my family, despite my travels, despite my all but abandoning her for the past few months, she still cared. I was one very lucky woman.

"Hey, whatcha doing?" Bea's sleepy voice interrupted my thoughts.

"Hey back."

She crossed in front of me and curled up on the couch. She was dressed nearly as I was, which was no surprise, seeing as how she'd raided my dresser for something to wear. On her, my tank top was almost too small. Bea was a lot shorter than me, but curvy and much more well-endowed. Since most of my pants would probably not fit, either in width or length, she'd opted for a pair of cut off sweats, which on me, reached mid-thigh, but on her were to her knee. Both of us were barefoot.

"Couldn't sleep?" she asked.

"Nope."

"Me, neither."

We sat in companionable silence for a few minutes.

"You thinking about anything in particular?" Bea asked, her voice soft in the stillness.

"Sort of." I rested my chin on my knee. I watched a spider crawl across the top of the window. I couldn't tell if it was inside or outside, but I couldn't bring myself to care.

What I really wanted was to go back to the Wild Moon and finish my discussion with Adam. I felt unfinished, as if too much was left undecided. I didn't know what would happen from here, but I didn't like not having an answer. Maybe that's why I'd volunteered to search for the kids, to look for Alex Robles. I hadn't asked to be involved, but I had been.

"You want to go back to the ranch, don't you?"

"You can tell, can't you?"

She chuckled and pointed at me. "I know you, Keira Kelly. I've known you for thirty years."

"That you have."

"Anything I need to worry about?" Bea asked.

"Not really." I sighed and straightened my legs, leaning forward in the chair. "Adam and I have some unfinished business."

"So go, take care of it."

"I can't do that. I promised to watch over you tonight, and I will. Adam will keep." And so would I. "Besides, no one's going to die because Adam and I don't get a chance to talk tonight and come to a resolution. He and I can talk later."

"Resolution?" Bea perked up at that, sensing the opportunity for some girl gab.

"It's nothing, really," I said, unsure of how to explain it without grossing her out. When Bea first found out vampires existed, her immediate reaction was to grab at the cross she wore around her neck. Now, six months later, she'd accepted my relationship enough to tease me about it, but I knew the fact of his being vampire still bothered her. "Adam and I are of a difference of opinion on something and we haven't had a chance to work it out."

"Again, so go. It's obviously bothering you," Bea said. "And, just as obviously, you're not ready to share with me, so I can't help."

"It's not that I don't want to share . . ." I began.

"Keira, really, I know you, remember? It's okay. You'll share when you're ready. Go on back to the ranch. Ignacio and I will be fine here."

"But that will leave you without a car," I protested. What else could I say? I knew this was a losing battle, my own stubbornness rarely a match for Bea's. I was a little uneasy about leaving her here, but she was right. Pete Garza didn't know where I lived and I was well enough off any beaten path that stumbling across my house was more than unlikely. I had no neighbors, no other houses near mine.

"Don't worry. I'll call Tio in the morning, he can come pick us up or send my nephew. Do what you need to do and I'll rest easier knowing that you did. Promise me one thing?"

"Absolutely."

"When you're ready, come see me and tell me what this is all about?"

"I will, if you'll promise me that you'll keep all the doors and windows locked and you will not, I repeat, not go outside until Tio gets here tomorrow."

She nodded. "Done. Now scoot, get on out of here before I call your brother to come get you."

I laughed and went to change clothes.

CHAPTER TWENTY-ONE

IT TOOK ME a few minutes to get dressed and head out to the Wild Moon.

As I drove up to Adam's, I noticed the porch light was on, but the house lights were still dark. Odd. Usually, once Adam got up for the night, showered and dressed, he went upstairs and turned on the living room lights. He'd sit there for a bit, reading through correspondence and getting papers in order, then walk over to his office for the rest of his work. Occasionally, he skipped the first part and went directly to the office, but he always turned on the lights.

My cell phone rang as I pulled up to the front of the house. I glanced at the display and answered it.

"Hey, Carlton," I said. "Kind of late, isn't it?"

"It's been that kind of a day," he responded. "Besides, I knew you'd be awake."

Not surprising. Even before Adam, I'd been more of a night person and tended to sleep days. "I guess you got my voice mail?"

"Yeah, interesting. I'm going to send out a couple of guys in the morning to go check out that old cemetery. I talked to Mrs. Wentz about it, but she didn't know it was there."

"Any other signs of the kids?"

"Nothing yet, but I'm not giving up on the runaway idea. I still can't put my finger on what's up, though."

"Hey, listen, I was up at Bea's earlier. Talked to a couple

of kids there." I quickly filled him in on what Crystal and Andy had said.

"Huh, well, at least that corroborates what you all saw out there," he said.

"Yeah. You get anything out of the other parents?"

"Mrs. Martinez thinks Brittany's been brainwashed by 'that bitch Missy Wentz' and Aaron Stahl mostly figures his nephew's old enough to do what he wants. So, I'm batting pretty much zero at this point." I didn't need to see him to know how frustrated Carlton was. The weariness in his voice made him sound old.

"I'm about to turn in for the night," he continued, "but I thought I'd make sure to let you know I got your voice mail. I've got a guy stationed at each of the houses, in case they call. I'll also ask Rick to see if he can swing by the Pursell place in the morning, maybe ask around again."

"Thanks, appreciate that. Hey, so you know, Bea's up at my place with Ignacio Robles." I filled Carlton in about what had happened earlier and about Bea's history with Pete.

"For heaven's sake, Keira," he said. "She never reported that?"

"I know, Carlton, but now's not the time to worry about that. It's a long time ago. I want to be sure that Pete's not going to bother her or Ignacio."

"Don't worry, I'll take care of that. I'll have someone drive up to your place and check in on them in an hour or so. I can't station someone there all night, since we've got a few guys, but we'll make sure they're okay."

"Thanks. Call me if anything happens," I said.

"Will do." He hung up.

I reached to open the door. A tap on my car window startled me.

"What the—" I whirled, dropping my phone. "Tucker, what are you doing here?" I picked up my phone, dropped it in my bag, then opened the door and he stepped back.

"You haven't gone inside." It wasn't a question.

"No, I got a call from Carlton, why?" I peered at my brother's face, which was in shadow. He wasn't smiling. Tucker reached a hand out and touched my shoulder, giving it a quick squeeze.

"Bea's okay?"

"Yeah, I couldn't sleep so she sent me home. Tucker, what is it?"

I caught him glancing at the house and his sort of neutral expression morphed into one of concern.

I got out of the car and made it to the porch nearly a full three seconds before my shapeshifter brother caught up. The front door of the house was unlocked and I started inside.

"Wait, Keira—" Niko's voice came from behind me.

"No." I stepped forward into the dark silence. Niko's hand landed on my shoulder, I twisted to move away but he was faster and stronger. He grabbed my upper arm and stopped me as I entered the foyer.

"Please, wait. Just a moment." I half turned, angry he was keeping me from going down to the bedroom. I knew that's where Adam was, despite the fact that it was still dark.

"What the hell is going on, Niko?"

"I'm sorry, it's Adam. He needs blood."

"I know." Obvious. What wasn't he telling me?

"Lance came by here about an hour ago, to drop off some mail. Adam was still asleep."

"Still?" My heart stuttered in my chest. "Niko, it's past one. Adam should have been awake hours ago."

"I know."

Niko's blue eyes glittered in the darkness. He was a very pretty man, red-gold hair framing a pale sculpted face. He and Tucker made a lovely couple. Normally, Niko's face was relaxed, if a bit wary, as befitted the man who served as second in command to the lead vampire. Tonight, it was neither. I saw true worry there, the kind of worry that gave me the cold chills.

"Lance called me immediately," Niko said. "I came over and tried to wake him, but couldn't. Then I tried to give him fresh blood, from a deer."

We both blinked as the living room lights came on. I glanced around. Tucker stood by the switch, arms crossed over his chest. He'd gone into protector mode. I'd almost forgotten he was here.

"Adam roused a bit when I painted blood on his lips." Niko's voice broke a little. "He drank some, Keira," Niko continued, his worry lines more obvious in the light. Niko had died a young man, but his many years of experience reflected in the cool blue of his eyes. This was no boy.

"Didn't help?" I asked in a whisper.

"No."

I barely heard the word, closing my eyes against it.

"You know he wouldn't take any from me," I said as I opened my eyes again, catching Niko's gaze. "I offered. Every night." And he'd refused, again and again. Was this what his stubborn denial had come to? "I'm willing to offer again."

"I know." Niko bowed his head in acknowledgment. "But . . ." He fell silent. I waited long enough to see if he was going to continue speaking.

"I'll go down now." I stepped away from Niko and headed for the stairs.

Niko's arm shot out again, blocking my way.

Both my hands flew up automatically. "What?"

"He's in really bad shape, Keira."

"I don't care." I pushed Niko aside and ran down the polished wood steps, the heels of my boots clattering and echoing in the stillness.

Damn it. Stubborn fucking vampire had gone and almost died.

CHAPTER TWENTY-TWO

I RUSHED to Adam's side, barely taking in the fact that he lay rigid on his back as if tucked into a coffin. A soft blanket covered him, baring his unclothed shoulders. I shivered. This wasn't the vampire I'd come to know. I'd often watched him sleep, fascinated by him, wanting to imprint his beauty into my brain. He was the third lover I'd spent any appreciable time with. Most of the others were for fun. The first man I actually *slept* with, as opposed to just have sex with, was Carlton. He'd been a sound sleeper and tended to drape himself all over me . . . constantly. I didn't mind at first, but soon got to the point where I started to feel claustrophobic. I soon realized that Carlton had seen my staying over as a declaration of "forever after." Our breakup happened a few months after my first sleepover.

The second man had been Gideon. Almost the opposite of Carlton, Gideon was a light sleeper who spent much of the night tossing and turning, occasionally reaching over to grab at my arm, touch my back or shoulder, never really relaxing into sleep. Often, after sex, I'd stay for a while, but eventually make some excuse and go seek my own bed in the maze of bedrooms in the old house. Because we were distant cousins, both Gideon and I stayed at the clan home in London, a centuries-old and ridiculously appointed mansion harking back to the turn of the eighteenth century.

Adam was more of the "sprawl all over and take up space" sleeper, but he never forced himself into my side of the bed. Instead, we often made room for each other, turning when the other did, sliding over to accommodate an arm or leg, touching lightly sometimes, other times spooning together. It never seemed a battle for territory, more a mutual comfort zone.

I suppose I never really paid attention to sleeping habits before now. Sleeping together was so much more intimate than sex. It was when you finally let go of all pretense, the façades that we build around ourselves. I could never let go of mine with Carlton; Gideon never let go of his with me. With Adam, all barriers were down. Not the first night I stayed with him, but soon after. I didn't have to pretend I was human, he didn't have to pretend he was other than vampire. So quickly we'd let all the warts show.

"Adam," I whispered as I crawled across the bed to him. He didn't budge, didn't move a muscle. I couldn't very well listen for a heartbeat or put a mirror up to his nose. I reached out, half afraid to touch his skin, expecting it to feel clammy, the cold of true death. He couldn't be totally gone though, Niko would have told me—wouldn't he?

I slid the blanket down, and laid my hand on his unmoving chest, skin to skin. I needed to know how much of him was still in there. Was this a case of retreating while trying to heal? Thing was, healing took energy, whether you got that energy from a juicy steak, a McBurger or a few ounces of fresh blood. This wasn't the broken hurt kind of healing, either. It went a great deal deeper. I didn't know how long Adam had been conducting his experiment, trying to survive on animal blood extracts mixed in wine. I knew the catalytic event occurred during World War II, but I had no idea exactly when he'd stopped taking living blood.

Adam's skin was so very cold. I closed my eyes and reached, using the metaphysical connection we'd shared longer than we'd been lovers. My barriers dropped, opening up, senses seeking whatever spark of Adam was left deep inside him.

Silence. The utter stillness of death unanimated. I tried again, letting everything drop, all defenses, all barriers open. The sound of my own breathing seemed loud as hurricane winds enveloping me, buffeting the void where Adam belonged. He wasn't totally dead; I couldn't feel any decay, but the icy emptiness echoed the loss of awareness as if he'd passed over. My body shivered in response. Immediately, I slammed shut my shields, not willing to follow him down whatever hole he'd fallen into himself.

"He's in a coma." Niko's voice jarred me back to reality and the present. He stood behind me, Tucker to his left and slightly to the back, as if to guard and protect. It hadn't taken my brother long to establish a relationship with this man. Not that I could say anything, I'd taken up with Adam as quickly . . . although I suppose our years of acquaintanceship in England counted for something. It didn't really matter though. Tucker's judgment was usually sound . . . unlike my own.

I scooted away from Adam's unmoving body and sat at the edge of the bed.

"Coma?"

Niko shrugged, his head cocked a little to one side, arms folded across his chest, a strange mixture of defensive posture and conciliation. Until he and Tucker became lovers, the two of us had barely been able to have a civil conversation. Last year, when I'd first visited the Wild Moon, his attitude toward me had even led to a fight between him and Adam. I never asked about it; Adam had never volunteered any information.

Now, Niko and I could speak together. I wouldn't call us friends, simply tolerant of each other's place in our respective lives.

"Self-induced. I think he's trying to regain his strength," Niko said.

"Damn it," I leaped from the bed, angry at myself. "I should have been here. I could have forced—"

"Keira." My brother stepped around Niko and took my arm, stopping me. "It wouldn't have helped."

"He's right," Niko agreed. "If he's in a coma now, Adam was in no shape—"

"To what?" I snapped the words out. "To take blood from me and live?"

Niko sighed and dropped his head, staring down at the floor. We all three stood silent for a moment, an eerie tableau at the side of what easily could be my lover's deathbed. The figure in the bed remained motionless, no more lifelike than if he were displayed at Madame Tussaud's.

"It's not that easy." Niko's voice was soft. He raised his head and looked directly into my eyes, his own blue eyes dull, their usual sparkle missing. "At this stage, he might not have been able to stop."

It didn't take me long to catch that particular clue.

"Fuck."

"Ditto." My brother's frown echoed my own.

This was not good news. It wasn't even not-bad news. This was worse than I'd imagined. Damn Adam's skewed sense of honor, anyway. If he'd started hunting with the other vampires, or allowed himself to feed a little from me regularly, this wouldn't be happening. At least, I thought so. I wasn't the vampire expert around here. I asked Niko.

He nodded, a slow movement, as if he were reluctant to agree. "Yes, possibly," he said, his words deliberate as if he were considering the answer. "Hunting seems to have revived everyone else. I think it would have helped Adam. In fact, I thought it was."

"Was what? How? He wasn't hunting." Now I was confused.

"Okay, look, this looks to be a bit of a tale. Why don't we all go upstairs? This is a little . . . creepy."

I barked out a laugh. Creepy? I stood there with a bloodsucking vampire and a hellhound. This wasn't exactly smack in the middle of normal.

"I mean . . ." Niko looked over at Adam. "It bothers me seeing him like that." That, I could agree, was an understatement.

Minutes later, the three of us sat in Adam's living room. Me on one of the overstuffed chairs, the two men side by side on the couch. Niko sat forward, his arms on his thighs, head bowed a little. Tucker tried for a more relaxed posture but failed. I could see the tension in his shoulders, in the slight grimace on his face.

"I'm not exactly sure where to start," Niko said. "It's complicated."

"How about the highlights?" I really wasn't being facetious or flip. I wanted as much information in as short a time as possible. The more I knew, the easier it would be to help Adam.

"You know that Adam made me, right? You know my story?"

"Some of it," I said. "He found you in the streets, dying, turned you and saved you."

Niko let out a soft sigh, his shoulders tensing a little.

Tucker put a hand on the other man's back, not moving it, a steady weight signifying his support. Niko's mouth turned up at the corners and he gave Tucker a look I recognized, yet had never seen on the vampire's face before: tenderness and gratitude. His usual arrogance had vanished, replaced by a quiet vulnerability.

"I was a whore," Niko said, his blunt tone allowing for no sympathy. "I never knew any family. The streets were home. Not even sure how old I was when . . ." His voice trailed off, then he continued. "I spent years doing nothing more than existing, trying to stay alive. I did well, actually. There were women, men, sometimes both at once, who liked pretty young boys. I was even good at self-defense, in case any of them got too rough. But there was one thing I couldn't stop."

He looked me in the eye, catching my gaze and holding it. The glitter was back, except now it wasn't the twinkle of amusement, this was the shine of something darker, something once buried and almost forgotten. It wasn't pretty.

"My then patron was a lesser noble who kept lodgings in London. When he was in residence, I slept in his bed. When he was following the court, I slept in the barn with the stable boys, the cats and the fleas. I had a bit of a nicer pallet than the others, but I knew my place. My patron threw me back out on the streets the moment the first bubo appeared. It was nearing winter."

A thin smile crossed Niko's face, his eyes narrowing, gaze losing focus a little as if lost in remembering. "Dudley's wife was still living then and he had not yet taken up with the Queen." Niko blinked and looked at me. "That's how we marked time then, you see. I had no idea of the actual year."

I nodded, acknowledging everything he wasn't saying.

Despite his youthful looks—he looked to be no more than twenty—there were many years behind this man. Years, experiences I hadn't known. Okay, well, fine. Used to that. Age didn't faze me.

Niko's voice grew even quieter. "A few days later, the one lump became many. I was in the alley behind a public house when I fell into the slime of the gutter. I don't know how long I was there. All I know is that sometime later, I woke up, ravenous, disoriented, in a fancy bed in a stranger's bedroom. I wasn't alive anymore, but was more alive than I'd ever been when my heart beat. He never hurt me. He was the one person I cared about for a long time."

Niko rubbed his hands across his face and fell silent.

The soft chirping of the crickets outside was the sole noise in the house other than the exhalations from Tucker and me. Niko didn't need to cross any Ts at this point. I got the picture he'd painted with such few words.

"Nikolai . . ." I began.

He straightened, despair gone from his posture, a bit of his old arrogance back. "Yes?"

"He calls you 'Niko,' and 'Nikolai.' You're English then? That's not an English name."

He shrugged. "It's one of my names. One he . . . I like."

"I'd wondered," I said softly. "You didn't strike me as being very Romanian. I wondered about that last year . . ." I didn't have to finish.

"The Gypsy village. Yes." Niko stood and walked over to a window across from where we were seated. The blinds were drawn, so I knew he wasn't looking out. I figured he was looking back.

"I took the name when we settled in Romania—much later. It was easier to seem more local, even though I didn't really look it." He shrugged. "Peasants and villagers rarely ask questions."

"Were you still together when he met me in London?" As lovers, I meant.

"No. Not consistently. Occasionally. We'd both moved on. He gained power and prestige. I became his lieutenant, or whatever. By the time we moved back to London, so many things had changed. So had we."

Niko looked at me with a curious expression, as if waiting for something—a reaction, perhaps?

At this point in my life, I more or less did the serial monogamy bit—at least up to now and in the three major relationships I'd had in my short life. I wasn't opposed to other arrangements should the subject ever come up. So far, it hadn't. Besides, how could I be jealous of something that happened before I was born?

"Either way, it's not important," Niko continued. "What is, is the fact that because Adam made me, he can often use me for energy. He can do that with most of his kin. Me, the others."

"Come again?" I was thinking the word "vampire" all of a sudden took on a whole new connotation. Feed from his minions? This was news.

"He's the king. For us, it's not simply a title. He has ties to all of us . . . actual blood ties. When each of us swears blood oath, it's exactly that. Adam takes a sip of our blood, we taste his. It creates a tie that can't be broken unless both parties agree. Then once a year, he'd take the annual tribute, a reprise of the original blood oath. In older days, he'd have been offered tastes from the young men and women of the village. He never did that when I knew him. I don't really think that part was necessary. Blood from us, though, is more than symbolic. Because of this, he's able to feed from us at a distance, maintaining his strength, his power as king."

I nodded at this. It made sense. Human kings of old did this all the time. My clan was no different, collecting our own version of tribute, be it money, services, goods. Nowadays, it was more symbolic than actual—a coin, some fancy baked goods, etc.—a token gesture of fealty.

Hell, my mother's people's history wasn't much different either, except their case was more akin to the vampire's. Stories of changeling children and young men or women being taken by the faery folk were often more than stories. It wasn't unusual for the Sidhe to demand tribute from the local populace. I didn't know what they did nowadays.

Niko's story was the vampire version—a sort of cross between tribute and a marriage bond—somewhat more of the latter, since feeding directly from another person was more about sex than blood. I got that. A tribute, in whatever way, was an integral part of the king-subject relationship.

"Wait a minute. You said 'take'—past tense. He stopped?"

Niko turned from the window and came back to the couch, allowing himself to fall heavily into the plush cushions, his usual grace abandoned.

"This happened long ago. Shortly after . . ." He didn't finish the sentence. No matter, I knew what he was going to say.

My brother said it for us.

"The camps."

Niko nodded. "It was something else Adam said he couldn't do. He told me one night, after he'd made the decision. I was arguing with him. He said he'd seen the destruction of the Nazis, what they took in 'tribute'—looting, lives, women. It was all too much. It sickened him—

sickened all of us. He couldn't allow himself to even remotely be associated with that kind of behavior."

"And now—this has contributed to his weakness?"

"I don't know." Tucker moved closer to Niko as the vampire bowed his head once again. "I wish I had answers. I don't."

"How long has Adam not fed from living blood?" My brother's question was as blunt as his caress of Niko's neck was tender. I knew he cared for Niko—despite that, Tucker was my kin, clan . . . my blood, my family. His primary focus was going to be me and my concerns.

"I'm not sure," Niko said. "Other than his . . . emergency feeding from you at the quarry . . . Adam stopped hunting, stopped feeding from us or from humans shortly after the concentration camp, but still drank animal blood as needed. It wasn't until—" He stopped suddenly, his gaze flickering over to me then away. He pressed his lips together against the words he obviously wasn't willing to say out loud.

Freaking hell. I was most definitely aboard this clue bus and I wanted off right now. I did not want this to be happening.

"He stopped drinking live animal blood because of me." The words came out of my mouth with no more emotion than if I'd been reading the back of a cereal box. Nine essential vitamins with every bowl. Except Adam hadn't been getting whatever was essential for his health and un-life . . . because of me.

CHAPTER TWENTY-THREE

NIKO NODDED, not meeting my gaze. "I'm sorry. I didn't plan to tell you. I know he never wanted to let you know."

"Fuck, Niko, why the hell did he do something so incredibly stupid?" My steps took me to the other side of the room and then back. I didn't even remember standing up. "Shit, shit, shit."

"Calm down, sis." Tucker crossed the room and took my arms in his large hands, effectively stopping me dead in my tracks. "Adam is a grown man. I'm sure he had his reasons."

"Yeah, reasons that make absolutely no sense and are obviously killing him. He's in a fucking coma, Tucker, or had you forgotten?" Tucker winced at the fury of my words. I wasn't moving away, wasn't struggling against his hold, but my body was shaking with the rage blowing through me.

"This is not fucking fair." I was nearly shouting at my brother. "I can't do this again, Tucker. Not again. Gideon used me, abused my trust, blamed me when he got in over his own damned head. Now I have a stubborn vampire who decides—without consulting me—that I can't handle him drinking blood, so he quits doing it? What the hell is this, anorexia by stupidity? Now he's dying and it's all because of me. I will not be a party to this, I can't. I just can't."

"Shh, *m'eudail*, quiet." Tucker's hands moved up and down my arms, a brother's attempt to calm me, to stop my infernal mea culpas. "It's not your fault. No worries. We'll call Isabel. She'll come."

I shook off his touch and moved away, not wanting to see his face, see the concern.

"Fine, whatever, not my fault. But no matter what, I'm *still* the catalyst. Damn it, what if we *can't* get in touch with Isabel? Even if we do, what if there's nothing she can do? Then what? I let him die?" I whirled around and stared at my brother who was standing next to Niko, who was still seated on the couch, no doubt reluctant to join in. I know I probably looked as if I was accusing Tucker, accusing Niko, but what I really wanted to do was to go right back downstairs and shake some sense into a co-matose vampire king who'd made a life-altering decision without consulting me—without even fucking *knowing* me. There was so much wrong there I didn't know where the hell to begin.

"I don't know, Keira," Tucker answered. "All we can do is try."

"Who's Isabel?" Niko interrupted.

"Our aunt. A healer. She's on walkabout," Tucker explained.

"Will she know anything about vampires?"

"I don't know, *a rún*." Tucker's left hand dropped onto the top of Niko's head, lightly caressing the other man's hair, displaying a softness I didn't knew he had in him. At least, not toward his lover-of-the-moment. I'd heard Tucker use endearments like this to family, usually to young ones or sometimes to me whenever he felt unusually big-brotherly. I'd never heard him be more than casually respectful or humorous to his lovers.

This was most definitely new behavior. I shelved these thoughts for now. I'd be talking to Tucker privately—later. When we had time to talk about other things—*if* we had time.

"Isabel's gifted," I explained to Niko. "She's more than a physical healer. She's about as holistic as you can get. A touch telepath and empath, mostly, with talent for healing. I'm not sure exactly what she does or how she does it. I don't even know if there's anything she can do for Adam, but it wouldn't hurt. We need the big guns here and she's it. Unfortunately, we've been trying to contact her . . . on another matter . . ."

"But you haven't been able to reach her?" The vampire stood and joined us. He started to speak, hesitated, then straightened a little and looked directly at me, probably for the first time since we'd first met. "Look, Keira, I'm sorry, I know you and I got off to a bad start. I admit I was a bit jealous. Adam changed a great deal after he met you. Not about the blood . . . everything else. Buying this ranch, deciding to come to Texas of all places. I wasn't sure it was a good idea."

"I don't suppose it was." I wasn't being fair and I knew it, but couldn't help letting my feelings show in my tone of voice. This wasn't a burden I wanted to carry. Who the hell had appointed me bearer of this stake-shaped cross? It was enough that I had to deal with being a family freak, being the cause of Adam's demise was not on my menu.

"Keira." I heard the warning in Tucker's tone. He knew I was acting like a child. Yeah, well, I was. So there.

"Yeah, okay, fine, sure. You were saying?" I met Niko's gaze and crossed my arms, going into defense posture mode. I stopped short of stomping my foot.

Niko shrugged. "I didn't like what Adam was doing and I blamed you. I apologize."

"Okay . . ." I wasn't sure what he was trying to say.

"Look, to help Adam, I think we all need to work together. I'm willing to bury the hatchet, as it were." He didn't hold out a hand to shake, casual touch wasn't part of the vampire etiquette. It wasn't with us either. He stood still, his hands clasped behind him, a semi-formal pose.

I studied his expression, trying to figure out if he was sincere. I couldn't tell much. No guile, no twitchiness . . . but how well can a vampire hide his true feelings? Probably extremely well, considering his age. If Dudley's wife wasn't yet dead when Niko was turned, that would put him around the four and a half century mark. People learned a lot over time, vampires or not.

"All right. I'll deal with this," I said, letting my arms relax a little, loosening my posture. I could cut Niko a break. Being obnoxious wouldn't help Adam. "What next?"

"What?" Niko looked startled.

"I get it, you're right. What do we do next?" I smiled a little, showing that I could as easily extend the hand of friendship. I didn't think he expected me to agree so easily. No doubt my dear brother had talked about my stubborn streak.

"Well, that's it . . . I . . ." Niko looked at Tucker, then back at me. "Thing is, I'm not sure."

"Not sure?" My voice started to rise again. "Then what the f—"

"Keira, enough. We need to combine forces and figure out what we need to do." Twelve hundred years or so of sanity and practicality spoke up. That is, my brother, the semi-sane one, actually decided to say something more or less logical, practical and to the point. Well, okay, semi-sane and not exactly twelve hundred years. The first couple of hundred he spent more in the "kill, kill, blood makes the grass grow" mode—all that Viking berserker type stuff. He got over it. Mostly.

"Niko, how long will Adam stay stable?" Niko looked at Tucker with something like surprise in his face. I think my own expression was damned close. "That is, assuming he is stable," Tucker amended. "He is, isn't he?"

Niko looked at each of us, his brow furrowed as if not knowing what to say or how to take this.

"Yes." He spoke deliberately. "As stable as he'll get."

"And that means?" I asked.

"Adam will likely remain like that for a while," Niko explained. "In the coma, he can't deteriorate."

"But he can't heal, either, can he?"

Niko shook his head, his hair masking his expression. "No," he whispered. "He can't heal."

"Can we leave him there long enough to wait for Isabel?" Tucker asked.

"I think . . . I hope so." Niko looked at us again, his eyes glittering. I couldn't tell if those were tears lurking. "I know about this academically," he said. "We've spoken about it. We learn that we can do this if gravely injured . . . put ourselves into a kind of stasis."

"Gravely injured?" Okay, so I was curious.

"We fought in many of your wars, too, Keira."

"Not *ours*, actually." My brother smiled a little at his own comment. "But I get the picture."

So did I. Like my own family, the vampires sometimes became a part of the human world—a necessary evil.

"And what happens then? How long can he stay there and what can we do to get him out?"

"That's the problem," Niko said. "Normally, we heal the injured by moving them to a safe place and then giving them living blood . . . usually from a donor."

"How much blood?"

Niko turned abruptly and walked away from our immediate vicinity. He seemed a little too interested in the window and not in answering my question. He didn't have to answer, because I already knew what he was going to say. His silence confirmed it. By the same token, I didn't really have to repeat my question, but I did. I wanted the words. I wanted to know exactly what we were up against.

"How much, Niko?"

He turned then, the threatened tears becoming reality, leaving tracks across his pale skin. "All of it."

All right. Not an option. I couldn't be killed by normal means, but I was pretty damned sure that draining all my blood might do it. I wasn't ready to volunteer any other sacrificial lambs, either. I'm sure we could find someone to volunteer. Suicidal idiots and fang hags notwithstanding, I wasn't prepared to go that far.

"I take it this can't be animal blood?" My brother was suddenly behind me, his large hand resting on my shoulder.

"I don't know, but I don't think so," Niko said. "I heard about this once, nearly a century ago, when we were hiding out. Before Europe erupted into war . . . the first big one. We'd all managed to escape becoming involved in the various quests for power—the Seven Years War, Napoleon— but Adam correctly reasoned we couldn't escape this one. We considered many options, including the Americas, but Adam knew of a place he thought would remain obscure and safe. A friend of his owned a large estate near Iaşi, in Romania. The gypsies and peasants took it all in stride. They were used to the tales of the Mountain Lords and a few more of us wouldn't upset the status quo too much. In any case, Adam thought we should all know what to do in case the war reached us there and we were hurt."

"So you'd be sacrificing peasants?"

Niko shrugged. "I don't know what his plan was. We never had to do it. Of course, Romania did enter the war—disastrously—and we faced grim times indeed. Fortunately, we were in a fairly isolated region far enough east to escape occupation. Adam had made sure to explain how much a measure of absolute last resort it truly was. He made us swear we'd never go down that path unless there was no other choice—and only if it meant we'd save the others by doing so."

I sagged back into the chair, my muscles suddenly unable to support my weight. This wasn't a story of what had been and what could happen. This was now. Last resort. This meant that Adam really thought he was dying . . . the real thing.

"Fuck." The word barely had any sound as it left my mouth.

Tucker crouched down next to me and patted my knee. He looked over at Niko, who was staring out the window again.

"You don't hold out much hope, do you?" Tucker's voice was barely louder than mine.

Niko came over to us, his movements slow and painful. The normally energetic vampire was walking like a human man of ninety. I couldn't look at him. As he reached us, he crouched down next to Tucker and took Tucker's free hand between his own, the slender pale digits a marked contrast to my brother's sturdy ones. The two of them were so different and yet so alike. The tall, slender, nearly ethereally pale redhead seemed no match for the taller, more muscular darker-skinned Viking whose own hair had been compared to a fierce flame. At heart, they were both predator, both comfortable in their nature, their being. Adam, for all his lordly elegance, tried to avoid what came naturally. As for me, there was no telling.

"I'm his second," Niko said, "Effectively, Adam's heir. I have no interest in running the tribe. I don't want him to die. I'm afraid I don't hold out much hope right now. The one way I know for sure to bring him back is the one way he'd never allow."

"Is he going to get any worse?" I had to know.

"I doubt it," he said. "At least, I don't think so. I know this can be done for several days without any damage. After that, I don't know. All I know is folktale and legend."

"Damage?" I didn't understand.

"Revenant." Tucker was about as blunt as he could get. Evidently, he was quicker on the uptake here than I was.

"Isn't there anyone who can help? Some sort of vampire council or healers?"

Niko looked down at the floor again, a habit that I knew too well. It was my own method of not wanting to answer. "We have no council, no ruling body. Each tribe is separate, self-sufficient. There is no one who can know. If we ask for help, if we let it be known he's out of commission . . ." He let the words trail off.

I didn't really need for him to draw me the whole picture. I was slower than Tucker, but I was finally getting with the program. If the other vampire tribes knew of this weakness, they could attempt a hostile takeover . . . and in the vampire world, I was guessing that this wasn't done with mergers, acquisitions and three-piece suits.

"So we wait?" I wasn't happy with the answer that kept cropping up but, really, what choice did we have? What was I going to do? Find some poor illegal alien and feed him to the comatose vampire? Even if I'd been that cruel, I knew any chance of Adam sticking around after that would be nil.

A thought occurred to me—Ignacio's missing brother. No, it couldn't be that, no way. Adam kept strict control over his vampires, especially now, after what happened last October. There was a greater chance of Texans electing another woman Democrat for governor than for one of Adam's group to be taking human lives. There was another possibility, though.

"Niko, is there any way outside vampires could be in the area? Not specifically at the Wild Moon, I mean in Rio Seco County."

"I'm sorry?" I could see the puzzlement in his face. He wasn't following my non–non sequitur.

"Alex Robles." My brother, on the other hand, had plenty of practice with my thought paths.

"Exactly," I said. "What if—"

"Hold that thought," Niko stood from his crouch. "I see what you're getting at but, believe me, even if Adam might not know, I'd know . . . and if I know, Adam knows. We keep a tight perimeter here. If there were any others in the area, we'd know."

"You're sure."

"Positive." The normal confident, if not cocky, expression was once again in place. I'd given Niko something to think about other than Adam.

"Okay, then," I said as I stood. "Then that's a place to start."

"Start what?"

"Looking for answers."

I didn't know exactly what we were offering or where

we were going or even what the hell we were going to do, but I couldn't sit around and bemoan the fact of Adam's coma. No matter how much I wanted to change it, right now, there was nothing I could do to alter the fact. Short of finding some voluntary sacrifice—and I was *so* not going there—we'd have to leave things as they were for now and hope that Isabel would get one of the many messages I had left and planned to leave.

In the meantime, the three of us could get off our respective asses and get to work. Niko had a ranch to run and vampires to interrogate and maybe figure out a way to get Adam out of this predicament. My brother and I would continue doing what we were doing: looking for Alex Robles or some knowledge of what happened to him after Jolene dropped him off. We'd take the daytime, Niko, the nights. Something was bound to turn up. Something had to.

CHAPTER TWENTY-FOUR

I WENT TO STAND by the stairway leading downstairs to the master bedroom. Everything inside
me screamed to go down there, to do the inevitable
and open a vein. I was fairly sure I could get him to
stop . . . maybe. At least it was something, some sort of
action, not this hand-waving and angst-ridden discussion we'd been having.

"Keira . . ." Tucker warned.

"I'm not going down there," I said, staying right where
I was. "But . . ."

"I know. But I can't risk you."

"I know."

Behind me, Tucker and Niko whispered together. I stole
a quick look at them, sitting close, sides touching, heads bent
together. Tucker had both of Niko's hands in his. I couldn't
help but envy them their closeness. Tucker raised a hand
and stroked Niko's cheek, his thumb wiping away a tear. I
turned away, my own tears threatening to fall unchecked.

This was not how this was supposed to go. When I'd
taken up with Adam, such a damned short time ago, I'd
been so free, so happy. In England, we'd been flirting, not
even friends, really, just occasional acquaintances who'd
see each other at various evening events. We'd never even
gone out together. And then he'd had the audacity to fall in
love with me, come to Texas to woo me and win me and I
was won. Big time. And now, this.

Finally, someone like me, who wasn't all about dark magick, who wasn't human and who wanted me for myself and not for what I could do for him . . . or her. So many of my previous liaisons with cousins had been about games—and not the fun kind. I hated games. I guess I'd been a little stupid not to realize that games could be played outside the clan. Why on earth had he decided taking blood would offend me? I closed my eyes, letting my shields down a little, reaching for Adam again. I couldn't help it. I wanted to reassure myself that in the time we'd been upstairs, he hadn't actually expired. I reached, my awareness sliding down into the bedroom, over to Adam. The same deathly stillness floated at the center of the room, a negative place in the overall energy of the— Wait. What was that? I concentrated harder. In the back of the room, a shimmer, like seeing something out of the corner of your eye. I lessened my shields even more, and there it was again. I reached for it, it wavered and was gone with a pop.

With a rush, I came back to myself. I whirled away from the stairs and promptly sank to my knees.

"Keira!" Tucker and Niko helped me up. "You okay?" My brother put an arm around my waist and walked me over to the couch.

"Wow, yeah, okay, but . . ." I turned to Niko, who was hovering over me, concerned. "Was Adam ever at that old graveyard at the edge of the property?"

"Graveyard?" Niko seemed puzzled.

"The place I told you about earlier, when I first got back tonight," Tucker said.

"Oh yes, that's right. Why?"

"Has Adam been there?" I repeated.

"I told Tucker I saw it when we first bought the land a

couple of years ago. I could tell it wasn't active, so I haven't been back to that area in a while. As far as I know, Adam would have no cause to go out there."

"What is it, Keira?" Tucker asked.

"I tried to feel Adam again," I began.

Tucker warned, "Keira . . ."

I waved a hand. "I know, dumb, but I needed to make sure he hadn't . . . Anyhow, I felt something down there. Like a shimmer. When I reached for it, it vanished with a pop, exactly like in the cemetery earlier." I looked at Niko, who'd sat in one of the armchairs. "Tucker and I think this might be a ward or perhaps some sort of energy field left by one of our clan when we were here. Whatever it is, I think we should check it out."

"First, sister mine, before we go haring off again and get whammied by that energy field, I think we should try Isabel again and, if we don't get her, then call Dad."

"Okay, you've got a point."

"Of course." Tucker smiled. "Look, Niko and I will go downstairs and check on Adam, make sure he's comfortable. You call. We'll be back in a minute."

I took the hint. He probably wanted a little private time with Niko. Fine, I could deal with that. After all, Adam's coma affected more people than me.

Isabel's voice mail picked up after four rings. Once again, I left a message, providing enough cryptic information I hoped she'd figure out this was urgent. As soon as I hung up, I dialed Dad.

"Keira, sweetheart, so good to hear from you, despite the time." His quiet baritone made me smile despite myself.

"Hi, Dad, ditto," I said. "And sorry about the late hour." Unlike me, my dad kept fairly normal daylight hours. "I'd love to chat, but we're in a bit of a pickle here and need some information."

"Shoot."

I gave him the quick rundown, from what happened earlier, Adam's coma and the energy downstairs. "Do you know if anyone left a warding behind or if we set one on purpose?"

"Hmm, doesn't ring a bell," he said. I could picture him stroking his chin as he thought. My father, bless him, could have easily passed as an absentminded professor, sans the requisite horn-rimmed glasses. I adored him, but his attention to magick and the doings of the clan often seemed to take secondary place to his interest in science and nature. "I remember going up that far a few times during hunting, but that was when we first came to Rio Seco. 'Bout a hundred years or so ago? Place was still in use then, so I had to be careful. Avoided it pretty much ever since."

I sighed in disappointment. If my dad avoided it, it was likely others did, too. Gigi may be the titular head and our matriarch, but in matters of the mundane and day-to-day, my dad ruled the Kelly roost—at least our branch of the family. Gigi's business rarely extended to such small things.

"Hang on a second, sweetheart, your brother's here. He may know." Dad dropped the phone onto a table. (I could hear the *thunk*.) A moment later, someone picked it up.

"Hey, gorgeous, what's up?"

"Rhys," I said. "Hey there. Did Dad tell you why I called?"

"He did and, yeah, I remember that place. Ianto and I used to run around there all the time, in between burials—especially after it got abandoned. Lots of deer up roaming around there. Gigi found out about it and put a stop to it. I can't remember exactly when, but I think you'd just come to live with us. Then, a few months later, she said we could keep hunting there if we'd erect the statue."

"I'm sorry, what?"

"The angel statue. Gigi ordered it carved and Ianto and I had to go put it up."

"Whatever for?"

"Hell if I know. I imagine she wanted to keep people from going there and getting into the cave. I know you used to clean graves there as a kid, didn't you ever wonder why the angel had no name carved into the base?"

"I did," I admitted. "I never actually asked about it. So there's a cave?"

"Yeah, behind the angel. I don't really know why she wanted the entrance hidden, but you know Gigi."

Yeah, I knew Gigi. And I was pretty damned sure she didn't have the twins put up a statue for the hell of it, not even to hide a cave entrance. Gigi wouldn't have been worried about attractive nuisances or other liability issues, especially on land she didn't own.

"Did *you* ward it?" I asked my brother.

"Me? No. I'm not good with that kind of thing. I don't remember if anyone else did. We put the statue in place, helped plant some trees and that was it on our end."

"Rhys, look, this is really important," I said. "I don't want to go into all the details right now, but who around there would know? Who can you ask?"

"Sorry, Keira, but no one else is around," he said.

"What do you mean?"

"They've all gone to Vancouver with Gigi for a big holiday prep meeting with some of our B.C. cousins. Gigi says this Beltaine will be extra special so she wants to do it up in a big way. Honestly, when Dad said you were on the phone, I thought that's why you were calling, to make arrangements for you and Tucker to come home, since it's less than two months out."

"Sorry, hon," I said. "I'd really forgotten how close it was." And I had absolutely no intention of celebrating it with clan, whatever the reason my double-great-granny thought it was so special. "How come you're not in Vancouver, then?"

"Dad and I stayed here because we're meeting with one of the area game wardens in the morning. He's one of our cousins and we need to arrange hunting privileges for visitors during the feast. You know how long all this negotiating takes. Look, I need to run, but I promise I'll ask around about the wards. I'll call you on your cell if I find out anything, 'kay?"

"Thank, Rhys."

"Okay, simple," I said after Tucker and Niko came back upstairs and I'd filled them in. "We go to the cemetery. Niko, you can have Lance and a couple of the others sit with Adam."

Niko grimaced and crossed his arms. "Can't," he mutters.

"I'm sorry—what? Why the bloody hell won't you?"

"I'm sorry right back," he said. "But it's not *won't*, it's *can't*. It's a cemetery, right? Even though it's not active, it's still used as one? We can't cross onto the grounds."

"Holy ground," Tucker answered. "I get it."

I shook my head. "I don't. Niko, you told me last year that the whole 'holy object' thing with vampires isn't true. That you're as religious as you were when you were human."

"We are," Niko said. "It's not that it's holy, it's consecrated. Cemeteries are specifically consecrated against us. It's not a religion thing so much as part of ritual. It's hard to explain, but most orders of service to consecrate a burial ground contain language that effectively keeps us out. Statements like 'set apart from all profane use'— we'd be the profane."

"That doesn't make sense. Why that and not a blessed cross or a church?"

Niko shrugged. "How would I know? I mean, why do we walk and talk and have sex and live our lives, but we're actually not alive? I'm not a scientist. I simply know that I can't enter consecrated grounds."

"Well, damn it," I said. "This is going to put a crimp in my plans."

"I have an idea," Tucker broke in. "Niko, directly behind and above *La Angel* is an outcropping, kind of an overhang. The entire place kind of sits in this little bowl of land. Would the consecration extend to the land surrounding it, or to the cemetery proper?"

Niko looked thoughtful. "Usually, it's the cemetery land itself. As with any spell or ward, there must be a boundary."

"There's a small iron fence surrounding the graves," Tucker said. "I bet that was the boundary. I bet if you go up onto the overhang, you can get close."

"Did you say 'spell or ward' in regards to the consecration?" I asked. "Could that have been it? A ward cast by those consecrating the cemetery that affected Tucker, me and somehow, Adam, since he owned the surrounding land? Could it be that easy?" It was an exhilarating thought. If Adam was affected by that, by Tucker and me blundering across the ward and triggering it, then he wasn't actually in a self-induced coma after all, and fixing it was a matter of removing the ward. And that, once I got family involved, was a piece of cake.

Tucker burst my shiny bubble. "I doubt it. We didn't encounter anything until we were actually at the Angel and I tried magick. Don't forget, you went in and out of there plenty as a kid, per Gigi's direction. Even if she had warded it, it's unlikely the wards would affect Kellys . . . and in turn, Adam."

I sagged back into the couch cushions. "No, you're right. That was too easy. Damn."

Niko spoke up. "There's no way those kids could have placed some sort of spell, could they? After all, Tucker told me they were there the other night, before you all went there."

Both Tucker and I shook our heads. "No," I said. "Humans can't do that kind of magick. They may 'cast spells,' but really, it's more like praying, or wishing real hard."

"But they may have woken something up," pressed Niko. "Something or someone."

"That," Tucker said, "is why we need to go back there. Niko, you with us?"

"I am."

CHAPTER TWENTY-FIVE

"I T'S AS I THOUGHT," Niko said, staring at the cemetery entrance. "I can feel the barrier from here. I won't be able to get in."

Tucker nodded as he pulled out a camping lantern, a flashlight and a tire iron from the back of the Rover. "The overhang is straight back, over to the right a little. If you walk around that clump of oaks over there and climb up, you should get there fairly quickly."

"Got it," Niko said, and disappeared into the darkness.

"I'm trying to decide whether or not I should go ahead and shift now and save myself the trouble," Tucker joked as we walked through the graveyard.

I poked his side with the tire iron. We'd brought it to see if we could remove some of the debris accumulated in the deadfall. The space behind the statue to the limestone wall would be tight, even if we did clear it away, as the two guardian trees had grown quite large over the years. A crowbar and some more muscle would have been better, but I didn't have the former and the latter were all unable to get to the statue. I wasn't about to involve any humans at this point.

"Maybe make sure to keep aware this time," I said. "If we're lucky, the reason you triggered it was like you said, the magick. Let's keep all our magick hands in our pockets and tackle this the mundane way."

"Aye, aye, captain."

WE STOOD TOGETHER at the right side of the Angel, con-
templating the tangle of debris, weeds and mesquite, the
light from the lantern casting strange shadows. "That's
going to hurt," I said. "I should've brought gloves or something. At least there's no sign of the energy."

"You think the other side's any better?" Tucker asked.
"I'll go check." He grabbed the flashlight from me, sprinted
around the statue and came right back. "Nope, even more
of a mess. Let's go for it, then."

Tucker handed me the flashlight. "You hang on to the
light, in case I shift. I'll stand back a little."

I held my breath and began to reach for the deadfall.
The night seemed to grow quieter then, still—as if everything around us waited, too.

"I'm here." I jumped back as Niko spoke. Looking up,
I could see a flash of his hair over the edge. I pointed the
light upward. Niko peeked over the side. It looked like he
was lying on the ground, his head craned over the edge.

"It's a little crumbly up here," he said. "There's a tree
root that's grown through the stone."

"Be careful," Tucker said.

"Find anything?"

"Nothing yet, we haven't started."

"Good luck with that."

I nodded my thanks. I took another deep breath, and
reached out again, my finger barely grazing a branch at the
top of the heap. We waited a moment. Nothing. I stepped
closer, tucked the flashlight under my arm and grabbed
onto the branch. Still nothing.

Tucker stepped forward. "Let's get to it, then." He
grabbed onto the other side of the branch.

A flash. A hum. My entire body shook with power unleashed and power restrained. I froze, gripping the wood, feeling as if I'd taken hold of a live electrical wire. Light and heat assaulted my senses. Next to me, through a buzzing like a thousand bees, my brother screamed, the raw sound morphing to a wolf's howl.

I dropped to the ground, spent, one hand grabbing for the ruff on the wolf's neck as my muscles turned to jelly.

"What in all the unholy hells was that?" I demanded, trying to stand and not thump back down on my ass in the dirt, barely managing to keep my balance as my wobbly knees began to return to normal.

"Tucker! Keira!" Niko called down to us. I found the flashlight on the ground and pointed it upward.

"We're okay," I said. "I think. Did you feel that?"

"Something," Niko said. "Felt a little like electricity, but mild, like a static shock."

"It was more than that down here. Tucker's shifted again."

"I gathered that from the howl," Niko said drily. "Is he all right?"

"Looks to be a little shaken," I said after giving my brother the once-over. He crouched next to me, trembling a little. The remains of his jeans and tee hung from his fur. He hadn't had a chance to strip this time. Good thing I carried a spare set of clothing in the car for him. "Niko, can you see down behind the statue?"

Niko shook his head. "It's too dark and the overhang is too fragile for me to try to move any further forward. Can you shine the light over the deadfall?"

"Not without touching it, and I'm not sure I want to do that again."

Tucker's snout nuzzled my knee as he looked up at me, sad puppy eyes accompanying a low whine. I didn't have to understand wolf language to know what he meant. I don't like it any more than you do. I petted his head absently. "Something's back there, Niko," I said.

"Keira, maybe you should both go back to the car. We'll go home and figure this out."

He had a point. But we were here and going back to the ranch wasn't going to accomplish anything.

Tucker nudged me again, wiggling his whole body, an antsy dance signifying his impatience. I didn't comprehend. Perhaps if I became a shapeshifter like he was, I'd be able to understand him when he was in wolf form, but for now I wasn't getting it.

"What?" My impatience showed in my tone of voice. The words came out a lot sharper than I'd intended. "Sorry, didn't mean to be so blunt," I said. "I'm—"

My brother gave a low growl, more annoyance than warning. "All right, already," I said, capitulating. "Show me what you want."

"Keira, what's going on?"

"I don't know, Niko. Tucker seems to have a notion about something. I don't speak wolf so I'm having a little trouble figuring it out. If he'd shift back and *tell* me—"

A low growl morphed into a whine. I stared at my brother. He crouched, belly to the ground, head raised as if reaching for something. Tucker's head ducked down, moving from side to side as a shudder ripped through his body. He raised his head and bowed it again, another ripple under his skin as his muscles strained against . . . what?

"Tucker?" I ventured.

My brother yipped once and then stood from his prone position, remaining silent, his gaze catching my own.

"What the . . ." My voice trailed off as I realized. He *couldn't* shift back. Tucker's shaggy head dipped and rose again, straining and pushing as if against an invisible net. Another shudder and whine as he failed once more to change shape. I stepped closer, hand out to touch, to comfort. He nosed my palm once, in acknowledgment. Rising from his crouch, he shook himself, caught my gaze once more and turned back to the deadfall as if to attack it.

"Damn it, Tucker," I said as I grabbed his fur and tried to pull him back. "This is not a good idea. If something there is keeping you from shifting back, we shouldn't go looking for it. And if you think I'm going to let you touch that damned barrier again, you're insane. Niko, I think you're right. We're leaving. Tucker can't shift back. Meet us at the car."

"On my way," Niko said.

Tucker's head turned, jaws snapping in warning, not at all close enough to actually bite. I jumped back. "For fuck's sake, stop that!" I smacked him across the hindquarters. "Are you crazy? I'm trying to—"

Tucker barked loudly and shot me a glance that had to mean "Shut up and help" and lunged at the deadfall. I made a grab for him, but he slipped by me and, with the force of a full-grown wolf, scrabbled at the debris, paws and jaw tearing at it.

Nothing happened. No energy attack, just the dust and dirt flying as Tucker began to demolish the barrier. "Niko," I called loudly. "Come back!"

I turned my attention to the wolf. "Okay, fine. That's the way you want to play this, Tucker? I can humor you . . . at least for now. But understand this, brother mine, any—and I mean *any*—sign that whatever is back there is more than we can handle, we stop and return tomorrow night with some reinforcement."

I stood still a moment, closing my eyes. The scrabbling

sounds stopped and a cold nose nudged my hand. "Shush, wait," I said. "I need to try something." Tucker whined a little and pushed his head under my hand. "It's fine." I reassured him. "I need . . ."

With a deep breath, I focused inward, concentrating. My normal mental shields still held, still the same. I couldn't feel any lessening. Concentrate, Keira, I thought. A brush of fur against my palm felt soft, gritty with dust. I imagined expanding my awareness outward a little, reinforcing my invisible walls. I saw them in my mind's eye, a latticework of solid light weaving stronger, closer together. Turning my attention outside myself, I felt around for any signs of *Other*, of the energy we'd experienced. Nothing. It was as if it had never existed. Yet, Tucker couldn't change back.

I opened my eyes and regarded my brother. He sat patiently next to me, gaze catching mine. "I don't know," I said. "I tried to see if whatever it was affected me other than knocking me on my ass, but I seem to be fine. I couldn't sense anything either. I'm not very good at this, you know." He rubbed his head against my thigh. "Sorry, Tucker, I tried. Something caused this, but as far as I can tell, whatever it was, it's gone."

I ruffled his fur. "You still want to check this out?" I motioned to the deadfall. Tucker nodded and trotted back over to it.

In a few minutes, he'd managed to clear away nearly half of the debris. His fur was matted and filthy, covered in dirt, dead leaves and small branches. Dust hung in the air, a result of his efforts. He grinned at me, or at least as much of a grin as a wolf could manage and went back to pulling at the deadfall. I joined him, wedging the tire iron into the tangle and using my strength with his.

"Are you two crazy?" Niko's voice floated down.

"Probably," I said, digging at a particularly stubborn tangle of mesquite and torn-up rope. "Tucker's bound and determined to get back here and nothing happened when we touched it again, so hey, here we are."

"Damnation," Niko muttered. "And I thought vampires were stubborn."

"I can hear you." I laughed.

"Well, I wasn't trying to keep quiet," Niko retorted. "Why don't I lie here for a bit. Seeing as how neither of you are exhibiting common sense."

I shrugged and went on prying at the tangle.

It took both of us the better part of an hour and the sacrifice of too much of my own skin, but we finally broke through. I set the tire iron down, uncapped one of the water bottles, took a swig, then wet my shirttail and used it to wipe my face a little. I was as filthy as my brother. I found a shallow depression in the angel's stone base and poured some water into it for Tucker to lap down. I upended the rest of the bottle over his head. He rewarded me by shaking off the water, much as any dog would after bathing.

"Bloody hell, Tucker," I gasped. "What was that for?" He rubbed his body against my leg in apology. I opened a second bottle, refilled his temporary doggy bowl, then chugged down what was left. As he finished drinking, I picked up the tire iron. "Okay, brother mine, let's go. Niko, we're going in."

I shimmied through the hole we'd cleared, my brother at my back.

CHAPTER TWENTY-SIX

THE MOMENT I stepped through to the other side of the deadfall, I knew why we'd come. Tucker had been right. Something was definitely "off." A chill silence weighted the air, the dusty heat of the Texas night vanished as if we'd gone through the back of a wardrobe into the winter of Narnia. I shivered as my skin buzzed and tingled, my jaw tensed against the low-level energy permeating the place. The energy buzz felt more like something I was used to, more like someone set up a protection, less like an attack. I relaxed a little, and looked around.

There wasn't much to see, the same twisted mass of dead wood and rotting branches behind us, the back of *La Angel* to our left. Across this tiny clearing, not ten feet away, more deadfall, as if Nature herself had grown to protect? Keep out? Keep in? Something.

A hunk of limestone lay shattered on the ground, obviously sheared from the cliff face. I looked up to see where it had come from. Like Niko said, the gnarled root of a live oak dug down into the wall, reaching for the water that wasn't there, its growth splitting the stone. Directly under the trailing end of the root . . . an opening. Nothing to write home about, not even as large as the shallow cave opening we'd seen earlier during the search. Except this one wasn't a shallow hollow. My brother Rhys had been right. This was definitely the entrance to a cave.

Instinctively, I grabbed for Tucker's ruff with my right hand, shifting the tire iron to my left and tucking the flashlight under my arm. Harder to see that way, but I felt better holding onto my brother.

A piece of cloth was caught on the shattered rock, faded denim from a work shirt, not jeans, too thin for that. I wasn't an expert, but I knew immediately that it hadn't been there long. The denim was faded, but still fresh, as if recently torn from its wearer's clothing.

"What do you think?" I asked. "Alex? The kids?" I shook my head as I watched the fabric flutter slightly as a gust of air hit it. "No, too faded, too worn for the kids. The twins wouldn't be wearing work shirts, nor would Brittany. Maybe Jimmy Stahl, but I doubt it. It's too hot. Didn't the notice say he'd been wearing a T-shirt?" I nodded to myself and to my brother who hadn't quit staring at the cloth. "No, not the kids."

I raised my voice. "Niko, we found the cave. There's a bit of cloth here, recent. It can't be more than a few months old."

"Alex Robles?" Niko asked.

"Maybe. If he came here, he might have been on the overhang, fallen down or something. He sure as hell didn't come through that deadfall. I think we need to go inside, see if he crawled in there."

"Be careful, Keira, Tucker. Remember I can't come help you if something happens."

"We'll take a quick look around, see if we see anything. We'll come straight back out." By *anything*, I meant remains. If Alex Robles had fallen from the overhang, survived and crawled into the mouth of the cave, it was likely he died there. That deadfall hadn't been disturbed in years.

Tucker and I stepped closer to the entrance, the low almost silent growl from my brother raising the hackles on my own neck. A sudden movement of air brushed my face, a tendril of my own hair, long since half-unbraided, tickled my cheek. I started, and tightened the grip on my brother's fur as we stepped inside. The cave entrance wasn't much wider than both of us if we stood side by side, perhaps five feet or so across at its narrowest, expanding to perhaps six or so about shoulder level. There were no remains. If Alex Robles had been here, he'd gotten out . . . or gone further in.

"Can you scent anything, Tucker? Could Alex have been here?"

My brother shook my hand free and crouched low to the rock-strewn dirt. As he sniffed around, I stood at the entrance, moving the flashlight around, examining the area. At first glance, the cave mouth wasn't any different from the thousands of other cave mouths throughout the Hill Country—not that I was any fan of caving, but one of my distant cousins used to photograph caves as a hobby. There were no signs of habitation—animal or human— just that lone scrap of cloth that had caught our eyes. The dirt floor was dirt, rocks and some debris, nothing indicating a human had been there.

The cave mouth itself wasn't very deep, perhaps eight or nine feet before the eight-foot ceiling sloped downward sharply and narrowed to a small dark passage, barely large enough for me to pass through. Not that I had any intention whatsoever of going any further or, for that matter, any closer. I'd joked about it before, but I was definitely extremely claustrophobic, especially in caves. Once, as a girl, we'd gone to Natural Bridge Caverns over near New Braunfels. I did okay for most of it, since the caverns were quite large. At one point during the guided tour, they'd turned out the lights. I stopped screaming half an hour after they'd brought me back outside. The idea of crawling into a dank hole in the ground with merely a flashlight and a wolf for company wasn't going to cut it.

"What the . . ." The breeze shifted again, smelling of cold and rain. The odor of stone reached me and my knees gave way . . .

"Hijo de la . . ." *His out-loud exclamation fades as he peers through the dark, trying to see down the narrow passage in front of him. His eyes itch, blurry with lack of sleep and the inevitable pre-crash jitters. He hopes the remnants of the high would last a little longer—at least until someone finds him. This wasn't how he'd planned to spend Sunday morning, especially after the night before. The party had been fun, but now, here he is, stuck in some cave on the ass end of someone's property; lost, cold and wet from the incessant rain. Going with that girl last night and letting the others go back to the ranch without him? Really, really brilliant. Thinking with his* cojones *instead of what was left of his brain, is what it was.* Estupido.

He blinks a few times, wishing he'd had the presence of mind to keep a bottle of Visine in his backpack. Over the past couple of years, he'd gotten good at dosing himself without even having to look in a mirror. Practice makes perfect. And it really did get the red out—at least most of the time. His eyes are raw, so dry he could almost hear the lids scraping over the eyeballs.

Pendejo, *he thinks. If he'd had enough sense to ignore that cute little* guera, *but he'd always been a sucker for busty blondes. Then she'd pulled out a small mirror and started to roll up a dollar bill. He'd had to stay after that.*

The crank had been nasty—brownish chunks that could barely be cut up with a razor blade. His nose is still torn up, even after half a bottle of nasal saline. But it had been worth it. The rush was great and the girl was better.

But today is fucking hell. This isn't what he'd bargained for those few years ago when he'd crossed the river to find work. Lucky for him—at least, so he'd thought—he'd found a job right away. He'd had to travel a ways north, nearly two hundred miles. Border crackdowns weren't helping any. Did help that he knew English, though. Priests were at least good for that and the foreman at the ranch seemed to like it.

He shakes his head again hoping his brain would. Wait—is that a light in front of him?

"Hello?" His voice disappears into the matte black. Nothing. He must be imagining things.

He sniffs, his nose beginning to run. Damn it. That shit had been way too harsh. Either that, or he'd have to cut back. He can't remember the last time he'd started a day without a little pick-me-up. Life as a ranch hand sucked, but there were compensations. It felt so damned good while he was doing it, but his body felt worse and worse when he crashed.

A big sniffle reminds him that he didn't even have a pack of tissues. A quick swipe with the back of his hand helps the runny nose. Shit. That wasn't snot. That was blood. He doesn't need a light to figure this out. He can smell it. Can sort of see it in the grey half-light of the cave mouth.

The wind picks up and drives the rain further into the cave. Damnation. He crawls a little deeper into the cave, around the first bend. It's darker here, but dry. Good thing it was here. For a minute there, after he'd fallen from the cliff, he thought it was all over. But the

*drop wasn't too bad and the rain made the ground muddy
enough that he only sprained his ankle a little. Still, how
fucking stupid.*

*He wipes his nose again, smears blood across his face.
Disgusting. It's not a full-fledged nosebleed yet, but it's
working its way there.*

*He blinks as the not-light seemed to flicker in the dis-
tance.*

"Hay alguien aquí?"

*The darkness seems to suddenly grow darker, all ambi-
ent light from the overcast day extinguished as if a sudden night had fallen. Immediately, the passage narrows,
its walls seemingly inches from his face. He reaches out,
needing to lean against the cave wall but can't feel anything in front of him. The coffin-sized space suddenly
becomes endless, a bottomless, wall-less expanse of pure
blackness, sucking away all light, all sound, all—*

What the hell is that?

Eyes. Those are eyes.

Bats? No, too big. They look like . . .

I gasped, suffocating in the dark pressure, my mind
whirling with flickering images. Rough matted fur scraped
against my face, my neck. I turn my head, needing oxygen,
needing . . . I coughed, grabbing onto my brother, fingers
grasping at fur. His side moved. Still alive. I tried to rise
up, to figure out what happened. Another breath and the
darkness slammed me again.

I CAME TO, groggy and with a headache the size of,
well . . . Texas, and wrapped in the utter darkness of the
cave mouth. Evidently, my flashlight was dead, missing or
broken. Damned visions. At least this was a useful one,
showing me Alex Robles had indeed been in this cave and

had seen something that spooked him. Being in this small dark space was enough to spook me.

Whatever had triggered the vision, this one was different from the others: fuzzier, less distinct. Could be he'd been here long enough ago that the essence, or whatever, had faded.

"Tucker?" I called out, feeling around the cave floor. Nothing. I got to a crawling position, trying to figure out the best way to deal with this. My brother (I hoped) was still in here with me, maybe unconscious, but here. Niko was still outside, but he couldn't come down to help. I couldn't see a damned thing, not even a lighter darkness so I could determine the direction of "outside."

"Niko?" I raised my voice. "You still out there?"

No answer.

How long had I been out? Was it dawn? Niko might have had to escape the sun or maybe it was still dark and he'd gone to get help . . . or maybe he couldn't hear me. It wasn't a great leap forward to assume that whatever wreaked havoc on me and Tucker could also block us in here and block all sound getting out . . . not to mention light. My kingdom for a freaking match or Zippo so I could find the flashlight. If I'd been smart, I'd have brought in the lantern with us. Smart was obviously not my middle name today.

I patted the floor around me. Dirt, loose rocks. Seemed like the same place I'd been in, so I hadn't been carted off by unknown cave magick. My head throbbed, as if a thousand tiny steel drum bands pounded out a calypso beat in my brain. Fucking hell. "Tucker, damn it, you better not be gone." Or be dead. I did not want to think that thought. No way.

Crawling forward bit by bit, I eventually came to a wall.

I'd probably traveled all of five feet. Hard to tell in near-sensory deprivation. If I concentrated, I could hear my own breathing and something that might be my brother. I sure as hell hoped it was him and not something else.

Keeping my right hand on the wall, I slowly rose to my feet. Was it smarter to try to walk the circumference and eventually find the outside opening or keep crawling? I had no freaking idea. Oh shit, maybe I'd hit my head harder than I thought. My cell phone was in my pocket. I fumbled for the phone and flipped it open. A green glow illuminated the cave area nearest me. At least it was something. No signal, though, so I couldn't call. Waving the phone around, I tried to locate Tucker.

There, a few feet away to the upper right of where I was. A foot. A human foot. Tucker had managed to shift back.

Using the phone, I made my way over. Thank goodness, there was the flashlight. I picked it up and flipped it on. Blessed, blessed light. I shut the phone and put it back in my jeans pocket.

"Tucker," I said, patting his arm, his shoulder. "C'mon, snap out of it." I shook him a little. "Tucker?"

A muffled groan turned into a mumbled curse. "What the hell?" My brother rubbed at his eyes. "Are we still in the goddamned cave?"

"Bingo." I sat back on my heels. "I tried calling for Niko, but got no answer. I don't know if he's gone for help or what."

"Here, give me a hand up."

I put the flashlight down, and reached for my brother, catching him under one arm and helping him to sit.

"Ouch," he complained. "Damned rocks."

I chuckled. "Yeah, well, being naked in a cave might be non-conducive to comfort, even for you, big bro. I can go out to the car and get you fresh clothes, but I vote we get off this damned island."

"I'm one hundred percent behind that." He got to his knees. "Except . . ."

"No, there is no except," I said. "We get up, go to my car and leave this horrible place. Then, when our dear great-great-grandmama gets back home from Vancouver, I will call her and ask her what the hell she meant by creating this fucking ward so that we keep getting zapped by it. I've had enough of this, Tucker. Honestly, I'd figured you would've, too, what with all the non-planned shapeshifting."

"We came here to see if we could find any evidence of Alex Robles," Tucker said, rising to his feet.

"Oh, no worries. Been there, done that," I replied. "While you were sleeping, I got another round of smell-induced visions. Alex was here, all right, cranked to the gills and wasted out of his mind. He fell from the overhang, sprained an ankle."

"You saw this."

"Yeah, full living color . . . more or less."

"Meaning?"

"This one wasn't as sharp as the previous ones. Not my standard Change-O-Vision near-HD quality." I thought about it a moment. "You know, it felt different somehow, more like watching a grainy several-generation deep VHS copy. Not as much of a full-fledged immersion vision as those I had before."

"Huh." Tucker scratched his head and looked around. "So where'd he go?"

Damn. Where had Alex gone? He obviously hadn't climbed out through the deadfall. The growth and debris there was way more than three months worth. I sincerely doubt he'd climbed up the overhang. It was possible, if you were a really good rock climber, but without gear and as much under the influence as he'd seemed in the vision, plus with a sprained ankle, I doubted he could have climbed over a pebble, much less up fifteen feet of limestone in the dark.

"Well, hell," I said. "I don't have any clue."

CHAPTER TWENTY-SEVEN

"**Y**OU THINK he went further into the cave?" Tucker grabbed the flashlight from me and shone it to the back, toward the tiny, tiny hole. Well, okay, not so tiny, but still, really small.

"I'm thinking he must have," I said. "Otherwise, his remains would be right here. Maybe he got stuck?"

"It's a possibility."

I took the flashlight back and shoved at my brother. "So, go check it out."

"You want me to go down there?" Tucker asked. "Seriously? Have you looked at how narrow that hole is? Definitely not recommended for naked spelunking."

"Tucker, really. Don't go inside, go to the edge, stick your head in," I said. "See if you can smell anything. After this long, it's likely to be bones and such, but you could probably tell."

Tucker shrugged. "That's a fact." He ambled over to the entrance, placed both hands on either side and leaned in . . . or tried to.

"Uhm, Keira," he said.

"What is it?"

"I can't get in there."

"I'm sorry, what?" I moved closer, pointing the flashlight in the direction of the cave entrance. "What do you mean you can't get in? Stick your head closer."

"I can't." Tucker stepped back. "It's like there's a barrier."

"Hang on, let me look." I peered past my brother, but didn't try to cross the threshold. "I don't see anything."

"I didn't say I could *see* it." He sounded cranky.

"Okay, okay, keep your britches . . . never mind, you aren't wearing any." I stepped to the edge of the opening and shone the light down. The floor sloped downward at a steep angle once past the narrow doorway. From this angle, it was hard to tell how high the interior ceiling was, maybe six or seven feet. Not utterly claustrophobia-inducing, but damned close. I turned away, intending to pick up a rock and throw it. A shimmer caught my eye.

"What was that?" I whirled back to face the entrance, pointing the flashlight.

"What was what?" Tucker asked.

"That shimmer. Didn't you see it?"

"Nope. Doesn't seem to be there now."

"No, it doesn't." I bent down, keeping my eye on the opening, and picked up a small stone, a couple of inches wide. I tossed it and it skipped merrily down the tunnel, disappearing around a small bend about ten feet down.

"Huh." Tucker frowned. "I swear, I could not put my head past that entrance. You want to try?"

"Not really," I said. "But if we want to find out if Alex Robles came down here, I'll go as far as stepping inside. How's that? Maybe Gigi warded this against you in particular—or maybe, against Kelly shapeshifters in general, seeing as how Rhys said he and Ianto used to come hunt out here. Those two are as bad as ten-year-olds, poking their noses in places they shouldn't. It could be dangerous down there and Gigi wanted them to stay out."

Tucker laughed. "That, sister mine, is a distinct possibility."

"Okay," I said. "I'm going in and taking the flashlight with me. I'll step in a couple of steps or so and, if all's well, I might go as far as that bend, to see if by chance I see Alex's remains."

"I'll wait right here."

I reached a tentative hand toward the opening. No resistance, no barrier. Flashing a nervous smile at Tucker, I braced myself and took a step through. A *flashbangflash* of light and it went dark.

"YOU CAME. You heard me calling you." The mellifluous voice chimed in my ear. I rubbed my eyes.

"Damn it," I said. "Did I black out again?" I blinked against the bright white light. Where the hell was I? Inside a cave, it seemed. Rock walls glistened with pyrite and other shiny bits. Above me, stalactites hung way above my head, not close enough to be menacing. Where was all the light coming from, though?

A melodic chuckle made me turn my head. To my right stood a tall, slender figure, dressed in shimmering white robes. Silver-gray hair fell from a high forehead, over its gown, past the knees. Androgynous to a fault, its steel-gray eyes looked at me as it asked, "Are you hurt?" The voice was soft, musical even, but I could feel the sharp edge behind it, as if listening too closely could cut you.

"Tell me I'm dreaming or having another vision." I put my arm over my eyes and started to count to ten.

"No vision, Keira Kelly," it said. "You are indeed here."

I sat up, then stood. Well then. Not so imposing after all. We were nearly of a height, it was a few inches taller.

"You know my name?" I crossed my arms. "Who the

hell are you and why did you bring me here? Wherever here is." I opened my stance a little, squaring off, giving it a bit of Kelly attitude.

"This is our place, our home. You are kin. I called and you came." It looked at me with a neutral expression on the pale smooth face. Even with my enhanced senses I felt nothing, could sense nothing. No, not a vision, definitely.

"Your place, my ass. This land belongs to Adam Walker." Not exactly, but I wasn't about to split hairs. What I knew of the Sidhe other than my not-so-pleasant child-hood memories could fit inside a very small thimble, but one thing I did know: Land ownership conveyed a hell of a lot more than it did for human land contracts and I wasn't about to concede ownership.

It nodded. "So it is the Walker who now inhabits the surface. He is one of the blood-drinkers."

"He is. And you?" I didn't relax, staring into eyes the exact same color as mine. I knew *what* it was, not who.

"Not a blood-drinker." The words were said with dis-taste, the speaker's mouth pursing as if to spit out the very thought.

"No shit," I said. "Sidhe don't drink blood, they take souls."

I squinted against the sudden flare of brightness. It was as I'd thought; the light came from it as well as from the glowing walls. Flashes of red-orange chased through the clear white shine. I guess I'd pissed it off. Good. I wasn't in the mood. Tucker was probably yelling on the outside of whatever the portal was that I'd crossed.

"Let's not play games," I said. "Who are you? What clan? Why did you bring me down here?"

"We did not bring you," it said. "You came. We called you."

"Excuse me?" I narrowed my eyes and crossed my arms over my chest. "Called me? How?" I looked around. "And unless you have a mouse in your pocket, who the hell is 'we'?"

"You are kin. We called. You came."

"Seriously, I have no—"

A whisper insinuated itself into my brain. "*Here . . . come . . . here . . .*"

"That was you? You're the one fucking with me."

"A crude statement but yes. It was I."

I wanted to wipe the smug smirk off its face. "You had no right. The energy barrier, the energy that hit us outside, that was you, too."

It nodded. "I apologize. I meant for you to come alone. Your brother's presence intensified the warding and it had an unfortunate side effect on both of you. Had you come alone, you would not have been affected."

"Oh, gee, glad to hear it. Now, why the hell did you want me to come here?"

From somewhere behind, a figure stepped forward, allowing me to see it . . . no, *him* . . . clearly. This was no Sidhe. I knew this face, who was—oh fuck. I knew him.

"Greg Pursell?" Dressed in robes similar to those worn by the Sidhe, the young man looked no different from the ten-year-old photo his stepmother had shown me earlier today. A young twenty, still nearly beardless. His eyes, however, told another story, holding sorrow and knowledge beyond human ken.

"Yes." He spoke in a soft tenor, voice not nearly as musical or other-worldly as the Sidhe, but not quite human.

"I saw a photo of you today, taken about ten years ago, right before you disappeared. You look exactly the same."

The Sidhe, who had yet to identify itself, began to

speak. Greg placed a hand on its arm. "Please, let me explain to her."

It nodded and stepped back.

"It was my dad," Greg said. "You say that picture was taken ten years ago?"

I nodded. "That's what Bitsy told me."

"Bitsy?" He looked puzzled.

"Your dad's wife," I explained. Oh, crap. If he didn't know of Bitsy, did that mean he didn't know about his parents' divorce and his mother's subsequent death?

"Ah. So. I suppose my parents split up then."

I nodded and took the coward's way out. No way was I about to tell him his mother was dead.

"Then, well, eleven years ago, I was diagnosed with leukemia."

"Not AIDS?" I broke in.

"What? No. Why did you think that?"

"That's what the rumor is," I said. "That you were gay, sick with AIDS and that you went off on a caving trip and then went missing. Some people say your dad kicked you out of the house for being gay."

Greg's laughed echoed throughout the chamber. "Gay, huh. Oh well. No, not gay, not that it really matters anymore. Not AIDS. I had a sense for fashion and I liked faeries . . . this kind." He motioned to the Sidhe. "I'm a bit of a nerd. Reading Tolkien, Charles de Lint, all sorts of fantasy tales. One night, after my diagnosis, I was sitting outside on the back porch at my dad's ranch, feeling sorry for myself and caught sight of a faery. At first, I thought I was hallucinating. Good pot." Greg smiled. "Except I wasn't. The faery came up to me and started a conversation. I was out there alone that night. It was late. I told him about how sick I was. He told me about his world."

"So you offered to come live down here?" Made sense if the leukemia was untreatable.

Greg shook his head. "No, I didn't know that was possible. I liked the company. All my other friends stopped calling me when I got sick. As if I could make them sick, too." He shrugged. "What can I say?"

"We're all pretty self-centered when we're twenty." Sometimes when we're a hell of a lot older, I thought as I looked at Greg's Sidhe companion. Did it—he—lure Greg here with the promise of eternal life, a sort of reverse-changeling?

"I did not lure him." The Sidhe approached me, hands out to his side. "I wished for a companion and I asked his father for him. He was not of age."

"You what?"

"I didn't ask for it," Greg answered. "Dad never told me about it until it was too late. One night, when Taffy here and I were talking, Dad came outside. I didn't know he'd heard us. I'd wanted to keep this a secret."

"Taffy?"

The Sidhe gave me an amused smile. "Daffyd," he said. "Greg had a problem with the Welsh pronunciation."

Greg continued as if we hadn't interrupted him. "What I didn't know, is that after I went into the hospital for the last treatment, Dad came back out to the ranch and talked to *Daffyd*." Greg emphasized the name, pronouncing it correctly.

"When I came home from the hospital, feeling way better than I had before, Dad told me that he'd arranged a fun visit. Pete, the foreman at the ranch and one of the other hands, a nice guy named Worry, were going to take me. I was excited, because I hadn't been anywhere in so long. Honestly, I don't remember much of the trip. I rode in the car with them, passed out and woke up here."

"Passed out—meaning drugged, I take it?"

Greg nodded. "Yeah, Pete had a couple of to-go mugs of Coke, gave me one."

"When did you figure out this was a one-way trip?"

"About ten minutes after I got here," Greg said. "Daffyd was waiting for me and explained what happened. I wanted to go back, but I realized going back meant dying. Staying here meant I could live."

"You say Worry Saunders was one of the guys? I remember him," I said. "He took off on his wife and kids a long time ago. When was that exactly?" I tried to think. I'd met him once or twice at Bea's café, then run by Bea's parents.

"I bet he disappeared about ten years ago," said Greg. "After Daffyd told me what was going on, I kind of got the picture. I'm guessing that Pete didn't want any witnesses."

I turned to address the Sidhe, who'd stood silent throughout this exchange. "And you, you did this out of the goodness of your heart?"

He looked at me, silvery-gray eyes glinting. "I am Daffyd ap Geraint. I came here for you. I stayed for you. I saved him because he was lonely, as was I. The rest of my people who made the journey with me faded quickly. There were four of us at first. I was the last, the youngest; I suppose the strongest. When the rock broke, I managed to find a way out, counter the wards and place my own. I found Greg."

"What do you mean, you came for me?" I was beginning to get a very bad feeling about this. Okay, so Greg Pursell didn't actually die, but came to live here. I suppose that it was a good tradeoff for dying of leukemia. Not exactly his choice, but he seemed okay with it.

"I am your cousin," Daffyd said. "My sire is Geraint ap Pwyll and your mother's kin. We came to watch over you. We found this place and came to live here. We have been trapped below for decades of your time."

I tried to wrap my head around all of this. "So you say you came to watch me. Why?"

"At the behest of your mother. It was not a simple thing to ask of us. The people here do not know us and do not leave offerings of food."

My mother. Wonderful, just bloody wonderful.

"Dad set it up," Greg said. "He made a bargain. Daffyd needed energy, Dad wanted me to live." Greg walked over to a rounded boulder that had been carved into the shape of a chair. There was another one next to it. "Come, sit."

I looked at Daffyd ap Geraint, who stood silent. Something in his expression made me think I really wasn't going to like this.

"Dad worked it out. Pete would have some waitress up at the Diamondback seduce one of the workers, usually someone who didn't have any family here, someone no one would miss. She'd party with him, pass out the drugs and when he was good and wasted, bring him over to the crossroads. Pete would make sure the guy got to the cave entrance safely, without falling down the overhang."

Daffyd spoke. "He is correct. The Judge, his father agreed to bring me one man every year. Sometimes, if they are young enough, I can survive with one every two years."

I shot up out of the rock chair and strode to Daffyd, confronting him. "You mean to tell me you, Judge Pursell and the others had a bargain so you could kill humans?"

The Sidhe's eyes grew colder and his brow lowered. "What are they to me? I am not human. You live with the drinkers of blood, yet you do not seem concerned with their way. You and I were never human. The vampires were once of the same species they now prey upon."

"I don't know where you get your information, buddy, but these vampires do not prey on humans. Nor are they killers."

"It is nothing to me." Daffyd motioned with a hand. "The matters of Above are not my matters. They are not my blood. If this practice displeases you, my apologies. You are kin and of my liege's blood. This bargain is no longer."

"You're stopping because I said so?"

"I would have reconsidered my bargain on your word, however, I no longer need tribute."

"Because . . . ?"

"Some two years or so ago, I began to feel a new energy Above. It appeared on occasion, would spike, then vanish for some time. It would then spike again for a short period. To my joy, I found I could tap this source and achieve nourishment—more nourishment than I could receive from the humans. This led me to believe the source was not human. Some months ago, the source reappeared and remained. I cannot identify, but it is not a Kelly. I cannot feed from Kelly. It is forbidden." Daffyd smiled and said, "It is glorious, this source." The smile transformed his face into something unearthly, nearly divine in its beauty. It's no wonder the Sidhe were called the "fair folk."

Two years, spikes of time, then steady. Not human. Well, other than two Kellys who, evidently, weren't kosher fare, the only other non-humans around Rio Seco County were . . .

By all the powers that may or may not be—this damnable cousin of mine was feeding on Adam Walker.

CHAPTER TWENTY-EIGHT

"GIVE IT BACK," I said through clenched teeth, ignoring the beauty shining from Daffyd's face. "Now."

"I do not understand." The shine faded and his beauty lessened for it. Good.

"The energy, the anima, whatever the hell you call it. You had absolutely no right to take it. Adam Walker, the one you're stealing it from, is in a coma because of you and may die. I thought it was something else, something I— No, never mind. That's irrelevant. Now give it the fuck back and I might not hurt you." My threat was very probably empty. I had no idea whether or not I could harm one of the fey. Did he know that?

"I cannot," Daffyd pronounced solemnly. "It is not reversible. Like food you eat, it cannot be restored. Can you make a dead cow alive after you have consumed it as steak? Can you put the lettuce back into the ground?"

"Way to be facetious," I growled at him. "Then what do you propose I do? How do I heal Adam after you've taken all his energy?"

"That I do not know," Daffyd answered. "I regret any sorrow this causes you."

"Regret? That's it? What good are you and why are you here?" I exploded, letting all my rage pour forth. "Meddling from my mother's family—the ones who wanted me around as much as a case of the plague. The ones who never thought I was good enough. I have news for you, buster. I could give a flying fig about being heir to my mother's whatever. I don't particularly care about the family who made me feel lower than dirt. My mother all but ignored me and then kicked me out. Good riddance. Why don't you go back to Wales and leave me and mine the fuck alone?"

Daffyd's words were ice. "Perhaps your Kelly connections may think this, but your mother Branwen did not ignore you. She wanted you. But she had no choice but to return you to your other family, since our court did not wish to raise a halfbreed to the throne. Had you stayed, you would not now live."

"Throne? What the hell are you talking about?"

"Your mother is heir to the lesser court. Her cousin is the queen."

"Well, lah-dee-bloody-dah. Bully for all of them. I'm fine being Keira Kelly, thank you very much. Now I want to get the hell out of Dodge so I can figure out how to save Adam, since you damn well can't, even though you caused it. I want you to stop."

"You do not realize."

"What?"

"Your place."

"My what?"

"Have you any idea why you were made?"

"Excuse me?"

Daffyd studied me. "My apologies. I must be clearer. Have you knowledge of why you were conceived?"

"Because my father and mother kissed each other and nine months later a baby came out?" I didn't feel like holding back the sarcasm. If this Sidhe, this so-called cousin, thought he could out-haughty me, intimidate me, he was sadly mistaken. My first lessons regarding my "place" in life scarred me, taught me to survive. Gigi, despite her (quite valid) velvet-encased iron fist helped mold the adult me: someone who took no guff from others. Daffyd ap Geraint, meet Keira Kelly.

"You jest with me, Keira. You must know this."

"Then stop beating around the bush and tell me straight." Not that any of it mattered.

"Very well. About four decades ago, my queen and yours signed an agreement. In the interests of furthering our bonds, and in hopes of producing a much stronger lineage, your father and mother were chosen. After your birth, all was well. You were a healthy child and female, strong and more filled with life than any of our own—and sadly few—young. We are a dying race. Few remain. My queen hoped that with this union, others would soon follow suit and bring new blood to our line.

"In your second year, my queen died and her daughter, your mother's cousin, took the throne. She had opposed the agreement and, once in power, banned all but the most traditional from the court. She couldn't banish your mother, as the lesser court protected her. However, you were shunned. I am sorry that this is so." He bowed his head, one hand to his chest. "When you neared your seventh birthday, your mother and I agreed you should be taken to your father. I followed and have been here since.

"No one knew we were here. One day, when you were cleaning graves, I ventured out, hid behind the statue in front of the entrance. I wanted to see you. Instead, someone saw me. By nightfall, the cave was blocked. The one other exit had long been blocked as the result of road construction. If I'd had my people, we could have carved new exits, but by myself . . . I am not strong enough, even at full power."

I fell back onto the rock chair. "*Gigi* walled you in?"

"I do not know. I merely know that the cave door was blocked and I could not escape. It wasn't until the rock cracked some years later I was able to slip out. I was weak, faded, but I could walk and did. That night, I wandered all over the countryside, unwilling to return to my underground home. We Sidhe live under the land, but we also love Above. That first night of my freedom, I met Greg."

Now this was beyond craptastic. Sure, this Sidhe had murdered several ranch hands, had drained Adam's energy to the point of coma, but my own family had walled him in? I really didn't get this. First Gigi erects a statue for some reason, then years later blocks in the cave and effectively sentences him to a lifetime . . . which for Sidhe, means thousands of years . . . underground without companionship, to eventual death by starvation? Who was the worse monster here?

"I . . . I don't know what to say," I began. "I can't—how did you survive all those years?"

"Why do you think I needed a human life every year after being freed? My incarceration drained me to the point of needing to replenish often. Before that, I could last years without taking a life. But there is no need for your guilt, Keira, daughter of Branwen." Daffyd bowed regally. "This was not of your doing. I must warn you, however."

"Warn?"

"The man, Pete. When I told him I would no longer require an offering, he was not pleased. He killed the man he brought in a short while ago, lured him to the barrier and murdered him. He buried him outside the cave entrance. When I protested, he swore he would get revenge. That he needed the money the Judge paid him to bring me the men." Daffyd shrugged, the motion liquid and graceful. "There is little he can do to me, nor to Greg."

What he said sunk in. "Wait a minute here. I'm all 'yay!' that you're not requiring offerings, but taking from Adam stops now. Immediately. No excuses." Would this bring Adam back? I couldn't know, but there was no way in all the hells I was going to let Daffyd keep sucking him dry.

Daffyd regarded me with a grave look. "If I do not feed, I will die."

I gave him grave a look. "If you continue to feed, Adam will die. I cannot forgive or allow that."

"Would you then have me return to the bargain? Return to human offerings?"

"Neither choice, Daffyd," I said. "This bargain stops now. Your feeding stops now. Go back to Wales. Go back to my mother and tell her I am fine and don't need a babysitter." Yeah, and while you're at it, stop by British Columbia and tell my great-great-grandmother the same damned thing.

"You are my obligation. I am under *geis*."

"Not by my doing."

"You would have me fade?" he asked, his silver eyes catching my own gray ones and holding my gaze.

I held silent, eyes staring into his. I would not back down, could not. Adam would not be sacrificed for this creature, this cousin not-of-my-choosing. We held matching stares for a long moment, two interminable beats of our hearts. I could feel the underlying power, both his and mine. He reached for me, mentally, a whisper sliding across the back of my head, then as swiftly lost in the charged air. He could no longer reach me. It was as if, now acknowledged and identified, his siren call, his mental bait-and-hook no longer worked.

"I know your name, Daffyd ap Geraint ap Pwyll."

"Freely given, Keira daughter of Branwen."

"Daughter of Huw Kelly," I corrected. "You are kin, but I am Kelly. If I'm your queen's cousin and my mother is heir to the lesser court, then you are subject to me, correct?"

"Perhaps."

"Either I am or I'm not," I said. "No two ways about it."

"You are—or will be. I cannot say more."

"Will be?"

Daffyd fell silent.

"Fine then, be that way. All I ask is that you stop feeding on Adam, any of the other vampires, or any human or non-human sentient being. I don't particularly care if you stay here or go back to Wales or decide to take in Antarctica, as long as you stop. Oh, and that you let me go back." There, was that enough? I'd heard so many stories about being trapped in Faery—whether it was eating, drinking or not phrasing your request properly—that I wanted to make sure I didn't miss anything. Of course, this could all totally be off base. My blood might be half theirs, but I had fewer clues on how real Faery worked than I did about vampires.

A slow blink, then a deep bow, one hand to his heart. "I hear and obey."

"So, it's a deal I can go, then?"

"Yes. I will no longer feed from the Walker, nor any of his kin, nor any human or non-human person. You may return to the surface," Daffyd said. "I am not now, nor ever will be, your captor. In calling you, I merely wished to speak with you. You heard me. This means you were ready to hear me."

"Ready how?"

"Your Change. A part of your other clan heritage. Your mother said that once this began, you would be able to hear us."

"Is that so?" I pondered this for a moment. I guess dear Mama knew more about the clan abilities than I did. Either that or Gigi and she had been in cahoots all along, though that didn't explain Gigi walling in Daffyd. My granny was going to have some serious 'splaining to do once I got in touch with her. "How did you know to call now?"

"Come, Keira. I will show you the way to the surface." Daffyd ignored my question entirely.

"Keira," Greg broke in. "Tell my dad . . . Tell him I love him and I forgive him."

"I will, Greg." I turned to Daffyd. "Will Greg . . . ?"

He seemed to know what I was asking. "Greg will continue, as I do and until I fade. Do not grieve for us, Keira Kelly. Perhaps I will no longer feed, but the energy I do have is strong and may last for many years."

"Okay, then. Greg, yes, I'll tell your dad." At least about the love part. I was not so sure Judge Pursell deserved the forgiveness. I could sort of see Daffyd's side in that he was absolutely right about one thing. He wasn't ever human, nor would be. Nor was I. Difference was that me and mine chose to live among the humans, be like them insofar as we could. They were not our prey. The Judge and Pete: murderers. No excuses. No denials. I wasn't sure what to do about them, but I had every intention of telling the entire story to my brother and to Niko when I got out of here. I was sure we could come up with some sort of justice.

I followed Daffyd out of the main chamber and down a long narrow tunnel. It, too, was lit with faery light, allowing me to avoid feeling claustrophobic, despite the closeness of the walls. We walked for a few minutes, then turned down a passageway with a ramp leading upward. At the top, I saw a shimmery light blocking the end. At first glance it looked like cling film, translucent, letting light in. At second, it was pure light itself, moving in waves, rolling white with flashes of color.

"There is your exit," Daffyd said. "On the other side is the cave mouth, where your brother is."

"Directly on the other side?" I asked, wondering why we hadn't seen it.

Daffyd answered the unspoken part of my question. "It is visible solely to those of the blood, and only if you are looking for it. Humans and others see a short tunnel that goes nowhere."

I started up the ramp, then thought of something.

"Daffyd, before I go. A couple of nights ago, there were some teenagers out by the Angel. Did you see them?"

He nodded. "Yes, they were outside, chanting. They came here, lit candles and incense. Then they screamed."

Like my vision. At least I knew I was batting a thousand. "Do you know what made them scream?"

"I do not. I feared approaching them. I did not wish to be seen. I can no longer cast an invisibility glamour."

"Why?"

Daffyd's mouth curled in a sad smile. This one didn't transform his features. "Despite the energy I took from the Walker, I am fading, Keira. It will soon be my time, and when I go, Greg will go with me."

"You told me you'd last years."

"I lied."

I studied his face. "Greg . . . he doesn't know. You're protecting him."

"Perhaps. Perhaps he knows. We are companions, he

and I. I tell him stories that enthrall him. He brings me a humanity I never experienced. It is comfortable."

It was my turn to bow to Daffyd. "May your journey be as you wish, cousin," I said, calling up a half-forgotten farewell from my early childhood.

"And yours also, cousin."

Daffyd turned and I stepped through the barrier.

CHAPTER TWENTY-NINE

"WHAT THE HELL happened?" Tucker demanded. "One second you were there, the next you vanish and, two seconds later, poof, there you are again."

"Two seconds?" Time shifting, huh? Although I always thought it was the other way around—a mortal spends a night in Faery, comes out to find a hundred years had passed. Maybe it's because I wasn't a mere mortal.

"Well, Tucker, all I can ask is: do you believe in faeries?"

"What the hell?"

"Let's go outside and collect Niko and I'll tell you both the whole story."

Tucker shot me a look, but complied. Niko was nowhere to be found at the overhang, so I pulled out my cell phone and dialed his number.

"Where the hell are you?" Niko barked. "I've been waiting at the car for at least an hour. I climbed back up on that cliff twice and couldn't find you. I was about to go get help."

"We're fine, Niko." Tucker raised his voice. "We'll be right there."

We got to the car and Tucker dressed in the spare set of clothes as I gave them the whole story.

Niko and Tucker both began to growl as they realized my Sidhe cousin was at the root of Adam's coma.

"He must be stopped," Niko exclaimed, and turned to leave.

I threw up a hand to stop him. "Nikolai, stop. Look at me," I said, using my best command voice. To my surprise, he stopped in his tracks and subsided. "What's done is done. We can't bring the energy back. And there's nothing you or any of my family can do."

"I can damned well try," muttered Tucker.

"And to what end?" I put my hands on my hips. "Daffyd ap Geraint is Sidhe, probably older than the both of you put together. If he desires, he can glamour the entire cave and vanish and none of us, including me, will ever find him. Then, he can go right on back sucking the life out of Adam, until he finishes with him, then starts on you, Niko, then Lance, then every single vampire in the compound until each and all are in comas or dead. Is that what you want?"

"How do we know he has stopped?" Niko demanded.

"Because he is under *geis* and he is my kin. Evidently, this means something to him."

"And because you are his liege," Tucker put in. "I know you avoided learning about Faery, Keira, but I didn't. From what you said, Daffyd has to do what you require. Your mother is his liege lady, as are you."

Niko stepped away from me, all traces of rage gone. "Then, if that is the case, this Sidhe will not continue to feed. I am satisfied."

"Keira," Tucker said. "Daffyd said Pete killed Alex?"

"Yes."

"That's it, then."

"What?"

"Bones. Buried bones . . . or remains. When we came the first time. That's what seemed off to me."

Niko gave my brother a strange look. "Tucker, if I might be so bold . . . it's a cemetery."

"Yes, yes," Tucker retorted. "Don't get smartass on me. You've been hanging around my sister too long."

"Moi?" I pretended surprise. Tucker ignored me.

"New bones—at least way newer than what should be there for a graveyard that's not been used in decades."

"So it wasn't the energy barrier?" I asked.

"Yes, that, too, silly girl." Tucker ran a hand through his hair. "I should have picked up on the bones, but they weren't . . . aren't on the surface. I think I felt them when I tried to ground myself. The bones disturbed the grounding."

"Should we go back and look?" I ventured, not really wanting to do this now.

"I don't think so, not tonight," Tucker said to my relief. "No one's going to get in there. We should regroup."

He was right. I wanted time to think things through, talk it all out. Should we call Carlton and tell him what the Sidhe said, but pretend it was a ranch hand that wanted to remain anonymous? Easy to get Lance or one of the other vampires to place the call from an anonymous phone line. Or perhaps decide to mete out our own justice, as we did with Boris and Greta Nagy after they'd murdered my cousin Marty and their own two henchmen? Either way, I wanted to go back to the ranch and figure out our options, including what to do about Adam.

As I was about to get into the Rover, my phone rang. My home number. I looked at Tucker and mouthed "Bea." The display said 5:04 A.M. Not an idle call at this time of night. I flipped open the phone and motioned for my brother to switch places with me so I could talk while he drove.

"Bea, what is it?" I asked as I climbed into the car.

Tucker climbed into the driver's seat. Niko got in behind us.

"Keira," she whispered, a frantic note in her voice. "I think Pete's outside."

"Pete?" As soon as the word left Bea's mouth, Tucker gunned the accelerator, using his night vision and sense of direction to get us out of the field and onto the road.

"Yes, Ignacio thinks so, too. I woke up, heard a noise. I thought it was you coming back but it didn't sound like your car. Sounded like a truck. I've tried to call the sheriff, but I can't get through. The line keeps being busy. Tried 911 but the service isn't answering."

"We're on our way," I assured her. "I'll try Carlton. Niko, call the main sheriff's office." I rattled off the number. "Bea, I'm sorry, I don't have any weapons there. Stay down, stay away from the windows."

"I'm okay," she said. "Ignacio has one of the fireplace andirons. We're sticking together in the back bathroom."

"You try Carlton on the cell, too." I rattled off the number. "Be careful. We're on our way.

"Damn it to fucking hell and back," I growled. "He'd better not hurt her."

I tried dialing, fumbling the first attempt, then not getting through on the second. I left a terse voice mail. Then tried again. "Niko, any luck—? Carlton, thank the . . . Get someone over to my place, pronto. Bea called, she thinks Pete's prowling around outside. She and Ignacio are there by themselves. We're on our way."

"On it." Carlton disconnected. There was nothing more to be said.

The drive to my house never seemed so long. In reality, we were there in less than fifteen minutes, ahead of Carlton or anyone else.

THE HOUSE was still. No lights, no sign of life inside or out. No battered pickup to be seen. I breathed a sigh of relief. "Maybe she was wrong," I said. "There's no place around here to hide that truck." I lived in a single house that sat by itself in a small cul-de-sac off a quiet, undeveloped stretch of land. No other houses in the vicinity. No place for a person bent on evil to hide a pickup.

"Keira . . ." Niko's voice held a note of warning as we alighted from the Rover.

"What is it? What do you sense?"

He shook his head. "Let's go inside."

I fumbled for the switch inside that governed a couple of the lamps inside the living room. Nothing. The familiar green lights from the DVR and from the DVD player weren't there. Not a good sign.

Before any of us could move, a sudden flash and beeping from all the appliances as they sprung to life. I jumped back, into Tucker, who steadied me. "Whoa, there, Keira. Must've been a brownout."

I nodded. "Yeah, makes sense." With the heat wave, the local electric co-op often practiced rolling brownouts to conserve power. "Bea?" I called out. "Ignacio? It's us."

"I smell blood." Niko and Tucker spoke at once, voices melding with the same exact words.

"Where?"

"Kitchen," Tucker said.

Inside the doorway, Ignacio lay sprawled on his back, blood smearing his head.

"Out cold," Tucker pronounced after checking his pulse. "Bleeding's stopped some time ago."

Niko disappeared, calling back. "I'm checking the bedrooms."

"She's not here," I said flatly. "He's taken her."

Ignacio stirred, mumbling. *"Señorita, cuidate."* He blinked a few times, as if to focus on our faces. *"Señorita* Keira," he said. *"La llevó. El señor Pete, la llevó."*

"He says he's taken her," Niko said, rejoining us. "He's right, there are signs of a struggle in the bathroom. There was a man in there. Not this man."

"You speak Spanish?" I asked him, my mind refusing to think of Bea kidnapped by Pete Garza.

Niko nodded. "I do. Enough." His head raised. "A car. I believe I would rather not have our illustrious Sheriff question me. I shall remove myself."

"Take care, *cariad*," Tucker called after him. Niko slipped out the back door and into the woods. Tucker and I helped Ignacio up and to a chair in the living room. We sat across from him, on the couch.

Less than a minute later, Carlton pulled up in the drive and debarked, walking directly in through the open front door, a deputy in tow.

"Pete Garza took Bea," I said bluntly.

"I've dispatched an ambulance, in case we . . ." Carlton said. He motioned to the other man with him. "This is Rick Asher, speaks fluent Spanish. Can Ignacio explain?"

The deputy gave us a curt nod and began to converse with Ignacio, whose voice cracked as he spoke. Tucker got up and poured a glass of water, handing it to Ignacio.

"He says Pete came in, broke through the glass in the small bedroom. He had a gun."

"Son of a—"

"Hush, Keira, let him talk." Tucker grasped my hand and squeezed.

Ignacio spoke to Rick a few more minutes. Rick's face grew more concerned with every word. "He says Pete was ranting about bargains and not keeping them. Something about giving them Alex and they didn't take him so he was going to take Bea." Rick looked at Carlton who was writing in his notepad. "Ignacio says that Pete had a gun, a pistol. He was screaming in English, then in Spanish, like he wanted Ignacio to know what he was saying. Said Bea would be a good substitute. Ignacio tried to help, but Pete whacked him with the pistol, then dragged Bea outside. He remembers hearing the truck drive off before he passed out."

"What time?" Carlton asked.

"He says right after Bea talked to Ms. Kelly."

"He can't have gotten far," I said. "We got here in fifteen minutes."

"From the Wild Moon?" Carlton sounded surprised.

I shook my head. "We weren't there. It's not important why, but we were at the old cemetery. You know, No Man's Land, back part of the Wild Moon. From there, it's not that far here."

"Okay, not important why, but why?" Carlton insisted.

I looked at Tucker who shrugged and nodded. Okay, then.

"We were meeting with a ranch hand, a guy from the Pursell place. He got in touch with us earlier this evening. Said he had information about Alex."

"Did he?"

"Yeah." I ran down the mundane version of Daffyd's story, leaving out any mention of the supernatural. I made the cemetery out to be a convenient place to meet far from the possible witnesses an anonymous source would fear.

Carlton shut his notebook and put it in his pocket. "Rick, call dispatch, give them the down and dirty. We'll need all hands looking out. Have someone go to the Pursell ranch."

"Carlton," I broke in. "Pete got fired. I don't think he'd be at the ranch."

"Maybe," he said. "But I'm not ruling it out."

"What can we do?" Tucker asked.

"Nothing." Carlton stared at the both of us. "Go out to the Wild Moon and get some sleep. I'd rather not have to worry about two civilians out there with some crazy who has a gun and knows how to use it."

I started to say something, but Tucker held me back and I shut up. No point in arguing. When Carlton left, I knew we'd go looking ourselves. By now, I was sure Niko had called the Wild Moon to elicit assistance. I had no doubt he was out of human sight, listening in.

Carlton pulled out his cell phone. "Rick, when you finish with dispatch, get Judge Morales on the line. I want a warrant for Carl Pursell." He dialed a number. "Mary, bad news. Yeah, he took her. Go on over to her house and sit with Tio and Tia. They don't need to be hearing it from Chris on the morning show. It's near time they get up to go open the café." He paused. "Right. Will do."

With that, he flipped the phone shut and sat down on an armchair.

CHAPTER THIRTY

"WHO ARE YOU?" Carlton said, staring past us out the front door.

Neither Tucker nor I looked around. We'd both heard Niko come up the porch and inside. Why the hell hadn't he stayed away?

"Wait, I remember you," Carlton continued. "You're from the Wild Moon, right? Work up there?"

"I do," Niko responded with a smile. He crossed in front of me and sat close in to Tucker, as if staking a claim.

Carlton studied him, me, then back to Tucker. As the clue bus hit him, his eyes widened, but he didn't say anything. I glanced over at Niko whose expression was indescribable—a cross between a canary-stuffed cat and twelve-year-old boy who'd pulled one over on his dad. Boys. Did they ever grow up?

"Now what?" I asked Carlton.

"Now, you wait and, in about two minutes, I'm going to go out that door and join my guys."

"Two minutes?"

"Yes, I'm going to wait for the EMTs, make sure Ignacio is okay."

"Okay." What else could I say?

"Once Ignacio is gone, you two go back to the Wild Moon. I'd rather you not stay here. Or go over and sit with Tio and Tia, keep them company." Carlton let out a long exhale. "It's been one hell of a night."

I looked at him. "That implies there's more to the night than this?"

"We found the kids."

"You did?"

He pulled off his Stetson and placed it carefully on the couch next to him and ran a hand through his hair. More gray there, I noticed. More than last year. He was getting older. Forty stared him in the face, along with a reelection this year. Was Carlton satisfied here in Rio Seco? In all this craziness, he hadn't once spoken of his wife, his kids, that they were missing him while he was working insane hours. I looked at his face, now weary with lines that hadn't been there six months ago.

"They've been camping out in an empty house over by the lake. Someone saw lights there and reported it. I've spent the last two hours talking to them."

"So?"

"You were right, they went up to the Angel to do some silly ritual thing Brittany got out of a book. When they were up there, they got freaked out, saw something."

Carlton had the strangest look on his face.

"Something?" I prompted.

He picked up his hat and began playing with it. I was familiar with this gesture. It meant he was uncomfortable.

"They told me some stupid story about a vampire and a deer and blood. Scared the beejeezus out of them and they went running off into the night. Got into Jimmy's truck and drove halfway around the lake, ended up at a house that the Wentzes own and usually rent out. No tenants right now."

Niko, Tucker and I exchanged glances. I had to fight to keep a neutral, yet interested, expression on my face. My brother and his vampire lover smiled back at

Carlton, as if the whole thing was oh, *très amusant.*

Carlton shrugged. "Kids. Anyhow, whatever scared them, they took off and didn't want to come back."

"What was that whole ritual thing about anyway?"

"You're not going to believe this. It was because a couple of them were dating," he responded. "Except not Missy dating Matt, but because Jimmy and Matt were boyfriends. Matt's father found out, kicked Matt out of the house. Missy went with him, and Brittany, who is friends with Jimmy, tagged along. They made up the whole three-wheeling story. They were going to run away to Austin or San Antonio, but Brittany had talked them into going to the Angel first. They hid out at an old fishing shed that Jimmy's uncle once took him to, then snuck back after dark to go to the Angel."

Carlton fidgeted with his hat, then continued.

"When they saw the 'vampire' "—I could hear the quote marks in Carlton's tone—"they freaked out. Then Jimmy's truck broke down halfway to Austin so they hiked over to the lake house."

"You all didn't check the place?" Tucker asked.

Carlton shook his head. "Yeah, I know, stupid, but Mrs. Wentz told us she'd been out there already. Turns out she knew what was going on and lied, trying to cover for the boys. She'd been planning to go over there and give the kids cash, but ever since Brittany's mom rang the alarm, there had been a nosy neighbor or a cop or someone with her all the time. About three hours ago, one of the local patrols over there noticed lights were on at the house. They knew it was supposed to be empty and knew it belonged to the Wentzes. They'd heard about the search, went over there and found the kids."

"Do they still think they've seen a vampire?" Niko asked drily.

"Nah, they realize now it was probably some poacher out doing some very illegal night hunting. They let their imaginations and the spooky place get to them."

"That's good." Tucker elbowed Niko in the side. Niko ignored him. I hoped that Carlton hadn't noticed this little byplay, or wrote it off as boys being boys.

"So what's going to happen to them?" I asked.

"I talked to Mrs. Wentz," Carlton said. "Her husband is still out of the country on business. She's agreed to set Matt up at the lake house for the time being and send over a housekeeper. Jimmy's going to stay with him, evidently. They've agreed to stay there and finish school and graduate. Then she's going to help them find a place in Austin. She said she'd deal with Matt's father."

"So all's well that ends well." I hoped that was so, for their sake. Poor kids, going out to the cemetery, hoping that a ritual would help them work things out so those two boys could be together. Then, catching sight of a vampire on the hunt. It was a good thing no one believed them. No doubt by now, they didn't believe it themselves.

The sound of a siren dopplered in, cutting off as the ambulance pulled in.

"I'll go talk to them," Carlton said, standing. "Thanks for all your help. Please, lock up, Keira. I'll have one of my guys drive by later to make sure things are okay. You all go on to the ranch or Bea's house."

"Thanks, Carlton."

Niko, Tucker and I got up and headed out to the front as the EMTs loaded Ignacio into the ambulance. Carlton got into his SUV and took off.

"*Señorita.*" Ignacio's weak voice came from the back

of the ambulance. *"Por favor, antes de que me lleven. El señor Pete dijo algo muy extraño. Algo como 'viviendo con los angeles.'"*

Niko translated. "He says before he leaves . . . he remembers that Pete said something . . . strange. Something about living with the angels."

CHAPTER THIRTY-ONE

"WE HAVE TO GO back there," I said to Tucker and Niko as the ambulance drove off. "'Living with the angels' is cryptic, but what if he meant *La Angel*? We should go back."

Niko interrupted. "I want to go check on Adam. Perhaps I can figure out how to help him out of the coma. I'm afraid going back to the cemetery with you would be fruitless. Besides, sunrise is due in an hour or so."

Tucker shared a warm smile with Niko. "Go, take care of him. We'll go see if we can find Bea. Why don't you send John and his son? Have them meet us at the cemetery. Tell them to bring weapons. If Pete's got Bea at gunpoint, I want a way to overpower him before he can harm her."

I leaned against my brother. "You know, this is one time I'd love for the Kelly clan to be here in full force. Pete Garza wouldn't stand a chance against the combined might of The Kelly."

"That's a fact." Tucker smiled softly and gave me a quick squeeze. "Let's go, sis. Niko . . ."

The two men exchanged a private look. I interpreted it to mean "take care of yourself and let's come out of this safely." I could go with that. Safe was the one way I wanted to finish up: all of us, including Bea.

"I phoned for a driver earlier," Niko said. "Go along, find your friend. Take good care."

The return drive seemed interminably long, seconds

like thousands of lifetimes for me to worry Pete Garza would slip over the edge from crazy to bugfuck and shoot Bea straight out.

"Hang in there, sis," Tucker said. "He didn't shoot her in the house, nor did he kill Ignacio. That's a good sign."

Better than the alternative, I supposed. "Tucker," I began.

"Yes?"

"I don't think I want to do this the human way."

Tucker remained silent as I left the main road and drove up what was once the drive to the cemetery, now long since overgrown. I flipped off the headlights, slowed the car, letting it come to a stop on its own, without brake lights. We were still about a half mile away and on the other side of a small rise. No longer full dark, the slow lightening of the sky heralded the sunrise.

"Okay," Tucker said as he opened the car door. "We'll do it your way."

We each picked up a Maglite and headed toward the path. "Don't use the light, yet," Tucker said quietly. "I don't know how far a human can see a bright light. It's still dark enough for a light to be conspicuous. I don't want to take any chances."

I nodded. "I'm fine, there's enough light for me."

The quiet enveloped us, broken by the chirp of crickets, the rustlings of small night predators scurrying to their daytime burrows. My eyes adjusted easily, more so than I expected. Despite the growing daylight, it was still pretty gloomy here. My brother nodded toward the narrow winding path that led up to the overhang.

"It's further, but I think we'll be better off than trying to sneak through the cemetery proper. Too much underbrush and such."

"Agreed," I said.

He handed me his Maglite and stripped, folding his clothes and leaving them under a tree at the fork of the path. "Remember where I parked these."

I smiled as he took one step and then another, morphing from human shape to wolf in a brief blink of an eye. This is how shapeshifting was supposed to happen, I thought. Not a forced occurrence, but the natural state of being one, then the other. In the night, he was most definitely in his element. I let him take the lead and I followed close behind.

As we approached the overhang, I could hear music, something . . . some sort of song? Tucker paused and tilted his head, listening. A truly wolfish grin appeared. Definitely Pete. I dropped to the ground, tucked the two flashlights in the back of my jeans and crawled side by side with my brother. A few minutes later, we'd reached the point where we could see over the edge, close enough to figure out Pete was most definitely down there, but far enough so he couldn't see us.

His truck was parked directly outside the cemetery gate, headlights on and the radio blaring some heavy country wailing "she done me wrong" ballad. Tucker crept out a little further, all stalker awareness. I sidled up next to him and, as best I could, crawled a little further forward. The truck headlights barely illuminated the area behind the Angel, but Pete had one of those big square heavy-duty lantern flashlights propped up next to him on a rock.

He'd dragged Bea through the opening Tucker and I had made earlier, propped her up against the outside wall of the cave entrance. Bea was trussed up like Penelope Pitstop, except Bea wasn't sighing melodramatically. Her eyes were open, wider than I'd ever seen them. Some sort of gag was tied across her mouth, preventing her from speaking.

Pete hummed along to the song, a snatch or two of the lyrics escaping from his mouth as he worked. At first, from this angle, I couldn't tell what he was doing, but as I crept a wee bit more, I could make it out. Shovel. Dirt. Hole. Pete Garza was digging Bea's grave.

I didn't have to look at Tucker to know what we were going to do next. We tensed, ready to jump off the cliff and land square on Pete. As I silently counted to three with my fingers, so Tucker and I could jump simultaneously, Bea struggled a little, whimpered. At the sound, Pete stopped shoveling, dropped the shovel onto the dirt and pulled a pistol out of the back of his pants.

"If you don't stop whining, woman, I'll have to whip you upside the head with this." He brandished the pistol in Bea's face. With a greasy chuckle, he slid the barrel down Bea's cheek in a grotesque caress. "I don't want to fuck up that face of yours 'fore I get me a piece of you." With a twisted smirk, he tucked the pistol back into his waistband and smacked Bea across the face with his hand. "That's a taste. Don't make me do it again. You gotta be sweet so I can have you 'fore I kill you."

His grin widened as her eyes shut tight. With a chuckle, he began to hum again as he picked the shovel back up. The moment he'd bent back down, shovel to dirt, we sprang.

Pete never saw us coming.

"Stop, Tucker—don't—" Bea gasped as I tore the filthy cloth from her mouth.

Tucker had Pete on the ground, all his weight pinning the man so he couldn't move. With a low growl, Tucker's mouth twisted into mean snarl. At Bea's plea, he looked at her, nodded briefly, then looked back down at Pete Garza and growled louder. Pete began to whimper. A drop or two of saliva dropped from Tucker's mouth onto the man's face. Pete closed his eyes and keened.

Good, I thought. Be afraid. We are your worst nightmare.

"You okay, *chica*?"

Bea nodded. "Mostly." I tugged at the knots of rope, trying to loosen her bindings. "I'm not having any luck here. Damn it."

"There's a knife. A pocketknife," Bea said. "Over there." She inclined her head to the left.

I looked around and saw a fancy Swiss Army knife on top of some coiled rope.

"He used it to cut the rope. Had too much." Bea's weak chuckle quickly turned into a ragged sob. "Oh, Keira, oh, my God, you found me."

"Hush, sweetie," I said, cutting into the ropes around her arms and torso. "You know I will always find you." The knife made short work of the bindings.

Bea rubbed her wrists and ankles. As soon as I saw she was okay, I gave her the now closed knife and walked over to Pete Garza. He'd opened his eyes again and was staring at me as I approached. His eyes widened as he saw my face. Somewhere between cutting the last piece of rope off Bea and walking the few feet to where my brother had Pete Garza pinned, I let all of the rage I'd held inside, all of the sheer predator ferocity that was in my nature seep through to the surface. This was the part of me I'd always had; whether it was the Faery half or the Kelly half, I didn't know, but it was the part that would do anything to find justice for family. Bea was family.

"You killed Alex Robles," I said to Pete. I kept my voice low and steady, quiet enough to satisfy even the pickiest librarian. "You hurt Ignacio Robles." I stepped closer. "You threatened my family, kidnapped my best friend and now, you will pay."

"No, please." Pete begged, his voice tight and high. "Don't."

I looked over my shoulder at Bea, who, instead of pleading with me to stop, was staring at me, eyes wide and frightened, nearly as scared as she'd been when Pete threatened her with the pistol. At that moment, I knew I'd done something that I might never be able to take back. I'd pulled back the veil and let the other part of me bleed through. In the thirty years she'd known me, Beatriz Ruiz had never seen it. From childhood on, I'd known that when in the company of humans, I had to appear and act human. It had become instinctive to be that way. That hidden part, the part that danced behind my eyes when I first started to Change last fall now sat on my face as if I'd ripped off the Keira mask and exposed something too vicious to look upon. Physically, I know I didn't look any different, but whatever Bea saw in my eyes scared her, and I realized I might never be able to fix it.

I forced my attention back to our captive. Tucker held still, waiting for my cue. Before I could say another word, a soft voice spoke.

"Keira, no."

Daffyd stood at the mouth of the cave. In the dark of the Hill Country night, surrounded by the natural aura of the faery, he embodied the legend of the shining ones. Long hair flowed free, strands moving in the gentle breeze, his posture regal as that of a heroic statue. He was Strength and Light and Justice. Behind him, Greg Pursell stood, his hands clasped behind him in patient waiting.

"I will take him," Daffyd said. "You need not make that choice for yourself."

I held still, clenching my fists as I forced myself back to what passed for normal. He was right. No doubt I could kill and dispose of Pete Garza and still be able to sleep at night. The man was less than a cockroach and deserved to be exterminated. But I couldn't do it in front of Bea. I couldn't let Tucker do it, either. She'd never forget, never forgive us. For that brief crazy moment, I understood the reason that Adam Walker quit drinking blood, why he'd stopped hunting. I returned my cousin's calm gaze and gave him a slight nod.

Tucker, seeing my acquiescence, moved away from Pete, and came to stand next to me.

"Go. You need to attend to Adam." The Sidhe motioned gracefully with his hand. "Once you are gone, I will ward the cave again."

"You'll keep your bargain?" I asked.

"I will."

"Good. Then we'll keep ours."

With that, I reached to help Bea up and we left. As we reached my car, I heard Pete Garza scream.

CHAPTER THIRTY-TWO

"WE FOUND HER, Carlton, tied up and alone at the old cemetery," I lied easily. "It was something Ignacio remembered that Pete said. When we got there, no sign of Pete, except for some rope and pieces of his shirt. We left it all there for you to look at."

I hoped our ploy worked. Tucker had shifted back, got dressed and escorted Bea to the Rover while I dragged the rope and the rag he'd gagged Bea with, which turned out to be part of his shirt, out to the front of the Angel. We were taking the shovel with us. I made sure to stuff some more debris and branches in the hole, effectively blocking the way to the cave. I was sure after Daffyd reinforced his ward, no human would bother trying to get back there.

"She's okay?" Carlton asked.

"Yeah, mostly bruised and banged up. He slapped her pretty hard."

Tucker, who was driving, said nothing and concentrated on holding Bea's hand. I'd had her sit in the passenger seat so I could keep an eye on her. I noticed she wasn't holding Tucker's hand in return, but letting hers lie limp on the console between them. She stared out the windshield and said nothing. Crap, I was afraid of that.

Tonight, Beatriz Ruiz had seen the Kelly siblings in all their freakish glory. It was one thing to know, to be told about powers and shapeshifting and all the things that made us clan; another entirely to see it with your own human eyes and have it proven to you.

"Does she know where Pete went?" Carlton's voice started to break up a little, get staticky.

"She doesn't," I answered. "She told me she was unconscious until right before we found her. Pete hit her, then told her he was going to rape, then kill her. He admitted to killing Alex Robles and burying him in front of the Angel."

A burst of static was my answer, with only one word audible: "hospital."

"He says we should take you to the hospital, Bea." I leaned forward in the back seat, patting her shoulder. "I think that's a good idea. Where do you want to go? The clinic over up by Two Pesos?"

"No." Bea shivered and wrapped her arms around herself. "No hospital. I'm fine. I just want to go home."

"Bea—" Tucker began.

"No, dammit," Bea said. "Take me home. Tia was a nurse. She'll watch out for me."

Tucker nodded and turned at the next intersection.

"Carlton, I'm having problems hearing you," I said. "Bea wants to go home so we're taking her there."

"'Kay . . . plan. Sending crew . . . daytime . . . bones." I interpreted that to mean he'd be sending in a crew in the daytime to the cemetery to look for Alex Robles' remains.

"Thanks, Carlton. Once we settle Bea in, we're heading home." I shut the phone and tucked it into my pocket. "Hang in there, *chica*," I said. "Almost there."

Tio Richard met us at the door, Tia Petra two steps behind, wringing her hands. Both of them smiled from ear to ear when they saw Bea in the front seat.

"You are okay, Beatriz. They found you!" Tia began to bawl.

Tio stepped up and helped Bea out of the car. "All of you come inside. I will fix you something to eat."

"No, Tio, please," Bea said. "I . . ." For the first time since we'd rescued her, she looked me in the eye. "I'm sorry, but I want to get some sleep. I'm not up for company."

My stomach roiled. *Company.*

"I'm sorry, Keira," Bea continued. "I need a little time, okay?"

I forced a smile. "Yeah, sure, Bea. I understand."

"Get some rest, Bea," Tucker added. "Tio, Tia, please call us if you need us."

"*Sí, gracias*, Tucker," Tia said. "*Muchisimas gracias a los dos.* Thank you for bringing her back to us."

I nodded and swiftly turned away, tears threatening to fall at any moment.

Tucker put the car in gear and we headed to the Wild Moon. Neither of us spoke to the other until we got to Adam's house.

IN A MIRROR of our arrival at Bea's, Niko met us inside Adam's front hallway, well away from direct sunlight. The day had dawned bright and shiny, such a contrast to our moods.

"No change," Niko said quietly. Tucker pulled him in for a hug. Sensing my own need, he let Niko go and did the same to me. I sank into my brother's embrace, letting the tension, anxiety and sorrow melt away for a brief moment as I tallied up the count:

Missing friend found safe and sound: Check. (Safe. But sound after everything that happened? I hoped so.)

Missing kids found safe and sound: Check.

Missing brother found safe and sound: Half-check. (Found, as in we knew what happened and eventually his remains will turn up. Definitely not safe, nor sound.)

Bad guy caught and put away for life: Technically, check.

Which left Adam, still in a coma and no signs of coming out of it, despite the fact that the cause of the coma no longer existed. The cause that was here in Rio Seco because of me; taking the life energy from the one person I'd found that I could be myself with, no family politics, no need to hide my inhuman nature.

"We need to go on in." Tucker spoke gently, disentangling himself from me.

I nodded and followed the two of them further into the house. I had to fix this.

"YOU ARE NOT doing this, Keira," Niko argued as he paced across the living room floor. "I told you, in this state, he won't stop, he can't. He'll drain you."

"That's a risk I have to take, Niko. Tucker, please, explain it to him." I curled up in the corner of the couch and closed my eyes.

"Keira, I understand your need, but you won't find me arguing *for* it," Tucker said. "I am not quite ready to let you sacrifice yourself."

My eyes flew open and I stood to confront my brother, who was seated in an easy chair across from me. "*Let*, brother? There is no 'let' involved. If I choose . . ."

Tucker exhaled sharply. "You invoke Choice, then?"

Choice: the tenet that I learned at my aunts' knees as I trained with them. Both healers, both committed to life, healing and happiness, they were the ones who taught me how to guide others to their deaths. In a clan of near immortals, one may choose the time and date of their final journey. It is our most sacred principle and none may deny it.

I faced my brother solemnly. "I do."

Niko stopped pacing and came to stand by Tucker. He didn't have to ask what we were talking about. Although vampires are made rather than born, they too can suffer the eventual ennui that comes from living centuries, millennia. I had never asked for details, but in a conversation one night over dinner, I had gathered the vampires had something similar.

I swallowed drily. Shit, Keira, this is it then. "I need you to know, guys," I said. "I'm going to depend on you to be there. I'm not saying I'm going to let him drain me dry if I can help it. I want you two to do your best to pull him off after he's conscious."

"We will stand by you," Niko said with a formal bow. "We are your seconds."

Tucker echoed Niko's bow and took my hand. "Niko stocked some fresh deer blood in the fridge. I'll bring it down."

ADAM LAY EXACTLY as I'd seen him last night, flat on his back, no sign that not two days prior he'd been awake, normal (for a vampire), as alive as he would ever be. I stood near the head of the bed, Niko to my left, Tucker kneeling on the bed next to Adam. I closed my eyes and whispered a swift prayer to whatever powers may be. Despite my resolve, I did not want to die today . . . nor tomorrow, nor anytime in the foreseeable future. What I wanted was for Adam to get enough blood to revive, Tucker and Niko to be able to restrain him long enough for me to get away and give him the pouch of deer blood. If this worked, he could feed from the deer blood and restore his health. Then, at some point in the very foreseeable future, he and I were going to have that talk we'd put off.

If this didn't work, he would be alive, I'd be dead and I hoped my brother and Niko could run faster than a newly revived vampire, as I had no doubt Adam would first blame them, and then himself. Of course, I'd be dead and wouldn't care.

I knew I was hesitating, but couldn't help it. Now I was here, on the brink of doing this and my hand wouldn't open the knife. It was the same useful pocketknife I'd used to cut Bea's bonds and Pete Garza used to cut the rope to bind Bea. A souvenir? Maybe.

With a flick and a gasp of pain, I brought the sharp edge to my wrist, slicing the skin. I held my arm over Adam's mouth, letting a drop, a second drop fall directly on his lips. I moved closer and squeezed with my other hand, forcing the drops to fall more quickly.

The silence from the three of us grew thick as drop joined drop and slid across Adam's lips, down his face and onto the pristine sheet below him. No reaction.

I squeezed again, biting my tongue against the sting. With a gasp, Adam convulsed, back arching as a spasm rolled through his body. His lips opened. Tongue flicked out and licked. An arm whipped up from the bed and grabbed my wrist, bringing it to him. He rose to a seated position, eyes still shut, bowed his head, opened his mouth and began to feed, his fangs sinking into my wrist as if the flesh was nothing more than cotton candy. I barely felt the pain.

I close my eyes and hold on as he drinks, drinks, drinks. Beside me, I feel Niko move forward, his body bumping mine as he tries to pry Adam off me. Adam is too strong. Tucker's voice reaches me, "Adam, let go!" he shouts, the words too loud in my ears. I go inside myself, trying to reach Adam, trying to find the bond that connects us. It is there, faint, pulsing with the beat of my own heart, of Adam's as it finds me. Adam. Adam, stop now. You can stop. *He growls at me, soundlessly. I hear it in my head. I gasp and arch, the pleasure rocketing through me as he takes more. Sex and blood, it's always about that. I cup my free hand on the back of Adam's neck and with what strength I have left I grasp his hair and yank. He fights me, latching on even stronger, his left hand holding my wrist to his mouth. His right arm wraps around my waist to hold me closer. My eyelids flutter as I begin to lose consciousness. The edges of my awareness darken, confetti lights flicker behind my lids, flashes of fire.*

"Hold on, Keira."

I think I hear someone say that.

"Hold on."

I dig in, hold. Focus, I think. Focus. It's hard to do when your brain is feeling like warm Jell-O. As Adam drinks deeper, I start slipping, as if I'm going to let myself fade, to let go. I fight again, but it's too much, I can't keep my grasp. Beneath me, my darkness beckons, that piece of me that woke up earlier tonight, that I let surface. I find it, embrace it, it melds to me, becomes me. I push it in front of me, make it take the force of Adam's hunger. I feel it fill me now, become whole with me. I no longer fade. A new energy surges through my body.

With a wrench and a gasp, I pull on Adam's hair again, and this time, his head snaps back, away from my skin.

I hold him there and quickly move my other hand to his chest, holding him back.

"Adam Walker," I said. "Stop."

Time slowed to a crawl as our gazes met. Green eyes stared into my own gray. With a rush and a snap, everything was back to normal.

"Keira, I'm—" Adam scrabbled back on the bed, moving as far back as he could. Niko, still behind him, grasped Adam's arms, enough to steady him.

"No, don't. Enough." I moved closer. "No more recriminations or guilt. You did not hurt me."

"I could have killed you." The look of horror on his face made me want to either slap him or hug him.

"Adam, I'm fine. Look." I showed him my wrist, which had stopped bleeding. I knew by all rights, I should be flat out on the floor, either dead or close to it, needing a transfusion. I wasn't.

"How did you?" He approached me with caution. "What happened?"

"The short version? One of my Sidhe relatives has been stalking me since I got here thirty years ago. When you showed up, he discovered your power, your energy was a yummy treat. I showed him the error of his ways."

Adam's brow furrowed. "Meaning?"

I sank down on the bed, letting myself relax a moment. Niko followed suit, sitting on Adam's other side. Tucker stayed where he was.

"It's a long, long story, Adam, and has to do with collusion, family politics and all sorts of stupidity," I replied. "I'll explain later." As in much. "Meantime . . ." I crawled closer to him and wrapped my arms around him. "You're safe. You're well," I whispered. "Stay that way."

He returned the embrace, tightening his arms around me. "Ditto."

We all four giggled as Adam and I relaxed. What a hell of a few of days. Tucker quickly gave Adam the highlights of all the goings-on. Niko sat and basked in Adam's presence. I was doing much of the same. Except, unlike Niko and Tucker, there was something I wasn't telling.

In the final moments when I let go, I knew immediately what happened. I'd Changed. And with that change, came a transformation I was absolutely not ready to acknowledge to anyone, least of all myself.

I finally knew why my Change process had taken so long, had been so unusual. With that understanding, came the awareness Gigi had known along. I was the Kelly heir.

CHAPTER THIRTY-THREE

B EFORE I COULD BEGIN to contemplate what the hell
I was going to do next as my great-great-granny's
heir, the slam of the front door and a clatter down the
steps heralded a visitor.

"Keira!" The happy tones of my aunt Isabel preceded
her entrance. Behind her, an obviously frazzled John, the
human day manager.

"Sir, my apologies. I couldn't stop her." John threw out
his hands in frustration.

I shook my head. "Better men than you have tried and
failed, John." My brother, who'd risen in preparation for
attack, sank back on the bed and let out a long laugh.

"Keira, well, it's about damned time," Isabel scolded.

"Shouldn't that be my line?" I retorted. "We've been
calling *you*."

My aunt *tsked* and walked over to the bed, fixing me
with her amber-eyed gaze, head cocked like a curious bird.
"You've Changed," she proclaimed. "Looks like old fang-
face here has his uses after all. Ta very much. Now, we
need to go."

I jerked up from my comfortable lean against Adam.
"What?"

"Go where?" Adam demanded. "And who the hell are
you?"

Isabel waved a dismissive hand. "I am her Aunt Isabel
and you are the reason she finally Changed."

Tucker stared at Isabel, then at me and Adam. Niko looked puzzled. John, smart man, had sneaked back up the stairs and away from this crazy mess.

"Adam is?" I squeaked. "I don't understand."

"It's a long story, Keira," Isabel began. No doubt, I thought. Everything's a long story today. "It's not told to you until you reach maturity."

"*You?* Meaning *me*?" I asked. "That sounded like a specific and not a generic."

"Of course." She harrumphed and placed her fists on her generous hips. I hadn't actually noticed until now, but she was dressed in some strange combination of Tuareg robes and gypsy skirts. She wore ankle-high fabric boots and her ears jangled with several hooped earrings. Isabel's long dark hair curled past her shoulders and halfway down her back. Two small braids fell down the sides of her face, each with a ribbon woven into it. My aunt, the fashion diva? Only if you were fond of Stevie Nicks in her velvet and lace days, I suppose.

"By 'you,'" Isabel continued, "I mean Changelings of the blood. You don't Change the same way as the others. By all rights, you should have been told once the symptoms began."

"Why wasn't I?" I demanded. Adam's arm tightened around my waist. He'd not let me go since Isabel had come fluttering into the room.

"I was on trek, on walkabout, in search of a plant and healing spell known only to the nomads of northern Africa," she said. "I received an e-mail from Jane catching me up on things about a week or two ago. She'd sent it months ago, but it was the first time I was near enough to civilization to get to an Internet café. Somewhere in Morocco, I think." She gave me a faraway smile.

"Isabel," I said sharply. "Your point?"

"Those of you who are of the Blood must force the Change," Isabel said. "It is not a natural, easy process. Last time this happened in my own recollection was your own great-great-grandmother, Minerva. Too long ago for most living clan to remember firsthand. She was but a child, a mere thirty-nine years. I realized this after the e-mail. I'd been studying some old texts as part of my research on the healing plant, and had come across the record some weeks ago. Then, voilà, I knew I had to come to you."

I let my head fall back onto Adam's shoulder. Great, just great. Changed for five minutes and she'd actually outed me to everyone present. I wanted to hide.

"Keira, I'm not sure I'm processing this all correctly," said Tucker. "But did she say what I thought she said?"

"No," I lied. "It's all a figment of your imagination. In fact, the entire last three days have been nothing but a really bad dream. In a few minutes, I'm going to go over there, take a shower and come back out and Adam is going to sit up in bed and tell me he had the strangest dream. And then we're going to go on vacation—somewhere preferably far away from all of this."

Tucker's laugh showed a little strain. "This isn't *Dallas*, Keira—and you're not Patrick Ewing."

I shut my eyes. "It could be."

"What does this mean, Keira?" Adam asked me gently.

It means I'm the bloody freaking heir to the Kelly clan and next in line to take over when my dear great-great-*grandmaman*, Minerva Kelly, known as Gigi to me and my brothers, decides she's had enough of the politics and business and running this circus known as the Kelly clan and abdicates. Then it's my turn. Hi, universe? Do not want this. At all.

Isabel answered him. "She's the heir, Adam," she said, her tone solemn. "Keira has Changed and is now adult in our family. Unlike the rest of us, she is not limited to one talent, one power, but has inherited them all."

Adam straightened behind me. "You are queen?"

"Not until Gigi steps down," I said. "And that's not going to be for a very, very long time." I mentally crossed my fingers and sent up a prayer. Please.

"Very well then." Isabel clapped her hands. "Now that everyone is all better. Time's wasting. Let's go."

"Where?" The word came out before I could clamp my lips against it. I should know better.

"I need you. Gideon is dying."

Here's a sneak peek at

BLOOD
KIN

**Book Three of the Blood Lines series
by Maria Lima**

Available November 2009

CHAPTER ONE

I SUMMONED A DEMON once. At least at the time, that was what I'd thought it was. I could probably chalk up both the summoning and my hesitation about its result to the fact that I'd been drinking and smoking a wee bit—okay, a lot—of something not quite so legal. One thing was for sure: the damned beast had smelled rotten, like it'd been rolling in a thousand dead skunks or a few not-so-fresh corpses.

In my world, demons were nothing more than tangible evil.

And right now, evil was about to raise its stinking, ugly-ass head again—in the form of my former lover, Gideon.

Don't get me wrong. I'm not talking metaphorical he-done-me-wrongness or a badass boy who turned his back on my loving redemption. Gideon was neither the heart-breaking villain of a country-and-western song nor the hero of a romance novel gone amok. No, Gideon was evil. He had chosen the dark side. His power lay in darkness. He could speak to the shadows, call the shades.

I'd been in love with him and trusting and he'd convinced me to drop all my barriers, to open my naive self to him completely so we could truly be "one." I fell for it like an egg from a tall hen.

When I touched his soul, what I saw and felt inside him scared me so badly I ran from London all the way back to Texas.

But Gideon was also family. Not closely related, but all Clan were cousins, aunts, uncles, all connected. Clan blood begat Clan blood. He was blood kin.

So when Aunt Isabel showed up declaring she needed my help because Gideon was dying, that I had to leave immediately for the family compound in British Columbia—I knew I had to go.

Of course Gideon wasn't the only reason I had to skedaddle to Vancouver. I'd also Changed yesterday, and not solely the capital-C Clan Change we all undergo when we come into our true Talent. I had to be special. I'd become the Kelly heir—yeah, *that* one, the one who only came along every so many blah-blah generations, etc. The one who didn't have only a single Talent, but got the whole supernatural shebang, all the Talents from astromancy to weather witching. Not something I'd ever imagined, nor wanted. Leave it to me, Keira Kelly, to be genetically unique . . . or maybe a genetic freak.

The previous couple of days had been insane in other ways, too—missing people, the one person I'd found that I could truly be myself with in a coma, my best and oldest human friend nearly raped and murdered . . .

The craziness had turned downright depressing, though. Said best friend, Bea, wouldn't even speak to me on the phone.

After yet another failed speed dial, I slammed the phone Bea would not answer shut and shoved it in the pocket of my backpack. A yelp came from behind me as I tossed the pack aside.

"Ay, watch it!" Bea's nephew, Noe, a gangly just-turned-eighteen-year-old loped into my living room, avoiding the pack, which had landed next to him.

"Damn. Sorry, Noe. I didn't hear you come in."

"No prob. I didn't exactly knock," he answered.

I kept my back to him as I tried to compose myself. Had Bea sent him to talk to me? To tell me to stop bugging her? I just wanted to explain to her why I'd done what I'd done. Why sentencing a man to death at the hands of a Sidhe instead of turning him over to proper human authorities had been my only choice. Noe knew none of this, however, only that his aunt and I were in the midst of some sort of disagreement.

"So, packing, huh?" Noe said as he settled onto a nearby chair. "You gonna keep calling Bea?"

I nodded and fiddled with the fastenings on a rolling suitcase I'd dug up out of the hall closet. Most of my clothes were at Adam's, but some of the cooler weather gear that I expected to need for my unexpected and unwanted trip to Canada were still at my house. The temperatures would most likely be mild, but I'd probably need warmer outer gear for nighttime.

"How'd you know I've been calling her?" I managed to say after a moment.

"You've only been calling the house and the café over and over for the past few hours," he said, leaving off the obvious "duh."

I rubbed my eyes, trying to avoid the tears that threatened. Thirty years and I still had no clue how to handle a fight with my best friend . . . and this one was a doozy. Less of a fight, really, and more of a complete dissonance in moral systems.

"You're heading to Canada?" Noe prodded.

"How'd you hear that?"

"I listened to the messages you left on the answering machine," he said.

"Yeah, of course you did," I muttered and put aside a

pile of receipts and other detritus that I'd dug out of my duffel bag. Last time I'd used this, Adam and I had gone on a trip to a fancy vampire hotel.

"You stopping by the house first?"

Noe tried to make the question sound casual, but failed miserably. Sorry, kid, I thought, you're too damn young to dissemble. Ignoring him for the moment, I turned to search through the center drawer of a small chest that I used as storage. It was a pretty cool item, picked up at a craft show sometime last spring. The vendor claimed it was some sort of antique Asian-style chest. I didn't care about its provenance and had bought it because it was unusual. Instead of hiding it away in my bedroom, I'd installed it in my living room, its washed-out red paint and metal accents complementing my other furniture.

"Damn it, where the hell's . . . there you are." I slid three passports out of the back of the top center drawer, found the red one and tucked it into a travel wallet, which I then placed inside the front pocket of my backpack. Nothing like doing busywork, pretending I needed to be more prepared, even though at this point, I was as ready as I'd ever be. No need for packing much as I had plenty of clothes at the family homestead. I wasn't planning to take more than this small duffel bag and my carry-on backpack, private plane or not.

I liked to travel light. Besides, if I really needed anything while I was there, it was a good excuse to take a day or two trip to Vancouver.

"All those different passports yours?"

"What—oh, yeah," I said, trying to keep my brain on what I was doing. Did I want to stop by their house? Bea was there, sure. No doubt getting some much-needed rest and recuperating from what happened last night . . . well, early this morning.

"Didn't know you could have so many. You a spy?"

I stared at the boy, all six-foot-something of him sprawled across an armchair, body all spare and rangy, whipcord lean in the way that only teenagers can be. "Spy?"

"Thought only spies had more than one passport."

I laughed despite my mood. "Only in the movies," I said. "I'm a citizen of the UK by birth, U.S. by family and Canada, well . . . I'm not really sure about that one, but I've had all three since I was a kid. Since I'm going to Canada, I'm going to travel on my Canadian passport."

"Huh. That's kind of cool." He threw a long leg over the arm of the chair and started to swing it, his natural nervous energy needing some sort of outlet. One hand toyed with the pull on the reading lamp.

"So what's up, Noe? You need something?" I tried to keep it light, keep my voice from breaking. I managed, but just barely.

"I came by because I didn't want her to . . . you know . . . she's—" Noe shrugged in that boneless way that teenagers do. "I came by to tell you that Tia told me to come see you and tell you that she's gonna talk to her."

Despite the run-on sentence and lack of pronoun attribution, I didn't have a problem parsing his message. "Yeah, thanks," I said roughly and turned away.

"You ready, sis?" My brother Tucker stuck his head through the door, one hand on the frame as he leaned in.

"Yeah." I picked up my backpack and slung it over my shoulder, trying to avoid looking at Noe. He'd done a good thing, coming out here to talk to me. Bea was the de facto matriarch of her small family, despite the fact she was about my age. Even her elderly aunt, Tia Petra, and uncle, Tio Richard, bowed to Bea's need to lead. She ran the house as well as she ran the café.

Bea and I had been friends for most of our lives. She'd been my first real friend, human and more accepting of my oddities than anyone outside my family. This estrangement was killing me.

"You leaving now?" Noe asked. "Without talking to Bea?"

Tucker started to say something, but I held up a hand. "We'll actually be here until tomorrow. Tucker's here to take me out to the ranch where we're spending the night."

"We were *supposed* to be leaving now," Tucker added. "But the pilot's delayed because of weather and can't get here until sometime tomorrow."

Noe stood up, brightening. "So you can come by, then, now that you have time?"

Surely Bea wouldn't turn me away in person, would she? "I'll be there in a while," I said.

"You got someone to take care of the house while you're gone?"

"We do if you're willing," Tucker answered for me as he picked up my larger duffel and hoisted it over his shoulder. "It'd be a big help if you could stop by every once in a while."

"Oh, cool. You mean me. Sure." Noe beamed. He was a good kid, mostly. Just a teenager with few prospects and very little money. He attended school part-time at the University of Texas at San Antonio and worked part-time at Bea's café, but there were few other legal ways to make ready cash around Rio Seco.

Tucker grinned at the boy's enthusiasm. "Excellent." My brother dug out his wallet and slipped Noe some bills. "Thanks, kiddo. You'll save me some worry."

"You know when you're coming back?"

Not a clue, I wanted to say, but didn't really want to go into all the reasons I was leaving so suddenly. "I'm not sure exactly," I said, "but I'll call, I promise."

I damned well intended to come back as soon as I could, but so much was up in the air, I couldn't predict anything right now.

Noe nodded and in an unexpected move, he wrapped his arms around me in a hug. "I'll tell Tia." With that, I took one last look at the house that I'd sort of called home for the past couple of years and walked away.

I TRIED TO SWALLOW but, despite having gulped down sixteen ounces of water before I stepped out of my Land Rover, my mouth was as dry as the Llano Estacado. Bea knew I was here in front of her small limestone house. The Rover had a distinctive engine sound, one we'd laughed about in the past. "You can't ever sneak up on someone, *chica*," she'd teased.

My hand clenched, fist tight. Damn it. Knock already, Keira Kelly.

The brown wooden door opened before I had a chance.

I cleared my throat, still unsure of what to say, but it was only Noe. "Hey," I said, a lame attempt at being casual. I failed as utterly as he had two hours earlier at my house. I'd gone with Tucker to the ranch, dropped him and my bags off and returned to town to try to mend fences.

"Tia says that Bea says she needs some space." He looked down at the metal strip across the threshold, his toe worrying at a bent corner. One hand was propped up on the door frame, the other stuck in the pocket of his loose-fitting jeans, waistband riding dangerously low on his hips, the top two inches of white cotton boxer topping the denim.

A skinny bare chest showed evidence of a recent workout. Tia Petra probably had Noe doing some heavy lifting at the café this morning. It was nearly three, the time I used to stop by my best friend's restaurant for a coffee, breakfast taco and a quick gabfest . . . just another afternoon in the life of Keira Kelly.

But all that had changed with Adam's arrival, Marty's death and now . . . oh, so much had changed now after Bea's near murder only one night ago.

"Space?" I repeated the word like a badly trained parrot. "She does know I'm leaving for a while?"

The boy nodded; a more miserable expression hadn't yet been invented. Noe was a great kid, eager to please, still a bit of a teen slacker, yet always there to help the family out. "She said she'll talk to you when you get back." He toed the metal strip again, one bare toe running a line across the ridges. He looked up at me finally. "You are coming back, right?"

I nodded, too full of questions, pleas, emotions I couldn't elucidate blocking my voice.

"'Kay, then." Noe nodded back at me. "She'll be here. You know she's still—" He blushed, a teen boy's embarrassment at girly stuff overwhelming his attempt to be the man of the house.

"Yeah, she's still my best friend," I said, my voice finally working. "Tell her, no matter what happens, I'll come back." I looked at him, Bea's amanuensis, the person who would report back to her. "Tell her. I *will* be back." I turned away, my eyes blurring. "I'll call her."

The door shut behind me and I climbed into the front seat of my car.